Laura Elvery is a writer from Brisbane. Her work has been published in *Meanjin*, *Overland*, *The Big Issue* Fiction Edition and *Griffith Review*. She has won the Josephine Ulrick Prize for Literature, the Margaret River Short Story Competition and the Neilma Sidney Short Story Prize. In 2018, *Trick of the Light* was shortlisted for the Queensland Literary Awards' University of Southern Queensland Short Story Collection – Steele Rudd Award. Laura has a PhD in Creative Writing.

TRICK OF THE LIGHT

stories

LAURA ELVERY

UQP

First published 2018 by University of Queensland Press
PO Box 6042, St Lucia, Queensland 4067 Australia
Reprinted 2018

www.uqp.com.au
uqp@uqp.uq.edu.au

Cover design by Josh Durham, Design by Committee
Cover image by Curraheeshutter/Bigstock
Author photo by Trenton Porter
Typeset in 11/15 pt Bembo Std by Post Pre-press Group, Brisbane
Printed in Australia by McPherson's Printing Group

The quote from *Summer of the Seventeenth Doll* by Ray Lawler on p. 143
is reproduced courtesy of Currency Press.

 **Queensland Government** This project is supported by the Queensland Government through Arts Queensland.

  The University of Queensland Press is assisted by the Australian Government through the Australia Council, its arts funding and advisory body.

ISBN
978 0 7022 6006 3 (pbk)
978 0 7022 6124 4 (ePDF)
978 0 7022 6125 1 (ePub)
978 0 7022 6126 8 (Kindle)

A catalogue record for this book is available from the National Library of Australia.

University of Queensland Press uses papers that are natural, renewable
and recyclable products made from wood grown in sustainable forests.
The logging and manufacturing processes conform to the environmental
regulations of the country of origin.

For Simon

Contents

Trick of the Light

Ray tells me that my cheeks are rosy. Our supervisors at the factory said the paint would give us a glow. My nickname was Plum when I was a girl, after my rosy cheeks, I think, or maybe I always looked like I had something stuffed in my mouth. I was a chubby little thing, and now people say I'm a 'big girl' but that doesn't matter to me as much anymore. I'd love to tell Ray about the name Plum. Lots of couples have nicknames for each other, and I could call him Sunshine, or just Sun, for sun rays. I like that. Sun and Plum go together beautifully.

This morning I walked to the factory, knowing I would see Ray tonight. Every day I paint hundreds of clocks, using brushes made of camel hair, which is soft and the strands lose their shape. The numbers on each clock are so tiny it's impossible to be accurate without a pointed brush. I pass the tip into my mouth, wet it, and shape it with my lips. Nettie insists she can taste the radium on her tongue, but no one else can. Nettie is dramatic, that much is for sure.

No one in New Jersey pays as well as US Radium. We earn seventeen dollars a week, which is three times what my friend Barb makes at the lamp factory. We paint the dials with the substance they call Undark, and it's magical really. All those poor soldiers in the war who couldn't tell the time at night down in the trenches, we helped them see. One of the supervisors told Nettie a story about a soldier over in France who was a hero because he charged the enemy at the right time. His commanding officer said 0230 and it was pitch black and the sky was clear and the air was cold but the soldier's radium watch face told him it was 0230. In the silence he leapt over the ridge and charged and made ground. During the day, the enemy would never have noticed it, but at night, the paint we apply with our brushes made of camel hair glows, secret, like stars.

At work I think about Ray and my family, and sometimes I think about those soldiers and how we helped them. Now that the war is over, all sorts of people are buying our compasses and clocks, our Undark watches. So I remind myself of that when my shoulders hurt a little from hunching over my bench, or when Mother asks me why I'm holding my forehead at dinner and I say it's because of my headaches, from looking at numbers so tiny. From being so precise, painting two hundred dials per day. It's magic. A person has to know the time.

'Grandma still has the newspaper clippings from the shark attacks,' I tell Ray. 'She loves showing them off.'

'Last time it was pictures of the *Titanic*,' he says. When he takes my hand, shivers move up my arm and along my shoulders.

A few years ago, in the summer of 1916, shark attacks made big news along the Jersey Shore. It was during the heat wave in July while families were on vacation. The polio made it worse, Father read in the paper, because everyone wanted to go into the sunshine and too many people were in the water. There was absolute panic over whatever was down there – some said they weren't even sharks, just fish or sea turtles. Barb and I heard about the attacks and spent a day laid out on our towels in her back garden. Barb's blouse was dotted with blue fish and her thighs were elastic brown in the sun. I borrowed her sunglasses and we talked about Jack Wade from the football team, and about Harold Barclay, who is handsome but whose mother ran away with a man from the brewery. Barb's mother brought us sandwiches on a tray. I said I wasn't hungry so Barb ate them all, and then she lay back on her elbows with her neck arched in the sun.

Ray and I step off the tram and he kisses me on the corner, six houses up from Grandma Rose's front windows. I want all the world to see Ray pressing his mouth to mine. I'm thrilled to think he could imagine nothing else during the tram ride but how I would taste for him on this corner. I am wearing my green dress with the cream sash and I'm glad the tram pulls away slowly and the passengers in the back can see.

I try it out for the first time. 'I think I'll call you Sun.'

'What? Why?' He kisses me again.

'It's a pet name I thought of for you. Like the rays of the sun. Something between us.'

'It's not very masculine. What's wrong with Ray?'

'Nothing. Nothing's wrong with Ray. I love your name.'

He slips his arm around my waist. While we walk the six houses I tell him about Nettie thinking the radium has a taste. But it's nothing more than touching your lips with water. Like when I was a girl sucking on the ends of my hair, the dark brown wisps changing shape as though they were alive outside of me, smooth against my lips, no matter how many times Mother told me I'd end up with a ball of hair rounding out my middle like a cantaloupe.

Ray touches my face. 'Your cheeks are rosy,' he tells me again.

I hear Grandma inside the house, fumbling in the hallway, and I call to her. 'Grandma, I've told you to leave those in the lock. What if there's a fire?'

A series of clicks. She opens the door and rocks from foot to foot. 'What did you say about a fire?' Milky with cataracts, her eyes flicker between us.

'Nothing, Mrs Bell,' Ray says. 'It's lovely to see you.'

Grandma pulls him in, down, closer than he'd like, I can tell, but he lets her kiss his cheek. She grips his hands as best she can, and then mine.

'How's your arthritis?' I ask.

'You know I don't like to talk about that, Vivien,' she says. 'I'm fine.'

Ray removes his hat and steps ahead of me into the hall. Set out on the table in the dining room are eight crustless rectangles of sandwiches lined up like railway sleepers. Grandma's teapot steams beneath its woollen cosy.

'Mr Doherty, you sit here. Or wherever you'd like, but perhaps here. Vivien, you take up that place next to your beau.'

'Nobody says beau anymore, Grandma.'

'A sandwich, Mr Doherty?'

I glance at Ray to reassure him. I've already told Grandma that we're going out for dinner. That her house is just a quick stop. Ray is taking me dancing.

'Thank you, Mrs Bell. Did Vivien tell you we're going dancing?' He halves the sandwich in one bite and talks through it. 'I'm going to need my strength.'

All around us, the scent of mothballs spices the air. Grandma has filled a vase on her window ledge with pansies.

She turns to me. 'How is your mother?'

'She's fine, thank you.' Thinking of Mother reminds me of my single bed under my own window ledge in the room I've slept in all my life. Ray shares an apartment on the other side of the Watsessing River with his high school pal Tom. I've never seen him, even though I've offered to stay at Ray's later, or go over earlier, so Tom and I can meet. Ray doesn't think it's important. When I first saw their poky bathroom, I imagined leaving my toothbrush there one day, next to Ray's and Tom's, a different colour, the three of them lined up. Ray has a single bed, pushed against the wall, and the bed clothes don't match and the door can be locked so there's privacy, too.

Grandma fusses because she's forgotten something, and she returns from the kitchen balancing a small white plate. Slices of an orange have fallen about on their backs like beetles. She points out the forks and knives beside our plates, dainty things, rarely used, carefully set out for Ray's benefit. My knife skips across the flesh and a squirt of juice makes them both chuckle. I finish it as quickly as I can, and wait for Grandma to offer me the other platter.

'No, thank you, no,' I say. 'We'll be having dinner soon.' I pat my belly and push back my shoulders. The skin around Grandma's neck is grey and it reminds me of wet cement that hasn't been smoothed. In her wedding photos, Grandma is beautiful.

She flutters her palms up in surrender. 'Now, I know you young people are looking to leave, but I promised Mr Doherty last time – didn't I – that I would show you the hat pictures.'

Grandma's father set up one of the first hat factories in New Jersey. Ray sits beside her at the table. I watch him point at newspaper clippings in the pages of her scrapbook and smile as he hears the stories that I used to love as a girl.

She looks up. 'How is the factory for you, Vivien? I hope you're not working too hard.'

'I'm fine. We're very busy. I should bring one of the clocks to show you.'

She waves my suggestion away. 'No, that would be a trouble.'

I tell her that it's time we were going and she nods. Her fork is shaky as she prods at the plate of fruit, begging Ray to eat the last couple of slices. I fold the napkins and Ray helps Grandma collect the dishes. I hear her thrill, the gratitude at his kindness, over the sound of running water in the sink.

At the front door, I stand still as Grandma puts her lips to my cheek. 'You're looking healthy, Vivien. I think you've lost a little weight.'

Ray waits in the hall, passing his hands around the brim of his hat. He acts like he hasn't heard. Grandma grips my arm too hard and soapy water from the sink drips onto my dress.

'Thank you for the tea,' I say.

As I step out onto the front garden path, I leave without kissing Grandma back, but Ray leans in for his. 'Here,' Grandma says. 'I want you to have this.'

Ray unfolds, once, twice, a newspaper clipping that she's pressed into his right palm. 'It's the one you liked,' she says softly. 'The velvet bonnet with the ostrich feathers. I think you should have it.' He tries to protest.

'I won't take no for an answer. Me and my silly hats.' She shakes her head at her own foolishness. 'I want you to have it.'

Ray thanks her again and I guide him down the path. He waves over his shoulder and touches his hat. When we are six houses down, waiting for the tram, I stand on tiptoes and hold his face.

'Wow,' he says. 'She's really attached to those, huh?'

'Darling,' I say. A word better than any nickname. It's dusk and there's a chill and my cheeks will be rosy. Soon we will be a young couple sharing a seat on a tram, heading out for dinner. Others, older people of Orange, schoolgirls of Orange, will have their heads down because they are going nowhere but home. Their bones will be weary, their feet sore. 'I can't wait to go dancing,' I say, my lips on his cheek.

Ray says, 'I can't believe she gave me this.'

On the tram he tucks the paper into his coat pocket. We eat pancakes at Dennisons, and then we dance. The cream sash around my waist comes undone and two songs later

Ray re-ties it. Deep in my throat, across my cheeks and along my jaw, I feel the glow of his fingers on my hips.

'Mother expects me in an hour,' I whisper. We stay to finish the song and then walk to the tram.

Nettie at the factory talks a lot about all her boyfriends. She wears her hair in braids and gets each boyfriend to unravel them. She says it makes them clumsy and slow because their big fingers are trying to untie the braids without knots. Nettie likes the wait, and making them wait, too.

We step through the front door of Ray and Tom's apartment. We pass the poky bathroom and Ray doesn't say anything. Perhaps Tom is out somewhere tonight. When Ray ushers me into his room, I stare at the bed pushed up against the wall.

'I have to work tomorrow,' I say. I expect to be talking, I expect to talk right through this, so he will have to cover my mouth with kisses and the whole thing can be a little game.

I touch my hair. 'I have to be at the factory early.'

I hope I am soft skin and slim hips. I hope I am the taste of peppermint. I hope I am aglow beneath his touch, haloed with my hair on the pillow beneath the window. I hope we are young forever and together in the dark.

'Do you want to lie down?' Ray says, his voice catching.

I wake up in my own bedroom, imagining that I am incubating something strange. Last summer, Jean at the factory thought she was pregnant, but in the end she wasn't. Or she was, and then she wasn't. We never found out.

When I dress for work I am covering a body that has now been seen. Our uniform is a smock that I always change out of before my dates with Ray. When we first met at the tram stop months ago, he was in his suit, the one with the dark blue lining, and I felt like a schoolgirl. He doesn't see me in my work clothes anymore, and I have become slender like Grandma says, and my skin is healthy. With the money I've made at the factory I've bought some nice things, like the green dress and the powder blue hat from Paton's.

Beatrice sits next to me on our row. Everyone agrees that she's the prettiest of all the girls, but her boyfriend, Stan, died on his way home from the war, and I no longer wish that I was her.

'Did you and Stan have nicknames for each other?' I ask.

Beatrice doesn't look up from her dial, but she pauses, her brush hovering above the three. 'I guess we never did,' she says.

'So you always called each other Beatrice and Stan?'

Beatrice's brush quivers as she dips it into the pot. She dabs the bundle of hairs against her lips, rounding them to a point. 'Yes. Just Beatrice and Stan. Always just like that.'

A lady in France discovered radium, and here we are – Beatrice, Dorsie, Nettie, May, Lillian, Jean and me at one row, and all the girls at the other rows – helping out the soldiers one year, and making lovely gifts for people the next. When the French lady found it, she said it pulsed. Dorsie showed me an advertisement from a company in East Orange that makes a liquid radium elixir to extend your youth. Doctors sell it in bottles, but we're here every day, surrounded by our jars of paint that are white in the light and green in the dark. I think of my grandmother's hands, crooked like bird beaks, and how Mother has to run hers under warm water before she can slice the vegetables.

After lunch I tell Beatrice that I'll see Ray again tonight. Mother is making roast duck and Goldenrod cake, and perhaps Ray and Father will smoke out on the porch afterwards. While I paint my dial, I rest my left hand on Beatrice's lap. Beatrice does the steadiest manicures. When she was in high school she wanted to be an artist, and Stan was going to build her a studio for her paintings. Beatrice's camel-hair brush tickles my nails, and she's finished in less than a minute. I turn to my right and bare my teeth to Dorsie. The radium mix goes on clear, and most of our supervisors don't mind if we have a bit of a laugh with it. I'll surprise Ray tonight, outside, after dinner, with my glowing fingers, my glowing teeth.

Replica

Monday

The skull isn't the real thing, just a replica. The price tag says £36,000 and I'm surprised more people don't have the same reaction I do. I mean, £36,000 is the annual salary listed on Monster.co.uk for a West End executive assistant at a Totally Unique Accounting Firm That Works Hard and Plays Harder.

Caroline, my boss, holds her hands together in front of her chest and looks in the same direction as Mr and Mrs Maxwell. Technically the Maxwells wear the same clothes I do – trousers and shirts – but Mr Maxwell has a nice tan, a real one, and Mrs Maxwell has pearls and a cardigan tied around her shoulders, which I guess makes it pretty clear how much money they have.

The skull they're looking at is made of plastic and coated in streaks of bright paint, although the original was a diamond one. It's by an artist called Damien Hirst: Caroline has met him, or they've at least been in the same room. Mr Hirst seems like the type of guy who is having a laugh. At the whole lot of us, including me, because I sell postcards of his works for one pound each, or six for the price of five.

I'm sure he thinks postcards of people's artworks are just about the lamest thing. A laugh a minute as he counts his money, or as someone counts it for him. Laughing because one day Mr Hirst sees a cow. Normal enough. Then the next day he decides to take that cow – it's dead now – and put it in his workshop. Then he grabs the chainsaw that's sitting on the bench. Maybe he isn't sure at first if it'll even work, if it'll be powerful enough. *Easy does it*, he thinks. *It might ruin the thing.* But he makes some tentative ... I don't know ... swipes at the cow, and pretty soon one side has been pulled apart from the other, right down the centre. It's a cow that never was split in two and now is. And on the inside he sees something he hasn't seen before.

Another thing he's done, and it's also upstairs in the exhibition, is take a different cow's head – except this time it looks skinned – and put it inside a big glass box. In the other half, he's put flies and some sugar for them to eat. So the flies are multiplying, a lot, and they're buzzing around this dead cow's head, and laying eggs in it as well. But because Damien Hirst has a sense of humour, he's put a bug zapper in there too. And people who've bought tickets for fourteen quid – which is my lunch budget for a whole week – walk past and nod or scrunch up their faces. You'd think it would stink, but it doesn't. Not at all.

Mrs Maxwell has said something funny, or Caroline's laughing anyway. It doesn't look like they're going to buy the skull today. The Maxwells have been in three times in the past two weeks. Mr Maxwell is over by the posters, standing with his legs slightly apart and running a hand through his white hair. Those posters cost twenty pounds each, and they're not even going to buy one of those. Mrs Maxwell thanks Caroline and Caroline thanks them back and says, 'Look, anytime. My pleasure. It's a great piece.'

Tuesday

Last night, I bought four frittata patties and one bag of beans and one of boiled potatoes on Tesco's three-for-seven-pounds deal. So today I have leftovers I can re-heat in the lunchroom microwave. Jason offered to meet me for lunch, but his work is twenty minutes away. And I'm cruel, but I'm not that cruel. He'd be here for ten minutes and have to go again. Out the front of the gallery, people sun themselves in their own patches of grass that they're very careful to protect. A small girl runs rings around her family, shaking the ribbon sticks we sell for six pounds in the gallery gift shop.

A lot of people who maybe don't have much money come to the gallery because it's free and no one needs to know that's why you're actually here. The toilets are always clean and there's lots of space for strollers. Lucy says that once she found a dirty nappy, like a really dirty one, wedged behind the taps in the bathroom even though there are bins everywhere. But Lucy is pretty posh so maybe she lied. She goes to uni and only works in the shop part-time. We're the same age, but it never seems like it.

When I was at high school, I thought I was going to be a psychologist or a photographer or work in a nice office. Because that's what kids like us did. The career guides at school said nothing about being gift shop workers. Today I ask Lucy how uni's been and she goes on and on about her lecturers and timetables and assignments until I have to pretend Caroline needs me in the stockroom. After lunch, Lucy tells me she had someone who was very interested in one of the skulls. She doesn't say it, but I can tell that the man was from the Middle East.

Wednesday

Jason stayed over last night, and we had sex, which was fine. He always takes a long time, mostly because he's looking deep into my eyes and whispering things. I just do what I know will work and he can't help it and then it's all over and we can go out to the lounge room and watch *Big Brother.*

This morning, Jason kisses me on the neck and closes the door softly as he leaves. The rule with my housemates is that you can have boyfriends to stay, but it's better if they're not seen and don't use any of the hot water.

I always want to lie in on my day off, but I never can. In the kitchen, I pull down my box of cereal and I see that Jason has paper-clipped a twenty-pound note inside.

At the Tube station, I say to myself that I'll put the whole twenty quid on my Oyster card, but instead I press the 'ten' button and put the change in my purse. A man who looks like he could have been Daniel Craig shuffles in front of me through the turnstile, and he reeks of piss and something like wet carpet steaming in the sunshine. On the platform he hunches forward with both feet on the edge. Around him, other passengers fiddle with their phones. I wonder who'd rush to the edge if he fell. All I've ever seen on the tracks are rats, soft brown bundles scritching and nosing inside chocolate wrappers. Rats must be used to trains thundering above. When people kill themselves on the underground, the station will announce something like, *Mechanical difficulties*. And even though you want to be sympathetic, it pisses everyone off.

A voice comes over the speaker telling the gentleman on platform one to please stand behind the yellow line. Daniel Craig doesn't move, and he's first on the carriage when it pulls up.

On the journey I think of the underground stations all around me – especially the phantom ones that have been closed and no one can get to. Sometimes I deliberately freak myself out by thinking of that scene in *Atonement* where the water gushes down the steps of Balham station during the war and everyone hiding down there drowns. That actually happened. When I think too much like that I want to get off at the next stop, unless it's Balham, obviously.

I emailed my CV through to a bunch of places. The only one who replied was a recruiter in Russell Square, who asked to meet me today. Katherine is dressed in a navy blue suit and a shirt with pink and white stripes. On her right hand are three rings, all with diamonds.

'Holly? Lovely to meet you,' she says, and I like her straight away. Katherine's blonde hair is pulled back with a little fringe she has to keep flicking to the side. I don't look as good as she does, but the ad didn't say anything about a suit. She leads me through a few doors, saying *Hiya* to about eighty people along the way.

'Is this all okay?' I say.

'What you're wearing? Yes. But if we get you an interview at the next stage, are you right to present as a little more corporate?'

'Absolutely.' I take a seat across from her. Both the door to the office and the meeting table are glass. The table is empty, except for brochures fanned out in the centre and a white orchid in a vase.

'Great. Let's get started,' she says, checking her watch. Katherine lists things about me as if she's a doctor and I'm a patient with symptoms. 'You're currently in retail? Two years' experience?' She asks if I enjoy working in a gallery.

'The gift shop is really interesting,' I say. 'I get to meet lots of new people. I like helping customers find what they want. Good people skills, answering the phone, things like that.'

Katherine smiles at me in a nice way. 'Excellent. That's what all the employers are looking for.'

I speak up. 'What I'd like, though, where I think I'm headed, is a personal-assistant or executive-assistant role. Somewhere in the city, maybe? I'm very organised and reliable.'

Her smile stiffens as she writes in her notepad. 'At the moment, Holly, that's becoming very difficult even for candidates *with* admin experience. Sometimes three and four years' experience is not proving to be enough. It's still hard out there.' She nods like we both understand the GFC equally.

I hope Katherine is just taking a long time to get to the part where she'll say, *But actually, Holly, I have a very small, very friendly boutique firm that would adore you. It's a bit glamorous really, but totally down to earth.*

Thursday

Today I'm too depressed to face frittata patties for the fourth day in a row so I go down the road and get a sandwich for lunch. The cheapest used to be the egg and lettuce at one pound fifty. Now it's almost double that. On the specials board out the front, one of the workers has drawn a cow — grinning and super fat so that all the words can fit inside.

The halved cows at the exhibition upstairs pop into my mind. Someone paid millions for those cows.

Friday

I know what the time is when it happens because Caroline asks me just as she finishes a stretch to the ceiling and then back down to her toes.

'It's twelve-seventeen,' I tell her.

'Oh God, I did yoga six hours ago and I still feel like shit.'

'Ha,' I say. 'I should do yoga. I need to do something.'

Past the locked cabinets with the skulls is the stairwell, and I see dozens of people moving back and forward and up and down the escalators. Two identical security guards dart past. Their hands grip their belts where they have batons, not guns. They run, leading with their shoulders.

Caroline bolts up from her stretch. Her face is red and her eyes water. She says, 'Probably the usual.'

A big scrappy fight among teenagers that's been dragged inside, or a husband and wife arguing about losing their kid. Security will end up taking them to a room and calling the police if they have to. That's what Caroline means. But somewhere further above us – maybe in a white room walled with paintings – a woman screams.

We look at each other. 'What's going on?'

Caroline says, 'I'll go for a wander. You stay here.'

There's more running and more people watching the running. I have to concentrate to sell a library bag and stickers to a kid who takes ages to decide what she wants.

'What's going on up there?' her dad asks me, stroking the girl's hair.

'Not sure. Sometimes people faint, you know, in the heat.'

He keeps smiling at me, his eyes resting for an instant on my chest. He probably doesn't even know he's doing it. His daughter, or whoever it is, has dropped to the ground to unwrap the packet of stickers.

'I'm Calvin,' he says.

'Oh. Hi. Have a good day.'

He laughs. Nice though, not mean. 'I see you're … Holly.'

'Yep. Hi.'

'Lovely to meet you.' He must stare at girls all day long like this because he doesn't seem embarrassed at all. His eyes trace across my neck. He's old, I guess, but not that old. Sort of looks like some teacher I might have had for a semester of History before he got transferred to a better school.

'Lots of great things in a shop like this. I must say I'm surprised.'

If he was a real History teacher he'd know that museums and galleries make all their money in gift shops – not from broken bones and chewed-up bits of loincloth.

Maybe he's hitting on me, but the movement outside is making me antsy, and Caroline's not back yet. 'You want to see something?' I ask.

'I'd love to, Holly.' He turns his attention to the girl. 'Bridget, baby, you stay there.'

Calvin says something weird like, *After you*, and he follows me. More commotion beyond the doors: everyone is keen not to miss a moment. A mother has stopped with her stroller in the dead centre of the walkway towards the escalators. Half a dozen teenagers are saying, *What the fuck?* to each other and texting on their phones. Calvin wears a small smile like he's feeling a nice breeze across his face. He seems to have forgotten the panic outside.

I tell him, 'These are Damien Hirst skulls. From the exhibition upstairs? Exclusive collectors' pieces. Just £36,000.'

'Wow.' Calvin touches his fingers to the outside. Only Caroline has the key.

'Yeah, loads of people like them.'

'What do you think?' he says.

'Well. They're exclusive collectors' pieces.'

Calvin laughs. Flash of white teeth. Flash of gold necklace beneath his throat. He touches his finger to my shoulder then onto the glass. 'But what do *you* think?'

I turn back to the cabinet and see myself and the chaos behind me, in the dark, concrete atrium where everyone is either frozen or rushing. 'I think they're beautiful. He's made something no one ever gets to see.'

In the reflection, Phil, the main security guy, points up and speaks into his phone. Bridget has gotten up from the ground and is toddling over to her dad.

'And they're so fragile. I guess like a real human skull.'

'Mmhmm. Very true.' Calvin seems to be losing interest.

A teenager dashes in through the back door of the shop. He looks at Calvin first, then sees me in my uniform.

'Oh my God. Did someone just kill themselves?'

'What?' Calvin and I say it together.

'That's what they're saying. Oh my fucking God. That some guy jumped.'

'Daddy?'

I ask the boy if he's serious. His face is sweaty and he has a bit of a grin, the way you look sometimes when the news is so bad you need to fight it off. He says, 'I don't know. That's what they're saying. Someone jumped.' Bones and a brain tumbling and coming apart at the feet of someone who glances up too late.

The restaurant is on the sixth floor. Caroline took me there for my birthday in May. She bought us bacon sandwiches and freshly squeezed orange juice. We sat outside on the balcony. We watched tourists below and boats on the river and a crane, all the way across the water, dangling over Liverpool Street. Some worker hitched to the long metal arm, risking his neck for another skyscraper.

Above us, the sun in the sky. Beneath us, the glittering, bright pavement.

Skin to Skin

Dylan watches Stephanie make milkshakes for the two blokes in Fluminis uniforms who have come in, stomping their feet on the welcome mat. One of them takes off his hard hat and cradles it. Stephanie jams metal cups onto the spokes, cocking her head to one side. She is showing off, Dylan thinks.

'Decided yet?' she asks.

'Yeah,' the short one replies. 'We'll get a coupla bucks' worth of chips.'

'Sounds good,' the other one says.

'Dylan?' Stephanie turns and finds his eyes quickly. At school once, their Drama teacher Ms Morris put them in a scene together. Something about a war and Stephanie had to hold on to his arms as though she loved him, so she dug in her fingernails until she left marks like staples. Across the room, Ms Morris had given them the double thumbs-up.

Dylan empties a package of chips into the fryer. He rocks the basket and a spatter of oil bites him on the cheek. 'Fucking hell.'

Laughter from the front counter.

'Don't worry about him,' Stephanie says. 'Oi, Dylan. We can hear you.'

Silence for a few minutes while the chips twist in the golden oil. He salts them hard and shakes them into a box. Doesn't spit into them. Dylan comes round, hands over the chips. One guy is on his mobile, drinking his milkshake. He motions for his friend to pay.

'You all right back there?' The Fluminis worker says it to Stephanie – a little joke. Stephanie has blue eyes and a heart-shaped face, long brown hair, and a dusting of light pimples around her nose and lips. She's blushing when she takes the man's money.

'I got some oil in my eye. It fucken hurt.'

'Dylan!'

'But that's nothing to you blokes, hey.' He points to the logo on the man's fluorescent vest. 'Your risky business.'

Heaps of kids' parents work for Fluminis. Dylan sees them turning up outside the school gates at three o'clock in work utes with the logo in dark blue on the side – three tentacles of river bending away from the 'm' in the middle.

'No injuries here, mate.' The man jingles his change and holds it up to Stephanie like a salute. 'Thanks for the milkshake, love.'

'Take some sauce,' Dylan tells them. 'On the house.'

The electronic bell bleats when they push the door open onto the street. He watches the men climb inside their ute, plucking chips from the box as they drive off.

In the afternoon, Stephanie takes a washer and tooth-brush to the milkshake makers while Dylan moves a mop underneath the tables. His uncle Jon owns the cafe.

Dylan overheard his mum begging her brother: *Just give him something to do.* Stephanie was hired at Barcombe Cafe two months later. She wanted to save up for tickets to Beachcomber Island in Fiji, where she'd go for schoolies with her boyfriend and her boyfriend's mates. She'd take any shifts, she told Jon, thumbing towards Dylan. Even with him.

He dips the mop into the bucket and thinks about the water that comes from the River Derwent. Heavy deposits of minerals: cadmium, copper, mercury, lead and zinc. Dylan avoids drinking from taps. He showers with a product he bought online called Toxin Corps. When his mum saw it beside the bathroom sink, Dylan told her about the barrier it promised to cover him with. She asked *Why?* a lot, and then, *How is it supposed to do that?* Standing in a towel wrapped around his waist with the water running behind him, Dylan told her that she should feel free to use some herself, but to please pay for the next bottle; it cost thirty-five dollars. At school he buys water from the canteen and cleans his hands with a squirt of hand sanitiser from the front pocket of his backpack.

Dylan looks out the window. Barcombe is small, only six or seven thousand people. He has lived here all his life. Across the road from the cafe is a tiny church. Beside that are wooden houses painted white and navy and butter yellow. Then there's a dental surgery with a ramp leading to the door, and the Federal Hotel further along, on the corner that leads to the wharf. In his mind, the metals make the nearby river turn silver and molten, stirred up by the Fluminis machines. Beneath the water, Dylan imagines the particles slipping past one another, swift specks whizzing by on muddied currents.

★

For his Drama assignment – a monologue – Dylan has decided to tell the story of what happened to him at his old school. He's told it so many times to himself, but this is when it really matters.

Ms Morris calls his name from the roll and he steps up to the low stage. She sits at a single desk at the back of the room, a pen in hand and a stopwatch around her neck.

'Ready? And, begin.'

Dylan sits on a chair, opens his eyes and spreads his hands wide on his knees. 'I left that school because they spat on me at church,' he says.

The black T-shirt they all wear for Drama performances itches at his nipples and at the skin around his armpits.

'It happened to me. Some boys had been giving me a hard time. Girls too. We went to Mass. It was a Catholic school, see, and they must have planned it to happen when the music was playing. I mean, it was an attack. Not a coincidence.'

He's forgotten what comes next. He can see the words typed out on the folded sheet in his backpack, right there on the floor. He tries to catch the next line, one of many hovering like insects.

It comes to him: 'And they all spat on me, one by one by one, and I just had to sit there while they pretended to be perfect. I couldn't wipe it, not right then. The principal said he'd do something, but he never did. And Mum didn't have any power with those people like the other parents, and so she asked me what I wanted to do.'

Ms Morris writes on her paper while his classmates study their scripts or pretend to doze. Lying on her stomach on the carpet, Stephanie watches him almost sadly, Dylan thinks. He hesitates and stumbles through the middle part of his performance, in which a girl at his old school told everyone about how she'd been pregnant, once, but then she'd caught the ferry with her older sister to get an abortion in Melbourne.

Stephanie raises her head. She doesn't look sad anymore.

'That's what she told us,' Dylan says, flustered by Stephanie's bright eyes.

He doesn't like to think about his thirst for water, but there it is, a sticky ticking in the back of his throat.

'I thought it was a low act, what that girl did,' Dylan projects into the silence of the room, 'but she treated it as though it was some sort of victory.'

He recalls his final typed lines and delivers them smoothly. 'And those two things – what happened to that girl with the baby, and what she did about it, and what happened to me, and what I did about it – showed me that there's no justice. Not really. Things are out to get you.' He has followed his own stage directions and approached the window. He puts his head in his hands. Freezes.

The applause from the class is flat. As he walks past Ms Morris's desk, Stephanie jumps up and strides towards the door. One of her friends follows her outside.

Ms Morris stands and watches them go. 'Dylan, stop. Was that true?' she asks.

'Parts of it.'

Ms Morris sets her jaw. She looks like she's trying to smile through something. 'Honestly, though, Dylan. I—'

'Parts were based on my real life. But I was a character. I made up the character.' He knows teachers prefer fiction over non-fiction. Cut too close to real experiences and guidance officers must be summoned. Revelations can only come in flickers.

She waves him away.

★

The next day, Ms Morris is on playground duty, and Dylan watches her stroll the ridge above the school oval with her hands behind her back. Ms Morris is tall, with a stoop and close-cropped blonde hair. He locates a plastic straw on the ground a few metres away, and makes a show of lifting it from the dirt and dropping it in the bin.

'Aren't kids the worst?'

Ms Morris smiles. 'Sometimes.'

'I mean, they can't even pick up after themselves.'

She passes him, folding her arms across her chest. 'You're a regular good Samaritan, Dylan.'

'Did you like my play, miss?'

Ms Morris makes a *hmmm* noise and makes to keep walking.

'So you hated it.'

Ms Morris tilts her head, like: *I didn't say that.* The first bell rings. 'Back to class, Dylan.' She takes off her hat and turns to go.

He calls after her. 'So you hated it?'

They have an audience now. Four or five students from his Drama class gather, almost in earshot, lazily fingering their phones.

'I can't believe you hated it. Miss?'

She stops walking. 'I think you knew that someone in our class had struggled with that very issue, and yet you chose to perform a monologue about it anyway. That's what I think.'

'About abortion?'

She wipes the word away with her hand. 'That's what I think. But, anyway. Come on, there's the bell.'

'Well, Stephanie should have thought about that before she fucked—'

Ms Morris wheels around and her words rush out. 'What kind of a shithead are you?'

Dylan clasps his hands above his head. He lets out a laugh and looks over to his classmates, who glance up from their phones. 'She just called me a shithead.'

His teacher's face reddens. 'Dylan,' she says in a low voice. 'No. I said, "What kind of a *student* are you?"'

'Oh, brilliant, now you're going to *lie* about it?'

'That's not what I said.'

'You think I'm a shithead.' He grins. His lips are dry against his gums.

Ms Morris is shaking her head, panic spinning through her eyes. 'Listen.'

Dylan saunters ahead of her. 'I know what I heard.'

Josh, short and affable and hopeless at Drama, takes a step closer. He grins too. 'Did you, miss?'

Their teacher's best smile. 'He misheard. Absolutely not.'

Josh doesn't falter. 'Sure thing, miss. He really is a shithead, though.'

It's not even a word Dylan's classmates use. But the rumour spreads anyway, and they hassle Ms Morris. *Admit it*, they urge. *It's funny because it's true. Just say it.* But she won't budge. Packing away costumes two days later, Dylan hears Ms Morris telling her favourite student, Jessica, that he has a strange imagination. Within a week, his peers have settled on a position somewhere between not believing him, and the vague idea that Ms Morris did say it, but she shouldn't get in trouble − she's only telling it like it is.

★

At the start of Biology, period one, the note on the whiteboard says: *Regulation of gene expression*.

Dylan takes out his textbook. 'Sir, why can't we study something relevant?'

Mr Shah pauses with the whiteboard marker poised at the start of a new note. 'Care to explain what you mean, Dylan?'

'Something that makes sense to our lives,' Dylan says. 'Like mining or water or minerals.'

Mr Shah taps the board. 'We're studying genetics. What you're talking about sounds more like the purview of Chemistry.'

'Why can't you just give me a simple answer?'

Among the class there are raised eyebrows.

'Excuse me?' Mr Shah's tone darkens. 'Because that's not what this term is about. You're always welcome to study whatever you want in your own time.'

'Yeah, okay, sir. Blah blah blah.'

'Dylan, are you trying to be difficult today?'

He fishes through his pencil case. His hands are shaking. 'Whatever, sir,' he says, willing himself not to cry like he did after those kids spat on him at church. 'If being difficult means wanting to be *informed* and not wanting to die from whatever shit is in that river. If it's illegal to ask questions about fucking *science.*'

The class is energised – not on their teacher's side exactly, but tickled by this spectacle. Mr Shah caps and uncaps his whiteboard marker. He raises his eyebrows, speaks calmly. 'Obviously you can't talk like that in here. Time to go. I'll phone Mrs Austin and tell her you're coming.'

Dylan shoves his books and pencil case into his backpack, heads for the classroom door. The clock above the whiteboard shows that it's barely ten minutes into the school day. 'Maybe you're all complicit, anyway. Maybe Fluminis is paying for all of this.' He sweeps his hand around the classroom, and everyone follows his gesturing to the metal storage cupboard with the kicked-in doors and the rusted taps for Bunsen burner gas. To the decapitated skeleton model up the back. To the rat foetuses in glass jars up high on shelves so the juniors can't reach them.

Jessica says, 'What are you talking about?'

Mr Shah raises a hand. 'Jessica. Don't.'

'Forget it.' Dylan palms the door frame. 'Stay ignorant, losers.'

He's at the front gate of the school, turning left, when he sees a familiar car. For a moment he thinks Mrs Austin has already rung his mum, who's rung her brother to come intervene – all in that short space of time. Dylan is slipping through other elements so easily, it could be possible.

He raps his knuckles on the car roof. 'Uncle Jon. Did Mum call you?'

'Whoa. Hey.' His uncle is sitting with one leg inside the car, and the other planted on the grass beside the footpath. 'Your mum? No.'

'What are you doing here?'

Jon glances past Dylan, towards the school buildings. He raises the mobile phone in his hand. 'Ah, just pulled over to use this. I didn't realise I was here at—'

'Can you give me a lift?'

'Why've you got your bag?' His uncle narrows his eyes. 'You in trouble?'

'Yep.'

'Your mum will find out, won't she?'

'Probably. It's fine. You can tell her.'

Jon smiles. He nods towards the empty passenger seat. Dylan jams his bag at his feet, shuts the door, wanting to drive away fast. He waits. He watches Jon unlock his passcode and check his phone again. Nothing. His uncle looks back at the school, then starts the car and merges onto the road.

'Had driving lessons yet?' Jon asks.

Dylan shakes his head. 'Too expensive.'

Jon knocks his fist into Dylan's leg. 'Ah, well, you'd better con me into some free ones, then?'

'Thanks. Yeah.'

'Better yet – or as well as, if you want – I'll line up some extra shifts for you at the cafe. Steph's quit. You'll be by yourself after school till I find someone else.'

Dylan pictures Stephanie's heart-shaped face, her imperfect complexion, strangely alluring. 'Why? Why'd she quit?'

Jon reaches between his legs. He pulls on the lever and his seat jerks forward. 'Didn't say.'

★

Minerals start turning up in Dylan's trouser cuffs, pooling in the fabric folds by his ankles. He crouches by the deep fryer at Barcombe Cafe, feeling breathless. With his thumb he pulls the hem out further and runs the tip of his finger through them. Sandy, but sharper and colder. The sound alone shoots pain through his teeth. It isn't a uniform mass – he extracts a misshapen nugget, then inspects his hand. Skin-to-skin contact isn't as dangerous as ingesting through water, but his mind throbs with the promise of scrubbing, later. Dylan cups the bottom of the trouser cuff and crunches the particles together in his palm.

Stephanie announces her arrival by humming. She is here to drop off her key. She stands above Dylan with her arms folded, the key pressed against her freckled arm.

'Can you see this?' Dylan points.

She's been ignoring him since Drama class. Her silence has been like background noise, as humdrum as traffic. Now it's a roar.

'There. In the cuff.'

Stephanie looks pissed. She shakes her head and plucks bunches of serviettes out of a metal canister. 'What a shame I won't get to work here with you anymore.' She's making a mess.

'I'm serious. Please.'

With a huff, Stephanie drops down. She forks three fingers onto the kitchen's sticky floor to steady herself. She peers inside. A few seconds. 'Is this a joke?'

'They're minerals. Bits of metal, shavings of it.'

'Bits of *metal*?'

'From the river. It's filled with poison.' A chink appears in his voice. What felt inevitable minutes ago now feels monstrous. 'Look!'

Stephanie scrunches up her face, rises and glares at him. She leaves the serviettes on the counter, next to her key. 'You're so full of shit.'

On his walk home, the sky looks about to break apart before a storm, the clouds quickened with seams of lightning. The rain begins three or four streets from his house. In the cuffs by his ankles, two handfuls of weight shift up and down as he begins to run.

There.

By the fence.

Underneath the letterbox.

Fine silvery shavings and nuggets are clustered in tiny piles on the concrete at the end of his driveway. They look like they've been pawed at by an animal. Dylan tries to steady his breathing. They must have washed up here: Barcombe is under attack from a river swimming with toxins. He thinks of his mum, coiled on the sheets in their house, stepping out of bed, touching her forehead, walking to the sink for a mouthful of water in a tall clear glass.

He opens the front door, giddy with a sensation like dread, but with something else, too. Pleasure: the anticipation of a shower. In the bathroom, he carefully tips the silver grounds from his trouser hems into the cubicle. He sheds his clothes. He squirts Toxin Corps into his palm and rubs. Water sluices down his arms and chest. He watches the drain swallowing the biscuit-brown liquid.

★

The next morning, before his mum wakes, Dylan checks the letterbox. No minerals, but inside is a typed letter folded into a white rectangle:

FOUND PRECIOUS METALS?
WE PAY GOOD MONEY FOR METALS!
IN YOUR HOUSE? ON YOUR PERSON?
YOU FOUND THEM? WE WANT THEM!
CALL: 0491 570 158

Dylan takes the cordless phone from the kitchen and sits on the balcony, in the spot where his mum goes to unwind after work by painting ceramic nativity scenes and miniature, bewildered possums that she buys at the markets.

He grips the paper between finger and thumb. He dials the number.

'Hello?'

'I got your letter,' Dylan says. 'I know this is a joke. I just want to know who this is so I can avoid you at school.'

There is muffled laughter. 'Um,' a boy says.

It isn't Stephanie, then, Dylan thinks, feeling light-headed.

'It's Bob. Bob Smith.'

In the background Dylan hears several voices punching through, making demands, tossing questions around. The wind rushes around trees and bodies, where his tormentor with the phone stands, probably at the wharf past the Federal Hotel.

His mum can't know about this, not after everything that's happened. Before the spitting at his old school, Dylan was so doomed, so lonely. Now he's almost glad to have no one but his mother and his uncle. He has his job at the cafe, and the plush void of the cinema once a fortnight when Jon takes him. That's all and that's enough. The prospect of freedom – no more school next year – is nothing but a void.

'Well,' Dylan says. 'You're obviously making that up. So, fuck you. And leave me alone.'

'Hey, whoa, mate,' the boy says. 'I'll pay. That's what the letter said, didn't it?'

Dylan whispers it: 'I don't deserve this.'

'Sure you do. You earnt it fair and square. Steph told me.'

That voice. The tautness. The odd high pitch. Stephanie's boyfriend, Briggsy.

'What luck,' Briggsy continues. 'What a find!'

'Stephanie shouldn't have told anyone.' Dylan eyes an empty water bottle on the table. 'She didn't—'

'You've got a shift later at the cafe, don't you?'

He refuses to speak. Refuses to think of the time Briggsy has invested in the letter and the payoff he'll be expecting. Someone in the background offers a piece of information that Briggsy snatches up.

'Six? After you've finished, come on down to the wharf to get your sweet, sweet cash.'

'I'm not doing that.'

But Briggsy's voice has gone.

★

Later, after Briggsy and Josh and Vossy have ordered two boxes of chips from Dylan and counted their dozens of coins across the counter, they watch him lock the front door and then they herd him, almost politely, past the Federal, towards the wharf, as he knew they would. Briggsy pops the boys' rubbish into the bin. He licks the tips of his fingers.

At six o'clock the river is the colour of granite. The setting sun makes corrugations on its surface.

Josh asks, 'Here?'

The river, Dylan thinks. He turns his back to them and walks to one side of the wharf. It's narrow, with wooden boards brown-dotted with bird shit and the dirty pretty scales of fish.

Briggsy faces him. He rests his elbow on a post and lets his wet fingers droop, to dry. 'It just really isn't any of your business what Steph may or may not have done,' he says.

'She *told* me.'

Vossy says, 'I doubt it—'

Briggsy shakes his head. 'She did not.'

And Briggsy is right. The information about the abortion came when Dylan eavesdropped on his mum, who clutched the cordless phone and talked with Uncle Jon on the balcony while the paint dried on a nativity scene. Lumpy donkey. Startled baby. Mary's head bowed in prayer.

Dylan feels the thirst ticking in his mouth again. He looks beyond the boys to the entrance of the Federal, where a procession of men in fluorescent vests and hard hats tilts towards the front door. He will not call out. When those kids spat on him during Mass, during the hymn, he could have raised his voice higher than the song, but he didn't. He wouldn't admit what was happening to him.

'Even your uncle thinks you're weird,' Briggsy says. 'He feels sorry for you.'

Last night: more metal shavings grown like webbing from his heels as he stepped out of the shower. A pile coned neatly in front of the keyboard in his room. More, still, this morning underneath his cereal bowl.

'Speaking of your uncle,' Josh offers.

Dylan says weakly, 'I brought the letter.'

Briggsy talks over him. 'Steph's my girlfriend still, no matter what your uncle did.'

Jon Perrett, born in Launceston, cafe owner, smelling of blackboard chalk and breakfast juice, dressed in running gear, eyes the colour of hops.

He shouldn't, but he does. He asks the question. 'What did my uncle do?'

Briggsy lowers his voice. 'What the fuck do you think? He's almost twice her age, for God's sake. She came to me when she found out she was pregnant, even though we were on a break. She came to me.'

Dylan can't see in front of him, can't see the river beyond the wharf, beyond his feet. He holds the letter, hardly feeling it in his hands, or the wind on his face. He can picture the pillowy bundles of serviettes in Stephanie's hands, and her face when she dropped the key on the counter.

'You need to know what he did.' Briggsy frowns down at the wooden planks. 'We're not going to hurt you now. But soon everyone will know.'

As Briggsy and Josh and Vossy walk away into the salty wind, Dylan hears the huge arms of the Fluminis machinery grind to life beneath his feet. His vision cleared, he sees inside the Federal, where workers on bar stools nose their beers and tap-tap the tips of their steel-capped boots together. Feeling returns to Dylan's fingers and toes, and to the area around his mouth, from which, indulged and full and flush, the metals start to come.

Pudding

The office is buzzing. Travis has just returned from the United States, but Customs quarantined him at home. Apparently, there was an Ebola scare on the plane, and we won't see him for weeks.

'Suits him, doesn't it?' Margot says. 'Lazy bugger.'

I have visions of being stretched out on the couch, napping while *The Walking Dead* downloads. I want an Ebola scare.

We conference-call Dahlia in the boardroom. Someone from downstairs delivers a dozen green smoothies in tiny milk bottles, along with a jar of stripey straws. Carrot muffins sweat beside them, untouched. No one wants Dahlia to see them eat.

Margot sidles up and takes my arm in her fingers. I can smell the deep paste of her fake tan.

'What do you think it'll be?' I ask.

She shrugs. 'Must be big.'

Margot heads social media for Dahlia, so she plucks her phone from her pocket and holds it aloft over the smoothies. After a second, she separates one bottle from the rest, shifts it to the corner of the frame like Tasmania, lays a straw across its mouth, taps her screen. She hashtags the photo while walking, passing Cheryl, who fingers Pantone swatches. With Travis out of the picture, Cheryl's in charge.

'Maybe it's a Christmas appeal?' I suggest to Margot. 'Or a new flavour?'

'What are Christmas flavours in Australia anyway?'

'They're the same everywhere. Cinnamon, nutmeg, ginger.'

'Cinnamon?' Margot winces. 'No one wants carbs.'

'Fucking quiet, please,' Cheryl says as the Skype logo bubbles on the big screen. 'Hello, Dahlia.'

Dahlia is smile-ready, dressed in a white business shirt and pink-framed glasses. I recognise a new colour in her hair. She is framed by a shelf of books: *Success through Self-Love. Juice Your Way to Happiness. Ancient Grains, Modern Wisdom.*

Dahlia holds her hands in prayer. 'Good morning, everyone.'

'Morning!' trills Margot.

'Let's start with a *Proof*, shall we?' Dahlia adjusts her glasses.

Margot is prepared. 'There's a woman, @fitchickforlyfe2, who's been posting some really inspirational pics about her weight-loss journey, her battle with hypothyroidism and her goal to adopt a kid from Uganda in the next twenty-four months.'

Dahlia raises an eyebrow. 'Uganda? Bump it up to *Proof.*'

Proof is Dahlia's blog. Each post is signed, *Health and Happiness, Dahlia xx.* Margot writes one to three posts per day. She has a degree in Creative Writing.

'Actually, maybe it's Ghana,' Margot whispers to me as Freddie starts talking quarterly earnings. 'One of those.'

Will crowds the conference cam with a notepad sketch for a flagship smoo-boutique in Bluestone. Dahlia is ruffled.

'Why am I seeing this on paper? Surely you can send it to me.'

Cheryl shakes her head at Will, and he sits down.

'We should move on to the main item on today's agenda. Christmas.' Dahlia says the word like *Dachau*.

Freddie eyes off a smoothie. He creeps towards the centre table, bypassing the straws, and tries to fit his top lip inside the glass rim of the bottle. A slug of blended kale and celery drips down his shirt.

'Shit,' Cheryl hisses. 'Here.'

Dahlia frowns as Freddie swats at his shirt front with Cheryl's tissue. 'Everyone markets Christmas,' Dahlia begins, 'as the perfect time of year to spend with your family.'

A curl of uneasy laughter moves through the boardroom. Dahlia and her husband are *mindfully withdrawing* from their sixteen-year marriage. If it gets out – and then that's Cheryl's problem – Dahlia and her husband are most definitely *not separating*.

Our boss continues. 'But it's also a time for helping others. One of Dahlia's central tenets of faith is that we have a responsibility to give back to the global community.'

Cheryl starts nodding. Margot too, while tweeting.

'Absolutely,' I say. 'It's what sets us apart.'

'So from the first of December, hidden in the base of five Dahlia cups across the country will be a token. A lucky patron at any Dahlia smoo-boutique has a chance to find one.' She counts on her fingers. 'They could be in a juice, smoothie, pudding or protein-ball cup.'

Will flips his notepad. His pen flits down the page.

Dahlia loves questions that she can answer. 'And these tokens,' I say. 'What do people win?'

'Erin. Great question.' She shoots a forefinger at me, then clasps her hands together again. At my interview three years ago, Dahlia asked if I wanted to change my life by drinking green juice every day for breakfast. I promised that I did, and I got the job. Every year, on my birthday, Dahlia gets Cheryl to wrap a copy of her autobiography, *Dahlia It Up*, and place it on my desk. Freddie tells me the print run was slightly ambitious. There are cartons of these, somewhere in storage.

Skype buffers for a moment, and the room stills. Twenty storeys below us, the office crowds on their lunch breaks will be tucking into Dahlia FruiTango Nut Balls and Dahlia MissBliss No-Choco-Choco Smoothies.

When Dahlia's back on, her voice is chopped up and stalling from the wi-fi, before exploding in a rush of syllables. 'It's called trickle-down economics. It helps our most vulnerable reach their full potential,' she says. 'A lot of countries are getting on board. Even Scandinavia.'

'That's good,' Will says, ripping out a page. He came to us straight out of uni and Cheryl's had him on probation for twenty-three months.

'So. The Christmas prizes. Picture this: five gorgeous smoo-boutique patrons brushing their hands through golden stalks. Selfies with old toothless men wearing those straw hats. Burnished by the sun. Laughing. Dancing in a *hacienda*. Sipping on Dahlia Sun BerrySol.'

Cheryl's thumb hovers over her iPhone. She drawls optimistically. 'The prize is an overseas trip?'

'The *prize*,' Dahlia says, 'is to become – for thirty healthful, spiritual and nourishing days – a *plantation owner*.'

Will half raises a hand. 'What's a—?'

'Not just any plantation – and this is the special part. Fields and fields of amarillo. Dahlia smoo-boutiques will be the first in Australia to sell it.'

Heads bob. Excitement radiates. *Amarillo*. Dahlia first raved about it two years ago: an ancient Bolivian pseudo-cereal that would be big. *Huge*. Zero gluten, but full of zinc, amino acids and healing properties. She has the amarillo flower tattooed on the inside of her wrist – just looking at it gives her strength, she says.

'Five farms we can help.' Dahlia holds a palm to the camera. 'Five winners, five plantation owners. Freddie assures me he can make it happen. Just a few calls to the embassy, apparently.'

'The consulate,' Freddie corrects her.

'Whatever.' Dahlia smiles. 'The *consulate*.'

Cheryl clears her throat. She's worried about insurance.

'Winners won't do any of the hard stuff,' Dahlia assures her, 'like, you know, ploughing. Instead there'll be stories on the blog of a winner eating rustically at a farmer's table, a photo of another winner waving at a cute kid working.' She churns her hands through the air of her refurbished office.

Cheryl is back on board. She jabs the air with a straw. 'Maybe there's a jungle nearby—'

'A ride on the back of a donkey,' I offer. 'Trekking up a mountain, fuelled by Dahlia-branded amarillo.'

'You got it. Helpful stuff. Global citizens.' Dahlia checks her watch, and I glimpse the tattoo on her inner wrist. 'Write them all down, Erin. Give them to Margot.'

Dahlia tells Margot to start dropping competition hints on Instagram and Twitter. She tells Cheryl to give me the new deadline for the website, and then she is gone, her face momentarily frozen before the call cuts off.

Margot tucks in close to me. 'Is amarillo trademarked?' She calls out, 'Cheryl, do we own amarillo?'

Will looks up from his notepad. 'Bolivia's in South America, right?'

Freddie is at Cheryl's elbow, offering the carrot muffins. She gives him an awful smile — *No, thanks, you're a dickhead* — so he asks me.

'Erin? Want one?'

I'm starving. 'No, thanks,' I say.

★

The new website launches, Travis doesn't have Ebola and Cheryl ends Will's probation by sacking him. Margot's social media blitz is working. At smoo-boutiques all over the country, Dahlia patrons line up in the dozens, caught up in a manic pudding-buying spree, frantic to see a token at the bottom telling them: *¡Ganaste!* Some patrons don't even wait till they've swallowed all their Pina-Cleanada Super Sips, but tip the remains into city garden beds where bald-headed ibises drink the dregs in snatches. Couriers deliver our new Pantone 7487U cups in locked boxes.

At her desk, Margot is pleased. She shows me a new photo: tanned, pedicured feet rest on a freshly painted verandah balustrade, an orange sunset in the distance. 'It's got 245 likes already.'

I look closely. 'Perhaps we should avoid the hashtag *plantation owner*?'

'Why?'

'It might be a bit problematic.'

'How?'

I don't know. What about non-Spanish speakers moving onto Bolivian farms? What about taking the family donkey for a spin? What about five 18-to-39-year-olds asking *Abuela* where the tequila is kept?

'I'm sure it's fine,' I say.

Margot taps her phone screen. 'Look. Over 300 likes.'

In less than three months the winners of the five tokens are on a plane to Santa Cruz, via Auckland, via Santiago, via Lima, seated in economy.

★

With his quarantine now over, Travis sends himself back on a plane – this time to Santa Cruz. On the advice of her life coach, Cheryl expresses (to us) her unexpressed anger at Dahlia for opening the competition up to five randoms. Anyone could've found the tokens, and who knew what they'd look like? But, as Cheryl notes, 'all five are pretty much babes'. Margot uploads stories about the five winners. All of them except for Hugh (whose angle is 'Aussie-grandpa-turned-clean-eating') are in their twenties. In their stories they express how they love to travel (Marlon aims to visit North Korea one day) but have zero tolerance for drama (Claudia and Rohan) or fake people (Verity).

They are good-time guys and gals. Travis poses with them at the airport, their Dahlia singlets knotted at the waist, consulate documents organised, and their suitcases packed with what we hope are sandals and cut-off denim shorts.

★

I've been watching Freddie re-heat his bowl of seafood paella in the microwave for several minutes. Every thirty seconds he stirs the rice, testing it, except each time he shovels a few forkfuls into his mouth before replacing the bowl and shutting the door. There isn't much paella left.

Yet again he presses the quick-start button. He smiles at me as I stand against the sink. 'We could all pitch in. Get a better microwave.'

'Sure.'

'Oi, is Freddie in here?'

We turn. Cheryl clutches the door frame. 'We've got a problem.' Panic teeters in her eyes. Cheryl once told me I'd have brighter eyes and better hair if I took her lead and enjoyed the benefits of thrice-weekly fatty acids found in cold-water fish.

'What sort of problem?' Freddie asks.

'You're here. Fucking come.'

Freddie nods, grabs his paella from the microwave. He takes a bite. 'Ooh,' he says, 'hot.'

'Erin? Quick. You too.'

Cheryl herds us behind Margot's desk. Margot has one headphone in and she's typing, frenzied, pissed. She points to one of the windows open on her monitor. I see the headline: *Baby donkey killed by 'prize-winning' tourists.*

A photo taken from above shows what I guess, yes, is a smallish donkey, on its side in the dirt, apparently dead.

Freddie's eyes widen, mid-bite. 'Are they our tourists?'

Margot nods, her eyes fixed on the computer. She alt-tabs so fast the images seem to strobe.

'Surely donkeys die all the time,' Freddie says.

'I thought they were supposed to be hardy!' Cheryl says. 'Someone fucking Google donkey life expectancy.'

I lean into Margot's computer. More photos of donkeys. 'They all look old to me.'

Cheryl spreads her hands out wide. 'And what even are they? A cross between a what and a what?'

Freddie drops the sucked-out tail shell of a prawn into his bowl. 'You're thinking of a mule. Donkeys are actually members of the horse family—'

Cheryl shoves him. 'Fucking must you?'

'What did they do?' I ask. I wonder if Dahlia knows yet.

Turns out Claudia and Rohan have become, as Cheryl puts it, *friendly*, and have, in fact, borrowed the family donkey for a trek up a mountain to watch the sunset and camp overnight and take photos of it munching on hessian sacks of amarillo.

'Well, there you go.' Freddie shrugs. 'It wasn't the selfies.'

'No,' Cheryl says, rubbing her temples.

'It was the amarillo,' I say.

Cheryl's phone rings. She listens, then tilts the phone away. 'It's Travis.' Listens again. Tilts again. 'Not good.' She puts the phone back to her mouth. 'Not fucking good.'

★

46

We all work overtime. We distance Dahlia from the donkey, distance the donkey from the amarillo, distance the amarillo from Dahlia. Margot releases statements on social media about Dahlia's thorough and transparent processes, about her credentials, both environmental and zoological, about the dangers of eating several sackfuls of just about anything. Cheryl sets up three minutes on breakfast TV where the hosts ask Dahlia if she will oversee both an internal and external review of the alleged incident.

Travis flies home for damage control. We're in the office after hours when he steps out of the lift, straight from the airport. He's apparently cultivated an idea on the plane.

'We will,' he tells us, 'leak the *mindfully withdrawing*. Move towards the controversy, not away from it. Pump up the breakfast spots. Dahlia looking terrific. Bunkered down, *processing* it all, in her kitchen. I'm picturing her hair in a bun, a chunky knit—'

'Not too chunky,' Cheryl spits out.

'—asking for privacy, saying how marriage is hard work, her hands cupped around a mug.' Travis demonstrates what that would look like. I stare, mesmerised, my eyes scratchy and dry.

Then, of all people, Freddie pipes up. 'What if, to get over the heartbreak, Dahlia adopts a rescue puppy?'

We stare at him till, finally, Travis pumps the air. 'A dog! Puppies! Plural,' he says. 'We'll call them Biff and Scrap and Squid and shit.'

Cheryl covers her face and nods. She won't say it, but Freddie's hit the jackpot.

Margot begins to plan an elaborate Instagram competition to choose the names.

Freddie's on a roll now. 'And we could run something called, like, Cups for Pups Day? And a dollar from all extra-large smoothies gets donated to a charity that raises money for, I don't know, dog treats?'

The donkey will be forgotten. Christmas will make way for autumn and twelve-dollar hot pudding pots. We'll choose a new Pantone to celebrate.

Mountains Grow Like Trees

Beth was at work when Danny rang. 'Bad news,' he said. 'About the cabin.'

'We can't go?' She opened her laptop with one hand and rested the phone between her ear and shoulder.

'Sorry. I have to work all weekend.' Danny blew air out his lips and Beth flinched. She turned down the volume on her phone.

Danny had lined up a weekend for the two of them, at their friends' cabin in the mountains. Beth had the grant application to write, Danny reminded her, and working in the office was doing her head in. All those interruptions. Beth looked at the grant then, information spread across a dozen tabs on her laptop screen.

'Babe, you should definitely go without me,' he said. 'Jeremy and Mel won't care.'

'I guess so.'

'Do you mind?'

Beth had visions of the time alone. The desk in the corner of the cabin, adorned with a large glass of wine. Her important but doable work framed by the window with the trees outside. She'd stay up late and get up early.

Buy the good cheeses from the deli on the way up the mountain.

She saved a PDF of the application and pressed print.

'You got a lunch break today?' Beth asked. 'Drop the keys round?'

She turned off the highway at Windham and pulled into the carpark beside the deli. The mountain air tugged at her lungs. This felt right. She pushed her sunglasses onto her head and snatched up a basket inside the doorway of the shop.

A teenager was shifting around buckets of flowers. 'We're about to close,' he said.

'I'll be quick.'

Beth decided on a wheel of triple-cream brie. Avocado and lemon were a good idea, along with the loaf of sourdough and the early-harvest extra-virgin in the bottle with the monkish tassel. Strips of prosciutto vacuum-sealed. A little pot of fetta marinating in rosemary and oil. She paid the boy and dropped her change into the canister for leukaemia research.

The bottle of pinot noir from the Macedon Ranges rocked on the passenger seat as she drove the two-lane incline to Mount Ludlow. The trees snapped in the wind. Beth's grant application was about the mountain pygmy possum: her team planned to investigate the patterns of feral cats who preyed on the possum in Kosciuszko National Park. A new benefactor, a woman from Adelaide who'd made millions selling voluntourism packages, had set up a national fund for dozens of environmental projects.

In the mountain cabin, Beth would find peace. From all the regular things, she figured: job stress and fatigue from five a.m. spin classes four times a week and weekends that bulged with weddings/thirtieths/fortieths. She'd find order in paper and pen – there would be no wi-fi. She eased the car around a bend in the road and came up close behind a motorcyclist. She checked her phone. No messages, but no reception either.

Behind her eyes a headache prowled. Maybe she could eliminate it before it took hold. Her grandmother used to treat headaches by soaking a face washer in vinegar and water and laying it across the patient's forehead, on a couch, in the dark. But Beth didn't have vinegar or a face washer, and it never worked as well as when her grandmother had done it.

She overtook the motorcyclist and turned into the driveway before he caught up with her. Inside, Beth unpacked the groceries. The cabin was only two rooms, really, with a kitchenette in one corner beneath the high beams of the main room, a fold-out couch where she guessed Jeremy and Mel's daughter slept, and a bedroom with pintuck curtains and an antique chamber pot that collected spiders on the dresser.

Beth handled the objects on the sideboard beside the kitchenette. A small teak chest held four Durex condoms, including two past their use-by dates. People with children had less sex; Beth knew that for a fact. She replaced the lid. Beside the chest was a wooden mallard, its jade head bristling, orange feet planted on a stack of paperbacks with stickers from the book exchange down in Windham (*Morbid*

Farewell by JT Pratt, *Judgment for Strangers* by William Orin Knowles, *The Amber Demon* by Maya Clarence). She missed Danny. She put on a long cardigan, sat on the couch, pulled the folder from her bag and laid a pen on top.

There was a knock. Beth's mind rolled out endless hostage-rape-murder scenarios while the red wine breathed.

'Hello?' She heard the fear in her voice.

Seconds later, another round of knocking.

She moved to the window and slid the curtain across a touch. It was a girl, a pretty teenager. Donations, perhaps. Or directions. Not robbery. Beth opened the door and the cold breeze swept in as she looked past the girl to her own black Mazda on the gravel driveway, half a kilometre from the road, and at least ten kilometres from Windham. The girl must be a hitchhiker. Though she wasn't dressed like one.

'Can I help you?'

'I'm Charlotte.'

'Pardon?' Beth shook her head.

'I'm Jeremy and Mel's daughter.'

Wasn't their daughter blonde? And not in high school yet, surely. Out for lunch at the beach at the beginning of their friendship – which must have been five years ago – Charlotte was still in a one-piece bathing suit that was pink-and-white floral, with a frilled skirt that trimmed her hips. That little girl had fussed the fish and chips around on her plate, occasionally dipping them into the tomato sauce. She'd pinched the chips and licked off only the sauce, which had sent Mel quite mad, and the group had finished the meal quickly. Beth had seen Charlotte once since then. Maybe twice.

This girl had light brown hair and small but noticeable breasts and fingernails painted dark purple. She wore a short dress with stripes and a sailor collar. She took off a backpack.

'Who are you?'

'I'm Beth. Danny's my ... he works with Jeremy. Sorry – what are you doing here?'

Charlotte sighed. Such effort. 'I caught a train and then a bus and then I hitched a bit. They told me I could come.'

'Ahhh.' Measured and dreary and adult. 'No, you see, it was supposed to be me and Danny, and then Danny couldn't come, so I drove here by myself.' An odd sensation came to Beth. The feeling of an uneasy mistake, like lateness. The panic of a dream turning up ill-prepared to teach a class, deliver a eulogy, drive a race car.

Charlotte shrugged. She nudged the doormat with the toe of a black ballet flat. She looked beyond Beth into the lounge room. 'I guess there was a misunderstanding.'

No. There wasn't, Beth was almost certain. Momentarily, her headache blurred her vision. 'Let me get my phone.'

The girl waited till Beth returned, and made sympathetic sounds when she said, 'No reception.'

'It's freezing.' Charlotte glanced up at the trees and patted her arms like she was in a play. 'Are you going to make me stand out here? I'm their *daughter*.'

'No – yes – of course not.' Beth figured she had to get reception at some point, even if it meant driving down to Windham to ring Danny, to *hiss* at Danny, and find out what was going on. Charlotte was looking at her squarely now. Beth couldn't read her. She recalled herself in high school standing at the door of her Science teacher's staffroom to ask if there was some way she too could go on the excursion – *a scholarship or something?* – humiliation torching right through her, leaving her with little else.

'All right, then. Yes, come in.'

Charlotte walked past Beth's open arm, popped off her shoes and wrapped herself in a blanket from the back of the couch. She stood in silence, while Beth checked her phone for texts from Jeremy or Mel. Beth wrote messages – polite, breezy, apologetic in case there had been a mix-up – that hung there, impotent.

'I'll make you a cup of tea?' Charlotte offered.

'I'm sorry,' Beth said in her best university-corridor voice, 'but I'm just not that comfortable. If you really are supposed to be here, then it's my mistake, and I should probably leave.' A thin ultimatum.

'We could just hang out.'

'Sure. But we should sort this out first.'

'I've met you before,' Charlotte said. 'With my mum and my dad.'

'Do you remember that?' Beth undid the straps of her handbag and dug inside for the box of Nurofen.

Charlotte dropped the blanket onto the floor and turned to the sideboard. 'Look at this wanker,' she said. 'A Buddha *and* a blue eye *and* a book by Christopher Hitchens?'

Beth stared, the headache taking hold. But a cloudy idea had also formed, seeded by the way Charlotte had said, 'I'm their *daughter.*'

'Mel's not your mum. Jeremy's not your dad.'

Charlotte held the book and stroked its pages across her palm. 'Okay, so I lied about him being my dad.' She giggled. 'And my name isn't Charlotte.'

'What are you doing here?'

'It's ... um, Vanessa.'

'Vanessa?'

The first lie had hardly burdened her, but now the girl was positively playful. She put her hands on her waist and tapped her belly with her fingers. 'Okay, that's not true either. It's Tennille.' She picked up the Turkish blue eye.

'You lied?'

'The bit about Jeremy. He's not my dad.' Tennille pressed the charm between her palms like a pat of dough. 'You guessed the truth, though, right?'

Beth was alarmed. She was almost certain she had not.

Beth perched on the edge of the couch. Jeremy and Danny worked on the road a lot, selling innovative digital marketing solutions to small-to-medium-sized businesses along the east coast. Jeremy was responsible for south of Coffs Harbour; Danny, north of there. Tennille and Jeremy had met at a service station, where Tennille worked, near the border with Victoria.

'We had sex a few days later – at a hotel around the corner from the servo. There was a green bedspread,' Tennille explained, 'and packets of biscuits poking out of the cups on the tea tray.'

Through the starry expansion of her headache, Beth decided on a single fact: she was more appalled about all this than Danny would be. 'Oh, Jesus.'

'It was pretty average,' Tennille said. 'The shit-hole green hotel, I mean. This place is better. Every time I come here I think how great it is.' She grinned briefly before a blank look paled her face.

Beth remembered a picnic hamper that Jeremy and Mel had delivered the first time she and Danny visited the cabin. A Jeremy gesture – the cloth-covered fairytale basket in the woods was him through and through. She felt repulsed. She remembered the photo he had shown her, years ago, of the mermaid costume he said he'd stitched for his daughter.

'And why are you here now?'

'I got my weekends mixed up. I thought Jeremy told me the fourth, but he must have said the fourteenth. Or the eighteenth. Something. I didn't actually hitchhike. My friend Blake from school dropped me off, but he had to go.' Tennille folded her arms. 'I bet you've already texted Jeremy to tell him I'm here.'

'I haven't, no.' That was kind of true. She'd asked him about his daughter – not Tennille.

'What would you say?'

'That a girl who says she's your girlfriend has turned up looking for you. Sound about right?'

'But you believe me?'

'Do you want to call your friend – Blake, was it? To come back for you?'

'No reception, remember. It's the most annoying thing about this place.'

'Right.'

Beth searched around for her wine glass. 'When I was little,' she said, 'my parents never had any money. But this one time they saved for ages to take us on a holiday, and they rented a unit at the beach where we found fish hooks in the carpet.' She took a sip.

'What?'

'You were talking about hotels. Mum had to pick them out with her fingers,' Beth said, 'and we couldn't take off our shoes. *That* was a shit-hole. I'd forgotten all about that till now.'

Tennille came close. 'We never had much money either.' She stood at the end of the couch, almost touching Beth's socked feet.

'Oh.'

'And I know the bit, too, about him having a wife and daughter?' Tennille said it like a question. 'No one's perfect, you know? He's just a big kid himself.'

'He really isn't, Tennille. You may be a kid, but Jeremy? He has *high cholesterol*. You don't need him. You're young and bright. Guys like Jeremy—'

Beth had meant to sound wise and kind, but Tennille stuck out her jaw. Her face reddened.

'Christ,' Beth said. 'I can't believe he's sleeping with a teenager.'

'I'm not going to tell anyone,' Tennille said. 'Well, except you.'

'And you're eighteen?'

'*Now* I'm eighteen.'

Beth groaned. She thought of Mel, working on her own career, something in recruitment, while Jeremy stopped for Diet Cokes and sandwiches along the A1. Beth saw Mel at work functions once or twice a year. Mel ran thirty-five kilometres a week and always looked like she needed a

57

drink. Now, Beth felt an affection for her that was sisterly and warm and elastic. This sort of feeling – and these glasses of wine – would get her through this evening and this conversation with Tennille. Something else would have to get her through the confession to Danny and past any suggestion that he already knew what Jeremy had done. Beth typed out two more text messages to Jeremy, knowing they wouldn't send, but wanting a record of how she felt right then.

Tennille wandered to the sideboard. She picked up the mallard. 'What's this?'

'You said you've been here before.'

Tennille nodded. 'I have. What about this?' she asked, patting the teak chest, not waiting for an answer. 'Whose is this, do you think?' She lifted the lid.

Beth watched Tennille's face for a pulse of what the condoms might mean to her, but she only tipped her head like a tune was rolling around in there. She put the lid back on and held up three pairs of earrings Mel had brought back from a trip to Africa. A pair of gazelles, a pair of leopards, a pair of black-eyed antelopes, all mingling ark-like in a dish with half a dozen mints. Tennille unwrapped one and popped it in her mouth.

Tennille had a string of questions for Beth.

Were she and Danny married? Why not? Would they ever have kids?

Had she ever met anyone famous? Did she believe in God?

Where did she work? Were she and Danny rich?

Had she ever imagined what it might be like to have a tumour? Specifically a brain tumour?

When she was a kid, what sort of food did they eat?

Beth saw a way out of the seemingly endless questions. She took a slug of the wine. 'Are you hungry?'

Tennille said, 'Yes, please,' in such a way, softly and immediately, that Beth was sure she'd never had much in her life. Beth motioned for her to sit at the dining table and wait while she made up two plates of food. She set one in front of Tennille, who tugged at a piece of wet-dry prosciutto.

Beth watched, her head achey. 'You eat it. Like ham.'

'I don't like ham,' Tennille said, letting it fall from her fingers.

Beth tried to flatten out her annoyance by pressing her tongue against the roof of her mouth. She thought of the mucky fish and chips at the pub by the beach. Charlotte's precociousness. This girl's backward snobbery.

'That cost at least a dollar, that strip alone,' Beth said, like a wanker with a Buddha and a blue eye and a book by Christopher Hitchens.

Tennille, squinting, said, 'Fine.' She poked the whole thing into her mouth. She exaggerated its passage down her oesophagus. 'See? All gone.'

'I can see.'

'I'm actually a vegetarian.'

'Seems that way.' Beth kneaded her temples. A smooth moan. She tried to attach a romance to the pain but she hadn't even been working hard. The red was almost gone and the grant application draft was still in its plastic sleeve.

Tennille said, 'Jeremy was a vegetarian.'

Pain arched between Beth's eyes. 'Please don't talk about him right now.'

'For like a week,' Tennille continued. 'But then I caught him eating a whole roast chicken from Coles.'

Beth laughed. Tennille was delighted and seemed ready to launch into more anecdotes. Beth swallowed her wine in one gulp. She needed air.

'Do you want to go for a walk?' She hoped the girl would want to stay indoors.

'Yes, please.'

Outside, the moonlight ghosted the short path behind the cabin that led into the bush. Tennille put on her ballet flats and a jumper and she took the lead. Her hair was tucked into her collar in a smooth brown wave. She really was gorgeous. Slight and open and light. Funny in her own way. A pretty little thing, Beth's mother would have said.

'And you're an actual scientist?' Tennille asked.

'I am.' Beth stepped over fallen branches. 'Conservation, wildlife. At the moment: possums.'

She slipped her mobile phone out of her pocket, held it high. Still nothing. The unsent messages to Jeremy were flagged with red exclamation marks. Beth remembered a creek, not far from there. She breathed deeply, hoping the freezing air might flush out her headache.

From up ahead Tennille asked, 'Did you know that people used to think mountains grew like trees?'

'Mountains?'

'Up and out.' Tennille mimicked the growth with her hands. 'Over time, which I guess is why nobody stopped to ask why they couldn't see it happening.'

'How do you know that?'

'I read it somewhere, Beth.' Her name sounded strange coming out of Tennille's mouth.

Beth had lectured at university, often students about Tennille's age. High-achieving kids straight from school who fell apart days before the first exam. Mediocre ones, resilient and cheerful, their notebooks filled with nonsense. She angled her phone skywards.

As they walked, Beth felt herself being swarmed by a heavy-underwater-drifting, truly drunk feeling, so she made Tennille sit on damp leaf-litter while she delivered a lecture on endangered possums that were once thought to be extinct. She told her about the moths they needed for food. Wild cats – Beth would later remember forcing a groggy point about wild cats.

'Your possums,' Tennille asked, 'will they survive?'

'They're not my possums, but I hope so.' Beth watched Tennille massage the earth with her hands. 'What does your mum think? Your parents, I should say. About Jeremy.'

'Try to imagine, Beth, two people who could give less of a shit what their daughter does.'

Tennille stood and headed off, quickening on the track, sticks snapping under her shoes. She placed her hands on grey tree trunks, from one to another, like an animal finding her way. *Up and out. Over time.* The mountain was an impenetrable lump of rock, isolated, alienating, frightening. Suddenly, Beth had great, expansive love for the girl. She even felt an atom of love for Jeremy because maybe he was nice to Tennille in a way that was new for her. Beth felt many atoms of love for true and steadfast Danny, and atoms of love for her own mother and father, who never had two cents to rub together, but who managed to send Beth and her brothers to school with firm-soled shoes, and who still asked their daughter to post them photocopies of all her journal articles.

The phone in her hand made a swooping sound. The messages to Jeremy had gone from unsent to delivered.

A sign.

You can't insist on signs, her mother used to say. You can't insist on clean hotel carpet or a holiday every year or Christmas ham that lasts past December or cars that never break down. Or a head clear of pain, or the fat of a bogong moth to sustain a possum through hibernation.

'Tennille, wait!'

A minute later, although it could have been more, Beth's phone dinged.

You taking the piss? I don't know what you're talking about.

By the time Beth caught up, Tennille had taken off her shoes and was standing as straight and pale as a reed in a stream of water that was cold enough to burn. Tennille pointed both hands down at the water, grinning. 'Whose idea was this? I can't feel anything. Not just my feet – nothing.'

'Jeremy texted back. He said he doesn't have a girlfriend.'

'Of course he'd say that.'

'What will you do now?' Beth asked. 'Would you like to stay?'

'I guess I'll stay, yeah.'

'I'll take you home tomorrow. I can't drive tonight. Put your shoes on, hey?'

They walked back to the cabin in the dark, Beth leading the way. Inside, Tennille looked towards the fold-out couch. Beth lifted a stack of bed linen out of the storage box that doubled as a footrest. She inhaled the air: it smelt like vinegar in the dim, warm home of her grandmother.

'I don't think you're a bad person,' Beth said.

'I know that,' Tennille said. She caught a pillowcase up by its corner and it unfolded like a flag. 'Neither do I.'

North

In the campervan heading north from Leeds to Whitby, Amy sat in the back passenger seat beside her brother, Robert, who was ill from eating the whole packet of Jammie Dodgers. Amy's broken left arm throbbed inside its cast. The scent of jonquils honeyed the air and she held her breath, straining across with her good arm to wind the window up.

Traffic was slow, one lane in each direction, passing through the Yorkshire moors. Finally, a parking spot at a lookout opened up and their dad shifted gears and pulled in next to a dozen other campervans. Amy climbed out and removed the gum she'd been chewing since London. She wrapped it in its square of paper to leave behind on the seat. She and Robert followed other tourists, other families, and stepped over a low, steel rope fence to gaze at the shallow hills. Dad handed his new camera to a teenage boy and asked him to take a couple of pictures.

Before this trip, Dad had tried to explain the part of the world he'd come from, where their mum's mother still lived. Amy hadn't understood what the moors were and, even standing here with the brittle, patchy purple, brown-and-black land falling behind them, she still couldn't say. She stood to the right of her brother and tucked her cast behind his back.

The boy took one photo, then wound on the camera for another, while their hair spun in the hot wind.

Back in the campervan they tuned into the BBC World Service because it was the closest thing to the ABC, which her dad had been missing.

'They used to listen to this during the war,' he said. 'Families would crowd around it.'

'Which war?' She pulled her knees up to her chin.

'The second one.'

Amy returned the gum to her mouth, relishing its plasticky suck, getting plainer and safer as the hours wore on.

On the radio, there was more talk of the massacre in that place called Srebrenica. Of machine guns and children starving in the midsummer heat. It had been a week since the murders. The whisper of something broken on the continent they were visiting.

'I'll turn it down a bit,' Dad said, reaching forward.

'How did they die?' Robert asked Amy. Strangely child-like, almost remorseful. She knew then that her brother had been having bad thoughts about those people.

They arrived in Whitby after lunch, lurching through the town's tight streets as Amy tried to follow the map laid open on her legs. The houses were white with brown roofs, and had cats in their windows. On the hill above the harbour stood the ruins of Whitby Abbey – they would go there, Dad promised. He was excited, his first time back home since he'd had kids. In the driver's seat, he ducked his head to show how small he and his friends used to make themselves to squeeze inside the abbey's stone coffins. Scaring each other with, *I vant to suck your blood*, back then always smoking, always drinking, sometimes bringing their girlfriends along to look out to the North Sea. He hoped he might see all those friends and girlfriends again. They'd meet up in town, while Amy and Robert were with their nan and cousin Pippa.

At the flat on Scoresby Terrace, their dad shifted suitcases inside as Nan kissed Amy and her brother. 'You're here, you're here,' she said. 'Just in time for the baby. Pippa's due any day now.'

Amy had seen her grandmother twice in Australia. Once after Robert was born, and then, with Pippa, at the funeral. Two years had passed and Nan revealed herself to be shorter than Amy remembered. In her letters, Nan often wrote about getting her hair set. This, then – a head of small, neat, grey curls – must be what she meant.

Robert put his arms around Nan's waist and sighed. 'I'm tired.'

'I want to see Pippa,' Amy said.

Their dad emerged, twirling the car keys around his finger. 'I'll take her over, Pat. I can drop her at Pippa's on my way.'

Pippa was dressed in her uniform from the pub, watching television. She lay back on the couch, her legs bent over pillows and her belly mountainous in the middle. Amy didn't know how to hug her, especially with one arm fixed in its cast.

'Just gone into labour, can you believe it,' Pippa said. 'Early days though, ha, so don't worry.'

Amy had expected screaming and swearing, blood and sweat. On the lounge room floor was a toy car playmat and a baby swing with its packaging stuffed into a box. To her right, in the kitchen, a man tipped a tin of baked beans into a frypan filled with egg. He stirred vigorously.

'This is Owen,' Pippa said.

Amy concentrated on Owen's face so she didn't have to look at the beans. Beside him stood a tall boy, blonde hair parted down the centre, blue short-sleeved shirt with a collar. He was like all the boys back home, but prettier, paler, cleaner.

'That's Owen's brother. Scott, this is my cousin Amy, the one who's visiting.'

'Hi,' Amy said.

'Hi.'

Owen opened the fridge and poured Pippa a glass of juice. She seized up, silent, then raised a watch to her face. 'Still the same,' she said.

Amy sat down cross-legged next to the TV. Scott lowered himself to the carpet beside her. She looked side-on at Pippa's black trousers – the baby right there, centimetres away, about to cross a threshold – and flinched at the flash of pain in her broken arm.

'Did you hear?' Owen asked. 'Pippa didn't even know she was pregnant till four months.'

'Three-and-a-half.' Pippa narrowed her eyes at Amy. 'Makes me sound like I'm not right in the head.' She sipped her juice. 'It happens. Hormones and the pill, and you think you're just getting fat. You've got all that to look forward to.'

'I'm only fourteen,' Amy said. She thought of Natasha and Rachel back home, who'd both had sex at least twice and who spoke at length about whether they would ever consider having an abortion.

Scott leant in close. 'What happened to your arm?'

In her mind, Amy batted away the truth. 'Netball,' she said. 'I play keeper. I went up for the ball and landed funny.' Her skin tingled with the lie, with his scent.

Owen tipped the contents of the saucepan onto a plate and moved to Pippa's side, rubbing the back of her head.

BBC News came on, and fragments flashed during the introduction. People ran from a train station in Paris. A comet had been discovered. UN trucks sat stationary beside fat green trees. There was Brian Lara, saluting the crowd, helmet in hand. Temperatures were due to rise in the north of England: children and the elderly should stay hydrated.

The three of them watched Pippa at the start of another contraction. She grabbed her breath in one big mouthful. Amy marked this moment in her life, there on Pippa's floor. The pain that she knew Pippa was experiencing – where did it come from? How did it start? Was the baby in pain? – coupled with the memory of her arm breaking last month after the fight with Dad over food, over how little she'd been eating. Robert had watched from the other side of the dining table, chicken bones scattered, their father sobbing. Amy's anxiety had been grainy and fibrous, and had never smoothed out.

She thought of her own mother going through the same thing as Pippa fourteen years ago, perhaps with the TV on and eggs on the stove. And, yes, Amy was hungry for her mother. She felt hollow.

'What do you need?' Scott asked Pippa. He spoke very kindly, Amy noticed. Pippa's eyes were shut tight and she whimpered. Still no screaming.

Then the contraction was over and Pippa resurfaced, shuffling forward on the couch to sit upright. 'I really felt that one,' she said. 'How's Australia? Nan's been talking non-stop about you coming here.'

'She and Dad won't get along.'

Pippa nodded. 'But it's you she wants. And Robert.'

'Don't know how you stand the heat where you're from,' Owen said. Amy's eyes locked onto the yellow egg on the end of his silver fork. She held her breath.

'It's hot here for two, three months, *max*,' he continued, 'and I want to top myself.'

'Love?' Pippa patted Owen's hand. 'We'll call the hospital soon. Amy, what're you doing this afternoon?'

'Nothing.'

Owen scraped his cutlery on the plate. 'Scott, take Amy somewhere.'

'Like where?'

'How about the ruins?' Amy asked.

As they were leaving, she waved her hand towards Pippa's belly. Whatever she wanted to express felt stuck in her gut, like food. 'I hope you have a good time,' she said, as though Pippa was off to a party.

They walked up the hill towards Whitby Abbey, talking about school, sport, the baby. The hot breeze swelled against their bodies on the last push to the peak, where they moved silently through the cemetery. Beyond that, Amy saw arches and the toothy blocks of the old stone abbey cut out against the denim sky.

'How old is it?'

'At least a thousand years.'

Below them, the North Sea spread its infinite body against the cliff. Amy felt very light against the wind. As if sensing this, Scott reached for her hand, held it, then slipped his arm around her waist, the first boy to do that. She felt even lighter.

It was almost dinnertime, she realised, seeing the shadows of the ruins arranged on the grass. She wondered what Nan was cooking for tea and whether Nan would fight with her, or be sad, or even notice if she ate at all.

Scott's arm still circled her waist, unmentioned. He touched the cloth of her sling.

'There they are.' Amy pointed at an outline, human-shaped, the remains of coffins, sunken into the grass beneath an arch. The slabs of stone put a briny taste in her mouth.

'Dad told me about these,' she said. 'I'm going to squeeze in.'

Scott looked at her as if she was crazy and then, differently, sideways, as if he was going to kiss her, which he did.

★

A day later, Amy stood beneath the light outside the flat on Scoresby Terrace. She wondered if Nan was still napping. Out all afternoon, Amy had met up with Scott again, this time at the pub where Pippa and Owen worked, a chalkboard announcing the baby's arrival: *Eight pounds eight and doing great!* She longed to tell Nan about Scott. Having come this far, knowing Nan so little, she might discover a lot in the telling, in the listening.

Across the narrow road, two police officers lowered themselves into a car. One wrote in a notebook. The other tossed his helmet onto the back seat. Amy watched them drive away into the gentle, stretched-out dusk that felt so different from the ferocious summers back in Townsville.

She knocked. Nan wrenched the door open and peered up, then hugged her. The hallway smelt of cleaning liquid. The sharpness of pine.

In the kitchen, Nan lifted the lid off a tin of sweets. 'Here,' she said, shifting the tin towards the fingers of Amy's right hand.

'No, thanks.'

'You're very thin.'

'They make me gag.'

Nan put the lid back on without losing eye contact. 'Your dad's in some trouble.'

'What? Dad is?'

'Put your things on the bed,' Nan said.

Amy stared.

'Go on.'

So Amy took off her cardigan because she had nothing

else with her and draped it over the edge of the bed. Three huge teddy bears in pink satin dresses were lined up on the pillows. A quick thought pressed into Amy, about how easy it was for adults to behave like children.

Nan called out, not waiting till she returned. 'He's going to find it hard to get back on that plane in a week. He's in some real strife, the silly man.'

'That's why the police were here?'

'You saw them, then? I'll not have this.' Nan reached for a tea towel on the oven handle and squeezed it. 'I thought, yes, I'll pay for their flights, even his. It's the only way to see my grandchildren. Eileen next door says I'm a fool. Course I'm a fool. I am. My daughter was. The smoking may have killed her, but what came before that—' Nan brushed her other hand across the bench and the tin fell to the floor. 'But I wanted to see my grandchildren.'

Amy asked, 'What did he do?'

Nan hitched up her dress and crouched down one knee at a time to pick up the sweets. 'He started drinking, didn't he, with friends from years ago. Came across people they didn't like. I shouldn't say any more since you're … But the police found him along the beach early this morning. Your dad spent the rest of the day locked up. Come all this way just to … A fool!'

That was one word for it. Years ago, at a theme park, when Robert was too young to say such things, he'd called their dad *a big fucking kid* as they watched him squeeze into a seat on a mini train that chugged around a track. Other people started waving, laughing, till Robert and Amy, too, started waving, started laughing. Maybe it would be useful one day. Maybe it would be exciting to have adventures with a dad as silly as that.

In the middle of the night, Amy left Robert on the floor of their bedroom, asleep. She padded down to the kitchen, which was small and smelt of bacon fat. She didn't turn on the light. In a pair of long, button-through pyjamas with frills at the wrists, Amy opened the fridge. Sweets, like those in Nan's tin, made her gag. So did seeds from strawberries and tomatoes and kiwifruit. Mushrooms hadn't been safe for years. She'd once vomited the carrot her dad had persuaded her to eat, so carrot was out. Any meat other than tiny bits of tinned fish chewed very slowly were out. Broccoli and green beans tasted like the earth, like dirt. Bright yellow cheese she felt in her stomach for days. Vegemite and honey stuck in her throat. There'd been arguments about uneaten sausages and, of course, the chicken. By the time they boarded the aeroplane for London, Amy was down to food that was white, cream and pale brown. She felt none of the panic her dad felt. On the plane she ate bread and rice, and mashed potato that was stirred through with salad dressing and licked from a spoon.

There was the sound of a key in a lock. One shoe, then another, dropped in the hall.

'Dad?'

'Amy, love.'

'What happened?'

He watched her from behind the fridge door. 'Nothing bad. Don't get upset.'

Amy nursed her left arm with her right.

'What did you tell Nan about your arm?'

'Nothing. She didn't ask.' She let that sit. She let him wonder at all the people she may have told. 'Are you banned from getting on the plane?'

The light of the fridge shone on his hands as he gestured wildly. He moved towards her. 'Banned? What did Pat tell you? I have the tickets. No, I'm not *banned*. We can go *home*.'

Amy lay listening to the sound of her dad's voice in competition with Nan's. Flat on her back next to Robert. Brother and sister. The easy conspiracy of being frightened, apart. She folded back the covers and went downstairs and out into the night.

At sunset, beside the pub where Pippa worked, Amy pushed coins into a payphone and waited.

The phone was snatched up after one ring.

'It's Owen.'

'This is Amy, Pippa's cousin.'

His words were slower and softer this time. 'Where have you been all day? Pippa's worried.'

'Is Scott there?'

He wasn't, so Amy gave Owen the message: ask Scott to meet her at the pub, as soon as possible. They both paused while the baby screamed in the background, and then Amy hung up.

She entered the pub and sat by a window. In a dish in the centre of the table were single-serve packets of mayonnaise and tomato sauce. Her mouth tasted coppery.

A vision came to Amy: a cottage in Whitby with a light on at night, fish on Friday and chips with vinegar. Helping Pippa push the baby in a pram down narrow streets. Boats bobbing on the water.

She would stay. With Scott. Yes.

A lightness in her head made her turn and she saw her dad walk past the window. He stood at a distance, not noticing her. He glanced at the sign above the door then looked away for a long time in the other direction. She liked to think he seemed worried, that he was searching for her.

But she wanted to be alone. To be at a distance from everything, to fill herself up.

She pushed her chair further from the window, and sat with her right hand in her lap. At the bar were two young men, handsome, lean as dogs, spinning coasters between them. Amy watched the men for signs of unhappiness, for signs of interest in her, for signs of peace. Yes, here was the town where her life would happen. And if Scott didn't come, she'd simply choose another one of these boys, and stay forever.

A Man About a Moon

Riding on the bike down Macquarie Street Hill with her mother. To the beach. To see a man about a puppy, about a puppy and a moon. Hug the towel close, because maybe the day will warm up enough for a swim. Straddle her mother's bike with her short, thin legs. Don't let go. Let her mother ride the bike as fast as she wants. Let her stick to high speed, to what she's used to when she cycles to work at the milk factory, when she cycles home with three pints of milk and one pint of cream, to stir through their porridge, to sprinkle with sugar – 'We need to fatten you up, Susan.' Wonder at the name of the man's puppy and the colour of its fur. Practise the name she might give a puppy if she ever got one, as the bike whizzes past the bait shop and the fruit shop and the big yard with the bright red heavy trucks lined up. Whisper, 'Here, Buzz,' to herself while she looks up at the soft creamy underside of her mother's neck that shudders along to the rhythm of the bike, while her mother stares ahead towards the sea. Wonder what her mother is humming. Hop down from the parked bike along the row of shops with their high white awnings and signs to attract the tourists. Button her coat and tuck the thermos of tea into the fold of her towel. Look for a man in a mustard-coloured jacket, who will stand out on account of the empty beach, on account of everyone being inside and excited on this winter's day. Try to forget the fever that's kept her home from school for two days. Tell herself to conjure 'bright thoughts!' in the wise and patient way she would train her puppy to return time and again to its mat. Keep her eyes open and take her mother's sweaty hand after she locks up the bike, and climb a short hill to cross the road to the beach. Wiggle her toes in her shoes across the sand. Locate the man in the mustard jacket, who smiles kindly at them and says, 'Quickly now. Let's not miss it' – the moon! Don't miss the moon! Notice how much nicer the houses are here, how they're not as tightly packed together as the houses on Esther Street, how there's room for great big wedges of midday sunlight to shine between them. Follow her mother, who tucks in close to this man and listens as he points things out on the walk, till they're out the front of a grand white house and there's a woman waving at them from beneath an arch above the front stairs and her mother is nudging her in the back, saying, 'Quick. This is it.' Meet the man's wife, who smells like lavender and says 'Susan' with a lisp. Shuffle into the man's lounge room to see a television on four legs and a puppy nosing about in the corner before it scampers over to prod its brown paws on her shoes. Settle into the couch with her mother and the man and his wife and the hot tea and a dash of milk from the refrigerator, shooing the puppy away from the lip of the cup. Test the voice in her sore throat, saying, 'Look,' to the puppy while an astronaut bounces on the screen.

Hear the television's beeps and a sound like the ocean rushing. See the ladder and the underwater shadows on the astronaut's glassy face. Feel her heart swell like the first breath in a balloon. To wonder what all the other children in her class are doing, now that school is closed for the day. To feel certain she's the only one whose mother has a bike, whose mother has a friend from the factory with a nice wife and a television. To look at nothing but the screen and the puppy in her lap. She knows the moon is in the sunny sky outside, but for the first time it's up there at the same time as it's down here.

The Republic

The plane lands. The man beside me, a solar energy salesman, unbuckles his seatbelt before he's supposed to and tells me once more: 'Enjoy your pilgrimage.' I packed only carry-on luggage, so in the terminal I go straight to the car rental desk, collect the keys, say no to extra insurance and yes to a GPS, and I pull out of Heathrow onto the motorway. I've eaten nothing since breakfast except some plastic-wrapped banana bread and a too-sweet juice that the salesman grabbed from the flight attendant and shook for me. I tap the address into the GPS and I watch cars and motorbikes and lorries edge past me in the motorway traffic. I think the route to the cemetery will look familiar, but it's been years. The plaque at Kit's headstone says, *As we loved you, so we will miss you.* Even as a kid, I knew that no adults in Kit's life, certainly not in his family, talked like that. I grip the steering wheel, hating the drag of the rental car's clutch. The cemetery closes in three hours.

★

Kit told it like this: Manchester United were on a plane to Brussels to play a semi-final and the plane hit turbulence and the pilot thought it would be all right, because he had Manchester United on board – no pilot is going to be so unlucky that he crashes a plane with the entire team from Man U on board, plus all the coaching staff, and the reserve players, and some of the wives, too. And the pilot is right: no one *is* that unlucky and he gets the plane through the turbulence and everyone gets an extra tomato juice and a bag of peanuts. But then, five hours later, the pilot is walking through Brussels, something like thirty minutes after he would have been walking had there not been turbulence, and a car mounts the kerb and hits him and he dies right there and then. And Man U wins three-nil, and they catch their flight back to England, and no one even finds out about the pilot. Well, his wife and kids and the bosses at the airline find out, but certainly not Manchester United and their coaching staff.

'Is that true?' I asked Kit as we watched television in my lounge room.

'One hundred per cent,' he said.

'But how do you *know*?' I said.

'I don't *know*. But it's true.'

Kit knew things were true even when they might not be.

'Did you know there are people who decide to become their own countries?' he asked, switching between shows.

'You can't just become a country,' I said. 'There are already all the countries.' But as I said it, I couldn't pinpoint the number. And if there was a number, why that number? Why not one? Why not a million tiny crumbs of soil sliced the whole way around the world?

'I'm just saying people do it, Cora,' Kit said. 'They set up their bit of land, and make a flag, and give themselves a name.'

'And then what?'

Kit shrugged. 'I suppose they wait to see if anyone notices.'

A week later, when Mrs Maslow asked who had brought along an idea for the class play, Kit and Alex and Srinath and Pilar put up their hands. Kit went last, rising to his feet behind his desk, though none of the others had done that. He started: *Did you know? There's this man, or woman maybe, who has set up his own land with a flag and laws and everything.* And no one did know, not even Mrs Maslow, who added Kit's idea to the fourth column on the blackboard, next to Srinath's idea for a play about kickboxing.

Mrs Maslow loved the possibilities for costumes and props, a hero and a villain. The opportunity was there, she said, to showcase the talent in the class, to be grown up, but also fun. The play would have something to say, in this multicultural age, about who people were and where they were from. She asked for a vote and Kit, still the only one in the room on his feet, shot his hand in the air. Then Alex and Srinath and Pilar and I and everyone else voted for his play. *The Republic*, he had said. *By Kit Oswald.*

★

'What is The Republic famous for?' Mrs Maslow asked from the front of the room. I looked around, but I didn't know what to say. I could tell my classmates felt it too, this small and curious uncertainty.

Mrs Maslow's feathery hair was silver. She held a piece of chalk between her fingers and tucked her top into the waistband of her skirt. No one answered.

'What do they make?' she asked. 'What does the landscape look like? Are there mountains?'

'Yes,' Kit said.

I turned to him. Others did too. How did he know this? The image of The Republic was right there, behind his eyes. I wanted to see what he could see.

'Okay. What else?'

Kit set his teeth to the flap of skin on the side of his thumb. When he brought it out of his mouth, his thumb was bleeding. In the past I'd seen Mrs Maslow hold his hands in hers and wrap his fingers in plasters from the first-aid kit. He did it when he was nervous, he told me.

'They're famous for a battle of independence,' Kit said. 'David and Goliath, and they won, because The Republic is an island and they could see the invading enemy coming on ships across the ocean.'

Our teacher nodded. 'Why are they being invaded?'

'Beer!' Kit said, and we laughed. Before Mrs Maslow could protest, he switched. 'No, wait. *Milk*. The place is full of cows. And the enemy are attacking because they want the cows, for cloning. Like Dolly the sheep.'

After lunch, Mrs Maslow told us to sit at our desks to design The Republic's flag. She reminded us that it was an island, with black and white cows that were desired by the enemy.

'What's your favourite flag?' Kit asked me. As he drew, he stuck out his tongue.

'I don't know. Don't have one.'

'Bet you do. Do you like ours or America's better?'

My answer was ready, even though I hadn't known it. 'America's. Definitely.'

'A good flag is important,' Kit said. 'You should be able to draw it from memory. See it from a distance. Stars are good, lines are good. Do plain colours, like green for land and blue for the ocean.'

He peered over and landed his elbow on my paper. 'Cora,' he said. 'That's a mess.'

'Oh.' The idea dropped into my head that I should never have tried this, that of course I was going to be bad at it. I folded mine, creased it severely in half.

'But it's just a first draft,' he continued. 'Do another one.'

I took his stack of draft flags – a whole *stack* – between my fingers. 'Show me,' I said.

Kit lived with his mum, who wasn't really his mum, and she was away from the flat a lot. Mrs Maslow used to give Kit glue and coloured pencils to take home. He wrote in journals that were nothing more than half-inch piles of paper stapled together from the stationery cupboard.

Kit's first drawing, the one on top, would be the winner. A green circle in the centre of a blue ocean. Five yellow stars were fanned out like a crown above.

★

The night of the play was cold, an icy wind hushing about my ears as I collected my costume off the clothesline: red and white knickerbockers, and a jacket with war medals that had been cut from a Weetabix box. I called down for

83

Mum and Dad, and on the drive to school we sang to the Spice Girls on the radio together.

Other classes performed that night as well. A scene from *A Midsummer Night's Dream*. A younger class had adapted *The Little Match Girl*. There were lights and a hot chocolate stand in the foyer of the school hall, and Mum and Dad sat and waved enough for Kit and for me, as Mrs Maslow pulled open the curtains.

Kit took centre stage to deliver the prologue: *Once upon a time, a group of brave explorers left their terrible land to set up a republic out on the ocean. The island became their new home.* Palm trees hugged the edges of the stage. The rest of us crouched as soldiers from opposing armies. I stood, stage right, in a freeze with my arms wide to show strength, caught in a moment of reverence for Kit, The Republic's leader.

Offstage, the flag hung from its pole: Kit said that the audience shouldn't see it till the very end. He knew about timing, about waiting for the right moment. Kit's life was all about getting nipped and chased and baited. He used to go walking late at night with older boys from his building. Together they would cross the bridge into town to press themselves into the dark, their jackets zipped up to their throats. As a pack, they plucked bits of trouble out of nowhere, looking for ways to get noticed. In daylight hours, Kit's adult brother Gerry stalked the neighbourhood with his shirt off, past the playground with dozens of little kids, his pit bull terrier chained around his waist.

The script that Kit and Mrs Maslow had written couldn't have lasted more than ten minutes. In the final scene, the battle of independence over and the invaders defeated, we stood in our army jackets, patting the spotted plywood cows. I felt a sheen of sweat and a trembling nervousness while I grinned out towards the blazing lights. Kit raised the flag and the audience cheered, and Mrs Maslow promised to give him the flag at school as a souvenir, since it had all been his idea.

But Kit was not in class the next morning. Or the next, or the next. Within days we found out his beloved Manchester United jersey was still in his room. Police officers, a man and a woman, came to class to speak to us. And then different ones came to our house, and asked me questions about a man Kit might have known, while I sat in Mum's lap, sucking the tips of my hair, and ticking with fear.

★

I pull up on the street outside Dad's house, ease my foot off the clutch. Lights are on in all four windows, except for my old room, upstairs, which is dark. Before I can knock, Dad answers the door, wearing his waxed cotton mac and striped pyjama trousers.

'How was your flight?' he asks, kissing me and smelling of tobacco and Weetabix with milk.

'Good, Dad. I'm pretty tired.'

'Of course, love. I've got your bed made up. Have a shower if you like.'

In the kitchen, he sets a plate of buttered toast in front of me and a mug of tea. I'd forgotten the metallic taste on the rim of all the mugs in the house. How I went through a stage where I refused to drink from them, instead sipping from Mum and Dad's wedding set of crystal goblets. Years later, after they'd gotten divorced – Mum in her new flat with a computer and a modem, and Dad still at the house with an adopted stray cat – I found the goblets in a box and carried them to a charity shop so Dad wouldn't have to. But I couldn't bear to leave them behind. I came back and hid them in the attic.

I nod towards his armchair. 'What's in the paper?' I ask.

'Ten thousand people die from air pollution in London,' Dad says. 'Every year.'

'Like from petrol? Cars and planes?'

'What a way to go.' He coughs, bumps a fist against his chest.

I think of all those other ways to go. A bomb at the heart of a red bus, its insides pulled apart in quick bites. An aeroplane plunging to earth, lit from within by panic. A body, left for dead, bleeding like an inky stamp on a beach.

'Your mum said to tell you she'll be home all day tomorrow. I'll drive you over there if you like.'

'Can't wait to see her,' I say.

'Good of you to stay here tonight, Cora.'

Beside me, Dad drums his fingers in one long line on the table. I cover his hand in mine.

'And the other thing?' Dad says. 'How'd that go?'

In the silence we notice the noise from the television and Dad eases out of his seat to mute it.

I say, 'It looked like no one had been there in a while.'

He nods. 'I should go up for the lad.' His voice collapses in on itself.

Here in the kitchen, I can't stop myself recalling the undergrowth scent of the cemetery, the chapel at its centre with a honeycombed roof and buckled walls heaped with leaves and branches. The cemetery was silent, dusk coming early in December – I'd forgotten how early. At Kit's headstone I took out the flag and draped it across my palms. I should have ironed it, and I wished I'd made the stitching on the five yellow stars tighter. But this was it: I'd be back on an aeroplane in a few days, heading home. I laid the cloth out like a blanket beneath the plaque. Stupidly, somewhere between Sydney and Abu Dhabi I'd told the solar energy salesman about the reason for my trip back to London. A murderer had been caught, after all these years, and convicted. I needed to get on a plane and hear him be sentenced. Put it to rest. When I pulled the notebook out of my handbag and unfolded the flag from between two pages, the salesman didn't try to touch it.

Dad rests his hands in his lap and stares at the uneaten toast. 'It's not like I'm busy,' he says. 'You've come all this way. That's not a holiday for you, love.'

Dad looks at me, huddled with sadness. Our cardboard-brown kitchen, when I was young, never felt big enough for all our dinner plates and teacups and electric frypans with broken, greasy handles pinning down my Maths homework. Now, when it's just Dad, the kitchen seems even smaller and far, far emptier, and I doubt he cooks much of anything for himself. I feel like we're inside an amber beer bottle that swims with a set of tiny chairs and table, and a tiny bread bin with its mouth wide open. And over on that window, the one facing the backyard, Kit might have run his knuckles before appearing at the door to receive a ham sandwich from Mum. He would have sat on the floor with his back against Dad's shins while we watched the football together.

You won't always feel like this, is what Dad said when Kit's body was found on the beach, at the base of a sand dune, tucked behind rocks. *Yes, I will*, I told him, horror burning right through me, picturing Mrs Maslow cradling Kit's hands. *Blink, blink*, my eyes went.

Dad spins a mug on its base. We watch its movements together. His voice is animated with forced brightness. 'I've just had the news on. That man is sure to get life,' Dad says. 'No loopholes. Witnesses and everything, although why you wouldn't say anything all those years ago is beyond me. That other prisoner he confessed to. Straightforward.'

Things should be straightforward. Drawn from memory, is what Kit told me they had to be.

Foundling

The baby bird falls from the tree right in front of us. Neil warns me we'll hurt it if we pick it up, but still he edges closer to the wet handful of feathers on the uneven ground.

'Martin, don't,' Neil says. 'If you touch it and the mother comes back she won't want it.'

'But she's not here, is she?' I say. 'What if she's dead?'

The bell rings for dinner and I realise how hungry I am. The sun is setting beyond the fence, where blocks of stone bulge from the soil like buck teeth.

The bird tilts back its head and utters desperate cries. Its eyes are blueberries stuck beneath skin.

'It doesn't have many feathers.' Neil wipes his nose on his sleeve. He's been sick for weeks. Matron says she's tried everything. 'It must be freezing,' he says.

I have my jumper and, underneath that, the grey shirts we all wear. I could take the baby bird to dinner with me, and eat with one hand and warm the bird secretly with the other. None of the other boys has ever brought a bird to dinner.

'We can't just leave it here alone,' I say.

'But it's nature,' Neil says, sniffling. 'If it's supposed to die, that's what's meant to happen.'

Neil likes to pretend he grew up on a big farm with horses and dogs, and sheep for shearing anytime you wanted. I tell him that he doesn't know anything.

The bird cries and cries. I lean down. It flops sideways and feels like a wet balloon against my skin. I should have washed my hands, but it's too late. I untuck my shirt and fold it up to make a pouch, hoping the buttons won't hurt it.

'Martin, don't.'

'There, there,' I whisper. 'I'll give you some of my dinner.'

At the table, I lower my head and pray while Mr Jarrett tells us to nourish our bodies and be grateful. I slip a piece of beef into my mouth, chew it, and pretend to cough. I still haven't washed my hands. The meat is soft in my fingers as I worm it beneath my jumper, above the waistband of my trousers, and into the pouch. I find the beak, but the bird is still, and my fingers can't wake it. I leave the meat there just in case.

On the wall near me are photographs of the Queen on her visit to Australia. In one, she smiles at a girl in the crowd handing her flowers. Beside the frame, a curtain flutters at the window and, outside, a bird lands and fidgets on a tree branch.

Here is the mother, back to look for her baby that we took.

I look at the mean and hungry faces of the other boys: they must've stolen birds before too. All the mother birds out in the garden must hate living here with us boys with our loud voices and heavy boots. And every time they have a baby to feed and love, one of us runs away with it.

★

I leave the orphanage before Neil does and I move to Sydney. One afternoon I'm sitting alone in the Botanic Gardens when a woman asks me for the time. Helen works at a big parking garage nearby, taking coins as people exit. She hates it, so she goes for long breaks out in the sun.

'No one ever wants to talk to me in there,' Helen says. 'Everyone's in a rush.'

I thought Sydney would be a good place to know nobody, but Helen takes hold of me and talks enough for the both of us. In her voice – in her answers barked at ticket collectors and vows laughed at the altar of St Peter's and sobs heaved when she gives birth to Danielle two days before my twenty-ninth birthday – there are pockets of relief.

We buy the old house in Parramatta, certain that we'll live there for the rest of our lives, taking the train to work, coming home for dinner, having a kid and a dog and a packed-up car in the driveway once a year for a trip along the coast. Except I have no family to visit up north in Queensland, no friends who are presentable enough for introductions – but Helen knew that before we got married.

I keep the letter locked in a drawer in the study. Every few months, while Helen sleeps, I set my glass on the desk and take out the single sheet of paper. Its letterhead of names sounds like top-order batsmen: Benson Dawson Cleave.

I have a case, they write. They will fight it and seek damages.

They want to hear from me. There are others.

★

Danielle cuts her first tooth, learns to wave and clap and crawl and walk, and Helen and I don't talk about much of anything except what the baby is doing, or what she needs, or what sort of mood she's in. Dani chatters a little, and babbles constantly. She points at objects with the confidence of a magician. One day she finds a feather on the kitchen floor and lifts it to her mouth. She whispers a little message to it. She strokes it across her lips. My heart waxes with love.

She says, 'Bah.'

'Not in your mouth, sweetheart.' I run the feather along the soles of her feet. I say, 'Tickle, tickle. Have you ever seen a feather before?' Her fat feet writhe, nuzzling the floor. Dani flaps her arms at me. My head feels heavy and tight.

Helen is convinced television is bad for children, so when she's at work, I take Dani to the park, or over to see the ships in the harbour. Once, in the lounge room, with Dani on my lap watching *Play School*, I look up to see Helen framed by the door, holding something.

'It's just *Play School*,' I say.

'Turn it off,' she says. 'I'll take her.'

In Helen's hand is a flutter of oddly cut paper.

'What's that?' I say.

She picks up our daughter, who squeals and fights the end of her fun. Helen leans in to my forehead. A rare kiss.

She passes me a newspaper clipping. The crease runs down the centre of a black and white photograph of boys seated at long tables, their heads bowed, their hands in prayer.

'You should talk about it,' she says.

I open my mouth.

'To someone.'

But less talk. With the poverty of silence comes the richness of withdrawal. A relentless process to unhook the incident from my mind even at the shops or in the shower or, sometime later, by a beach on school holidays, while Helen digs channels with a stick so Dani can see the water approach and feel it spill onto her feet. Later again, driving on the freeway alone, unable to sleep, I crest a rise and a billboard emerges – an ad for toothpaste, a huge photo of teeth – that reminds me of danger all around. Here am I, a foreign object, a foreign body. I just need to do the unhooking. But aren't I safe now?

Helen and Rod meet at a Christmas party. Rod talks a lot. By Easter, Helen and I are separated, and they are engaged. For Dani's birthday, Rod gets her a purple unicorn lamp for her new bedroom, and he tells me I'm welcome at the house anytime.

★

I get up early and catch the bus into the city, past the coffee place where I used to take Dani. She works in the city now, and I could give her a ring. *Remember that Italian cafe where you'd sit at the counter and the owner gave you chocolate frogs?* But she knows about the hearings and would ask if she could be with me, and I want her far away from all the damage.

Through the windows of the bus, the city is raw and eager. To the fearless commuter beside me, I must look like a common flake, slumping into my seat with my head against the window, breathing strangely.

On the steps of Macquarie Tower, just a couple of blocks from the Botanic Gardens where Helen and I first met, I feel people glancing at me, thinking, *Is he one of those poor boys?* I look old, and my jacket isn't necessary in this heat. A charity bloke taps me on the elbow, makes it seem like I'll be doing him a favour to take the extra coffee out of his hands.

'Hey, mate. You want this?'

I shake my head, but my hands feel empty and enormous, so I take the cup.

He nods beside me, sharing my gaze towards the glass doors. He's about Dani's age, with a beard and a tattoo running the length of an arm.

'Been to one of these before?' he asks.

He's figured it out.

They told me I was lucky to have a bed at the orphanage – that my mother had died. But she could be any one of these women going past on Farrer Place, clutching her handbag, pulling a grocery trolley through the peak-hour crowds, taking off her glasses to knead the tender points on the sides of her nose.

Saying she'd died didn't mean anything.

'First time,' I say, wanting to leave it there. But he's given me coffee and not left me standing alone, so I add, 'Long-time listener, first-time caller.'

He chuckles, lifts the cup to his lips and cools it with

his breath. 'Well, if you need anything, I'd be happy to sit with you.'

They've named him on the news. He died eleven years ago, so I guess they're allowed. A file photo catches him stepping out of a white car. His face is slack, his mouth half-open, an unpleasant taste there.

I speak to the dark liquid in the cup. 'I'm not testifying, or anything like that.'

The young man smiles kindly and takes a sip.

★

I lick my fingers clean. The bird really is dead and I'll need to get rid of it. If I wrap it in a shirt and leave it under my pillow in the dormitory, it'll never stay a secret. Jeffrey or Graeme will say it's theirs now. Terry will threaten to chop it up with the hair scissors, one snip at a time.

I look up. Neil has gone, and one of the older boys is already wiping down his table. Placing the bird back beneath the tree might be enough to revive it. And tomorrow, when I go to check, maybe the grass will be empty – the baby bird gone, high above me, soft and fed and warm with its mother. But if it's still there, still dead, then Neil and I can bring a paper bag and collect stones to make a cross.

I touch my belly. A hand touches my shoulder.

'Sir?'

'Martin, what have you got there?' Mr Jarrett's mouth is filled with white dentures that are too big. His blue eyes are puckered around the edges. Terry reckons Mr Jarrett gave him the cricket score once, the time Meckiff had been no-balled four times and Benaud had given him the chop.

'Nothing, Mr Jarrett.'

He stands me up and prises my hand from my stomach. The dead bird dives to the floor.

'Did you take it?' he asks.

'Yes, sir.'

'Was it dead?'

'No, sir.'

'And now a mother bird has lost her baby.'

'Yes, sir. But it's nature.'

'You have to make this right,' he says. 'Pick it up. Come with me.'

We walk the halls till we're outside, heading towards Mr Jarrett's cottage at the end of the garden. Maybe the bird needed something other than the beef from my plate. The corner of a washcloth dipped in milk. A worm wet with dirt, writhing in the centre of my palm.

Mr Jarrett's blue eyes drop down to mine. He pulls a handkerchief from his pocket and takes the bird, lays it on the table and palps my shoulder.

'You shouldn't have taken the bird,' he says.

All the doors and windows in the cottage are open. Through the doorway I see a bathroom, where I can ask to wash my hands. The place smells like mothballs, and the quilt on the bed is stretched tight.

Taking Things Back

It's the twentieth of December and Kayla's little brother, James, finds a department store bag abandoned. Kayla is in a nearby shop, browsing leggings and sports bras. James's hands are sticky from his Bubble O' Bill. Kayla comes back out into the shopping centre, having bought nothing.

'Whose is that?'

James looks up from where he's crouching beside the metal bench. 'I saw it when you went in there. No one's come back for it.' He moves the wad of gum around his mouth.

'Well, leave it,' Kayla says.

'Wonder what's in it.'

'Doesn't matter. Leave it.'

'Let's return it and get the money.'

It strikes Kayla, as she watches her brother stand up, that he could in fact be a total petty criminal at night, out with his friends, and she wouldn't know.

Still. 'You reckon?' she asks.

Shoppers move around them, in and out of stores. Scalloped green wreaths stuck with red and gold baubles hang above their heads. Kayla moves to the bench.

'Give it.'

She peers inside the bag and pulls out a book, then a long grey box. She finds a receipt.

James is thrilled. 'Did they pay cash? How much?'

'Seventy-one ninety. Cash.' She knows how easy now it is to get the money. No real obstacles; it's as good as having the notes and coins in her hand. Maybe the department store will make them sign a bit of paper to be sure they aren't criminals (which they are), and ask questions to check they haven't stolen anything (which they have).

In an hour, or a bit less, Shannon will collect them outside the pet shop on Sullivan Road. Shannon made it clear she'd rather not have to fight for a car park at this time of year, and Kayla wants to stay on her good side. She and James are eight foster families in, and Shannon's house has a pool and two TVs and a sweet white dog and a nasty ginger cat that Kayla secretly plans to win over. Unlike their last three placements, Shannon has no kids of her own. Kayla and James have a bedroom each. Kayla has to share hers with a filing cabinet that blocks the balcony – a Juliet balcony, Shannon says, whatever that means. But for once: privacy. Kayla wanted to warn Shannon about James and all his newfound masturbating. But her New Year's resolution is to let her brother become more independent. If he were a baby he wouldn't need all those boxes of tissues.

James twists the handles of the carrier bag around his fingers. 'We could buy something for Mum.'

Kayla looks longingly at her little brother. The blood is pooling at his fingertips. He's the only person in her life she can hold eye contact with, comfortably, endlessly. Often, on the days when there wasn't enough food for a proper lunch each, James would find her in the playground — Kayla made friends no matter where they turned up — and hand over chips or part of his sandwich. Her habit was to try to hide it, but James never cared who saw and who knew.

Something for Mum. The flimsiness of such an idea — boxed chocolates, a pot plant, a set of bath towels embroidered with daisies to impress visitors — alongside the enormity of what, exactly, their mum needs.

'Fine,' Kayla says. 'Done by two-thirty. Okay?'

They enter the department store, passing throw rugs and shelves of rice cookers and green picnic cups stacked into the shape of a Christmas tree. They head to the nearest counter and wait. A round, black-clad woman motions, smiling, for them to go over to her register. Kayla lifts the bag to the counter. She releases the receipt from her fingers.

'We'd like to return this, please.'

'Oh.' The woman's smile thins.

'We only just bought it.'

The shop assistant slides out the book. It's a romance, Kayla figures, noting the man in a cape beside a horse, and the windswept woman beside them. Rubbish, her mother would call it, forcefully.

'There's more?' With her hand inside the bag, the shop assistant eyes them. A magic trick. A game of lucky dip. Her hand finds the box. She pulls it out: stainless-steel salad servers. 'Anything the matter?'

'Just changed our minds,' Kayla says.

'And the receipt's all here, is it?'

Kayla pushes it closer. 'Can we have it in two halves?' She thumbs towards James. 'Like, half each, exactly? To spend?'

The woman finishes with the receipt, circling and initialling and crossing out. She squints at them with the money in her palm, sliding the register shut gently. 'Maybe the bank near the food court can help you. This is the best I can do.'

They have seventy-one dollars and ninety cents. Kayla walks ahead of James, towards the food court. She turns around, hands him a twenty, ignores his protests. She heads to Tricky Donuts and buys a hot bag of fresh cinnamon ones where the grease has shone the outside translucent. The boy at Tricky Donuts agrees to give her the change she asks for, and she passes James the rest of his portion of cash. He salutes her and wanders off.

Kayla stands by a heavy fern in a silver pot as she posts the doughnuts into her mouth one by one. She has twenty-eight dollars and forty-five cents left.

Past the escalators there's a young guy in a bright green T-shirt, collecting for charity.

He reaches both hands towards Kayla, then presses them together in a soundless clap. Other shoppers weave past. 'How's it going?'

'All right,' Kayla says, stopping by the table. The photos pinned to the booth show newborns, pink and lustrous, stuck with tubes in humidicribs.

The man arranges himself next to her. 'They look so helpless, don't they? But such fighters.'

Kayla nods.

'Imagine how frightening that must be. Can you imagine?'

She can, but says, 'Not really.'

He brightens. 'You're good to stop. Anything you can spare will go straight to helping babies and their families, like these ones.'

Kayla opens her purse and slides all her coins into the slotted bucket on the table.

'Thanks so much,' the man says.

She has twenty-five dollars left.

At a stationery shop, Christmas carols thread through the frigid, processed air. Jubilant children write their names in glitter on pads of test paper.

'Here you go.' A girl in an apron hands Kayla a toy-sized basket. 'So you can keep your hands free while you shop.'

Kayla sees a menu planner that comes with a free pencil. She wonders what her mum is cooking these days, what it's like to cook for one, or if she even bothers with frypans and chopping up garlic and tasting sauces from the end of a wooden spoon. Shannon cooks Italian one week. Greek the next. This week it's something she calls Tex-Mex and James is excited. Kayla drops the plastic-wrapped notepad into the basket.

The girl returns and touches the basket handle. 'Take that to the counter for you?'

It had seemed inexpensive and sensible and sort of cute too, with its outlines of pies and cakes and bowls of spaghetti, but the notepad will take up more than half the remaining money. Kayla feels panicky.

'Paying cash today?'

'Yeah.'

On her way out, with twelve dollars and five cents remaining, Kayla notices clear plastic tubs on a table. She rubs erasers shaped like watermelons and pineapples through her fingertips. The erasers are two ninety-five each. They make her think of the soft lollies her gran kept in jars in the pantry to be brought to the couch during the footy. Gran bit the heads off lolly pineapples and pressed their yellow bellies between the pads of her fingers, whispering *C'mon, c'mon* at the television. She offered the decapitated sweets to Kayla and James, a joke, because who would eat them after that? Gran wouldn't give up anything if she could help it.

Even at the worst moments – the ones back in 2012 that people still ask her about – Kayla wanted to stay with her mother. *Is that right?* her father wanted to know. At times her life had its freedom. At other times: claustrophobia, meanness, despair. Kayla used to think she'd rather be close to her mother than far away. Once, in the car on the way to their next house, after whatever dilemma it had been that time – the bed bugs; or the small but fearsome laundry fire; or the rotting deck their kitten had fallen through, surviving – Kayla asked her mother if she felt any sadness about leaving.

'You can't feel sad about things that are awful to begin with.'

'Okay.'

'They're just houses, Kayla,' her mum said, even though together they'd snipped photos of flowers from magazines

102

to arrange across the front of the fridge. They'd bought birdseed from the service station and watched from the kitchen as rosellas landed on the patchy grass below.

'It meant something to Gran,' Kayla said quietly. 'Having a house. And now she's lost it.'

Her mum, running a palm around the steering wheel, said, 'See?'

Kayla checks the watch that the foster care agency gave her for Christmas – purple, and a bit juvenile, but owning this thing against her skin makes it special. She excuses herself past shoppers, jogging down the escalator to the ground floor. In a brightly lit store with nothing but white and tan clothes on featureless mannequins, she takes a leather belt into her hands. The tag says *$129.95.* In a beachwear shop, Kayla tries on a sixty-dollar wide-brimmed hat. In a jewellery store where she is the only customer, Kayla tells the man with a diamond earring that she's looking for something for her mum. He explains cut and clarity. He doesn't ask how much Kayla has to spend. He says, *Have a think.* He tells her she's a wonderful daughter.

In a dim shop spicy with incense, Kayla touches the corners of her lips and pinches away grains of sugar from the doughnuts. Soon, Shannon will be hopping into her red hatchback to circle down her suburban hill towards the freeway.

Scanning, Kayla eyes a set of glass shelves. Ceramic figurines of animals are set inches apart from one another. She picks up a black and cream cat the length of her fingers. It plays with a ball of wool in its paws. Kayla thinks her mum will like it and she's satisfied with the clink it makes when she sets it down to pay. Prettier, more solid, more *gifty* than a notepad, the cat leaves Kayla with a single coin. The shop assistant wraps the animal roughly in white paper.

Another Christmas, years ago. Kayla remembers James in her lap. He had a solid, heavy body. Their oftentimes hunger showed in other ways: James sniffled and murmured with a cold. He was maybe eight or nine. Old enough to let suspicions about Santa Claus stop him from getting too loud or excited in front of Kayla. But this chaos of wanting and needing, and the rhythm of frustration about just *why*, exactly, other kids got things all year round, kept her brother quiet, and hopeful that Santa was real. He rested his head back against Kayla's chest while they watched a movie. Their mum had gotten a job cooking at a nursing home, but then she'd gotten sick. Kayla thought surely there'd be another job before Christmas. Best not to talk about presents or the beach or pavlova. No one but James had mentioned a tree. The decorations he'd made in the final weeks of school sat on top of the TV.

Kayla heard a key in the lock and then saw the sliver of her mother's tiny body against the midday light.

'Good, kids, you're here. Quick. We're moving out.'

Kayla felt her face burning. 'No, we're not.'

'Get some clothes. Here.' She unfolded green supermarket bags into Kayla's hands. 'Help him, please.'

'Where are we moving?' Kayla asked. 'Somewhere better?'

Their mum started to take her shoes off, but kept them on. 'Sure. Somewhere better.'

'Why right now?'

'Now, Kayla. The essentials for now. I said *help him*.'

James dropped from her lap. Used tissues tumbled to the floor. 'Maybe a holiday?' he asked, almost convinced.

Their mum stopped and stared. 'Not a holiday. Not like that, mate.'

Kayla headed for her room. She thought she would like to take a look at Gran's bright, beautiful jewellery coiled in the biscuit tin inside her wardrobe. She thought she would like to take it with her.

'This is a good thing,' their mum said. 'Kids? This is a good thing.' She picked up the remote and turned off the movie so she could say it again, louder.

Kayla circles back and up the escalator where the charity guy is talking to a young couple in front of the photos of premature babies. She slips the five cents into the bucket.

A notepad and a ceramic cat tussling with a ball of blue wool are all she has to show for the hour. Kayla wonders if the person who'd bought the romance novel and the salad servers is still in the shopping centre, and if the lost bag has been remembered: steps retraced on square tiles to dodge *CAUTION: WET* signs and stubborn toddlers in a frenzy outside toy stores. Kayla figures that the items were presents for someone, and she tries not to think what will be wrapped in their place.

Apparently Gran left them a bit of money when she died, but she was their dad's mum, and Kayla didn't think to press the point after he said he was using it for something else. It was one of those things he said he'd pay back. ASAP, he said. But his car needed fixing ASAP, too. Her mother sobbed sobbed sobbed as though all the time she'd spent not crying – and Kayla couldn't remember seeing it before – she'd been thinking about it, wanting to, and here was her chance. From then on, her mother took her chance often. Kayla lay on the couch with her head turned in the direction of the kitchen. She listened to her mother through the doorway and tried not to think about the packages of pasta and tins of tuna and beetroot slices that came in the food bank cartons, or the regulation black leather-upper shoes her new school demanded by the end of the holidays. Instead: the vivid green of the football field, high and bright in the sun. Gran's soft fingers plumping the lollies. The tang of sugar in the air. The ball soaring between two posts. Something to play with. Something to hold.

Out in the sunshine, Kayla crosses Sullivan Road to get to the pet shop. She sees James waiting, his chin tilted up to gaze at the kittens and guinea pigs playing. 'I spent it all,' Kayla says. 'I've got nothing left.'

James pats his pocket. 'I didn't spend any. It's all there. I'm just going to give it to her.'

He's always been a gentle boy, always with cold hands that reached for hers in the bed they'd shared in the weatherboard house years ago. Their dad had covered the missing window panes with plastic bags that rustled in the night, sounding like mice, right by her ears.

She stares at him, feels her eyes sting. 'That's actually

very smart of you.' Swallowing, she shows him the menu planner, and explains what's inside the palm-sized paper package.

'I really think she'll show up,' James says.

'Who? Shannon?' Kayla surveys the road. 'Of course she will.'

'No – Mum. For the visit tomorrow, at the agency.'

'She might,' Kayla says. 'She probably will.' No apology messages on her phone yet. Every night before a contact visit Kayla turns her phone to silent.

'And she'll like the menu thing and the cat. But she can use my money to buy whatever else she needs.' James pauses. 'Unless we should buy something for Shannon.'

'Nah. She doesn't need anything.' Right on time, Shannon's red car turns the corner at the bottom of the road, and Kayla says, 'Wave, James. So she can see us.'

La Otra

Sarah pulled an apron and a pot of paintbrushes from the store cupboard. Her friends Monique, Henrietta and Tess floated into the classroom. Monique blew her a kiss and Sarah caught it, swiping at it with her paintbrush in the fumey air. Their Art teacher, Ms Farrell, called the roll and fielded questions from her nineteen Year 12 students as they moved through the studio hefting portfolios and papier mâché busts of Frida Kahlo. Yes, Ms Farrell was coming to their formal. No, she would not be getting her hair and makeup done. Yes, she thought the whole thing was a bit ridiculous. Yes, yes, her love for her students outweighed any politico-social concerns she had about the Australian high school formal industrial complex. But for now, girls: Art.

The eighty-minute class moved gently. Sarah called Ms Farrell over. 'Miss, what do you think? I'm trying to revoke the power of the male gaze by subverting the perspective of *The Birth of Venus*.' Ms Farrell nodded, took the paintbrush from her and added some texture to Venus's tendrils.

'I think you're trying hard to play nice,' Ms Farrell said.

'What do you mean?'

'No need to play nice all the time. They'll put you in quarantine if you're not careful.' Ms Farrell cleared her throat and leant in. 'What do you reckon she's thinking, Sarah – Venus?'

Sarah had wondered herself. '*Where are my clothes?*' She started to laugh.

Ms Farrell never laughed. 'What else?' She touched Sarah's hand.

'I think she seems tired.'

'Everyone's tired.'

'Of being looked at.'

Monique, immaculately groomed, impossibly perfumed, came up and put her head on Sarah's shoulder and said, 'I'm going to miss Art the most. I don't know what I'll do without it.'

Ms Farrell smiled warmly. She took Monique's portfolio from her hands and flicked through its pages.

'I'm going to miss *you*, miss,' said Henrietta, whose triptych based on representations of weaponry in *The Hunger Games* had sold particularly well at the school auction in term three. Someone's father, probably Henrietta's, probably a barrister, bought it unframed to hang in his offices at Waterfront Place. Loudly, he declared Henrietta's effort entitled *Arrows+Other Arsenal* to be a 'remarkable cohesion of feminist iconography and really, really great line work'. Sarah had rolled her eyes at Hen. She watched Hen's father, his lips at a plastic goblet of unwooded chardonnay, eyeing Ms Farrell in her black dress, rubbing one bright blue-stockinged foot against her calf. A bitterness had risen in Sarah's throat.

Ms Farrell assured Henrietta that she would miss her, and all the girls, after graduation. When the bell rang at the end of class – their penultimate class together – the students gathered in close. With charcoaled knuckles and clay-stuck fingernails, they patted Ms Farrell's soft, wrinkle-pleated arms.

'Till next time, till next time,' Ms Farrell said. 'And if you don't wash your brushes properly, *I kill you*.' The girls' laughter twirled above their heads. It was first period and they lingered in the warm room. Outside, kiln-fired ceramics projects rested in the docile sun.

Finally, Sarah hung up her apron and waved as she began to leave. Other girls, ahead of her, one by one, called, 'Bye, Ms Farrell.'

Her teacher raised her voice. 'Sarah? Can you stay for a moment? Monique, Henrietta, Tess? I will write you all late notes for period two. I have something in mind for four of my very best.'

They settled on stools in front of Ms Farrell's laptop. She turned off the lights and hit a key on her computer.

'I was wondering if you'd heard of this man?'

Diego – no last name – was a Spanish-born artist who had been commissioned by the state to produce an artwork for the western boardwalk at South Bank. Ms Farrell tapped a few keys and a photograph appeared projected onto the whiteboard. She clasped her hands together and faced the girls.

'He calls it *La Otra*.'

Monique, Henrietta and Tess gasped. Sarah gazed at Ms Farrell. The girls were very late to their next class.

★

Sarah invited her friends to her house because it was the closest to South Bank, and also the closest to the new liquid nitrogen ice-cream place they'd been meaning to try. Her mum buzzed Monique, Henrietta and Tess up to the apartment. They spilt out of the lift, all short denim and swinging hair. Their chests were criss-crossed with bags, like bandoliers.

'My word,' her mum said. 'Are you staying for the night, or for a month?'

'Just the night, Mrs Birch.' Henrietta patted her fat duffel bag. 'So much homework.'

'Good girl, Hen. You'll be an ophthalmologist yet!'

Sarah kissed her friends hello. They said *yes please* to her mum's offer of fruit toast and Earl Grey. She'd leave the goodies outside Sarah's door. Tess was given a sticky note with the wi-fi password, and Sarah led them to her room. Beneath the pendant light the girls offloaded their luggage onto her bed. Tess marvelled at Sarah's scarlet formal dress hanging in her wardrobe. Monique said, 'Hen's got a new flame at the train station,' and Henrietta confessed everything: the part about the boy writing down the names of Hen's favourite books and then the part about the boy copping a ticket from a transport inspector because he'd forgotten to tap his travel card.

'He reckoned it was worth it,' Monique said. 'But I don't think it was.'

'Do you like him?' Sarah asked.

Henrietta shrugged. 'Does it matter? He wouldn't leave me alone.'

They settled into a silence that was thrilled and expectant.

'Okay?' Sarah asked, and the others nodded.

Sarah tapped on her laptop. Here was the photo Ms Farrell had emailed her. And here were another nine photographs that Sarah had taken this afternoon – *on recon*, she pointed out – of Diego's sculpture by the Brisbane River.

'*La Otra*, hey,' Tess said. She slid off the bed and checked outside Sarah's door for the tea, but came back empty-handed.

'I'm appalled,' Monique said. 'And you know I love being appalled.'

Sarah addressed her best friends. She explained her thoughts as potentially reactionary, but no less valid because of their emotional sheen. She needed to weigh up the artist's right to freedom of expression with a citizen's right to police and resist that expression when the piece of art was imbued with so much *fuckhoundedry*.

A knock on the door. 'Toast!' Tess screamed.

When it was time to go, they all ducked to the loo, then Monique stacked the plates for Sarah's mum. They gathered their bags and balaclavas and they bunched together in the lift, four warm bodies breathing deeply. An installation of bravery in an air-conditioned metal cube.

★

In *La Otra*, Diego-no-last-name had created a functional bronze sculpture for the people of Brisbane. At the base of a grassy hill that led to the river, a life-sized faceless woman perched on all fours on a low concrete plinth. She was round-bottomed, trophy-hipped, aglow in the moonshine to be molested by ibises. Naked, but for the scent of the grass and the river that settled on the small of her back. A seat for someone. A bed for someone. A shining folly seen from above by a mother marsupial with bauble eyes as she acrobated electrical wires with a baby on her back.

Sarah circled the sculpture, her second time here. She felt her own, transmitted version of Ms Farrell's fury. From a young age Sarah had known the fever of male eyes on her; she thought it was as common as flowers. Sarah laid a hand on the crown of the woman's scorched bistre-brown head. A sign was bolted to the plinth. It read:

Diego: *La Otra* ('The Other')

Earlier, Ms Farrell had said *Here* when she unlocked the storeroom with the key she kept clipped to her waist. She turned her back while Sarah, Monique, Henrietta and Tess raided a metal cupboard for cans of spray paint.

Monique set her bag on the grass. She wondered aloud about sitting on the sculpture. 'I shouldn't though, should I.'

'Probably not,' Henrietta said. She tossed Monique a can of purple spray paint, labelled with a sticker of the school logo.

A can of green in her hand, Tess tried to choke back nervous giggles. Sarah pulled a balaclava out of her duffel bag, and then a hammer. A jogger listened to his headphones as he shuffled by on the path below the sculpture, oblivious to the hammer, oblivious to the girls.

Monique watched him leave. She shook her can of paint. The marble rattled in its throat. Sarah made dents with her hammer and Monique and Hen and Tess ran loops around the plinth to tinsel the burnished woman with white, green and purple.

'Hey!' a voice called out. 'Stop there.' A security guard swung torchlight down over grass, over river.

'Go, go,' Sarah called.

She thought of Mary Richardson and the photograph of the *Rokeby Venus* that Ms Farrell had also shown them. She thought of Mary's little axe, hidden in a suffragette's sleeve. Such pleasing slashes on the glass, on the canvas. Mary Richardson trying to scramble away through the gallery, a fever at her throat. Sarah raced towards her friends, and her feet pounded the wooden boardwalk all the way home.

★

Sunshine Gardens had phoned the school formal committee with bad news about the drop-off zone out the front of the marquee. Due to earthworks, nothing larger than a four-wheel drive would be permitted to deliver students to the waiting crowds on the night of the formal. No limousines. No Hummers. No decommissioned fire engines.

The girls in Ms Farrell's period-four Art class were taking it well.

'Probably better for the environment.'

'Just showing off, anyway.'

'Less is more, right, Ms Farrell?'

Ms Farrell looked up from the buttery slab of clay she was slicing into strips with wire for her next class. 'I agree wholeheartedly. What a fine, bold group of girls you've turned out to be.' As she glanced around the studio, she made eye contact with Sarah at the opposite table. She and her friends hadn't yet found the chance to talk to Ms Farrell alone, not since the destruction of *La Otra* was complete.

Sarah nodded deliberately.

Ms Farrell's lips parted. She mouthed, *Very good.* She raised her voice to the whole class. 'Please remember to staple your—'

A voice came over the PA system. 'Would the following Year 12 students please come to the office to see Mr Young …'

As each of their names was read out by nice, asthmatic Jackie in the office, Sarah, Monique, Henrietta and Tess set down their tools. Not unusual for one or two students to be summoned. But four – and best friends, at the same time – was deeply curious. Scraps of gossip from their classmates rose around the classroom until Ms Farrell said, 'All right, that's enough. Sarah, Monique, Henrietta and Tess? We will clean up your things while you're gone.'

Ah, Sarah thought. Their teacher, then, knew that they wouldn't be back.

The principal's office was down the steps and one building over with gazebos and gardenias around it. Beyond that the groundsman on the ride-on mower droned over scrolls of the green grass, and beyond that was the train station and the occupied freeway. Beyond that: South Bank. Beyond that: Spain.

'Bye, miss,' Sarah said to Ms Farrell. She wondered when news of their crime would reach her mother in their apartment, and Henrietta's father in his glass-walled office overlooking the river, his phone within reach. 'Miss? We'll see you at the formal.'

115

Out the door and down the steps into the courtyard, the girls walked two by two, arms resting on each other's jacket sleeves or fingers meeting to touch in the swish of their skirts. Sarah recalled the scratch of the balaclava against her cheeks and the hammer in her hand and the wolfish yelp she gave as it swung. Nearing the principal's office, Tess dug around in her pocket, pulled out a cigarette and dropped it into a bin. Past the canteen, Henrietta took off her glasses and held them up to the light. Here, some years ago, at this corner, she'd bitten into a pie and her final baby tooth had fallen out. Sarah looked at Monique's red hair that quivered as she strode the final steps to the principal's office, tendrils of it curling like perfumed Venus, newly born.

Love, Listen

Dad calls, says he wants to take me to the cricket. He's already bought the tickets, or someone at the nursing home helped him buy them. I take a cool shower, slick my arms and neck with sunscreen, and wait for him outside the ground. Police officers direct traffic as fans spill out of buses and cross the road. Small children wearing team caps bounce on top of their fathers' shoulders.

At the gate, security isn't interested in my reasons for smuggling in a litre of Mount Franklin. But I'm pregnant, I say. She is, Dad says. Look. The woman makes a face like she's never heard of human reproduction and points to the red bins.

Dad leads me through the turnstile. Wally Lewis got pelted with cans at Lang Park twenty years ago, he tells me. He nods towards the other side of the river. Bunch of animals. And now cans and bottles are banned. He raises his voice. Even for pregnant women.

We find our seats and Dad realises his mistake. Row H in the eastern stand. We'll have shade for three-quarters of an hour and then full sun for the rest of the day. He looks in horror at my belly. He'll roast in there, he says. I tell him we'll be fine. If the place doesn't fill up we can sneak into someone else's seats. We've done it before, I remind him.

We step down the cool concrete that is strewn with rubbish even though the game hasn't started. Dad helps me past the lift-up seats and holds mine down for me, takes my Woolies bag of provisions minus the Mount Franklin. Love, listen, he says. I'll get you a drink. I reach for my purse. Nah nah nah, he says. He comes back with bottled water and a tall cool beer, half gone. We cheers our drinks together. Do you know why cans are banned? he asks. Footy fans – that's why. Back in the eighties, they pelted the refs after they sent Wally Lewis to the sin bin.

I think, let him say what he likes.

We win the toss. Dad isn't a fan of our new opening partnership. He reckons one of them is perfectly bloody boring, can't talk to the media, a total nobody, no one knows who his wife is. And the other fella has a spot on one of the morning shows, will spruik anything on television. Cars, deodorant, Aussie beef, bathroom sealant. A real windbag. But with a pull shot like Ponting's.

Above us the shade slides away and the sun swings over our shins, but I don't acknowledge it. The baby gives three good kicks and his foot ripples beneath my palm. Dad knocks off the foam of a second beer and taps our Row H tickets on the seat in front. How's our little tiddler doing in there, he asks. I rub my belly. Oh, he's loving it, I say. Listening to the crowd. Snug as a bug.

Love, listen. Dad points. See up there?

Dad leans in close, takes a sip. Fixes me with his stare.

Yours truly, he says, darting his thumb to his chest, hit three sixes in a row all the way up there.

I play along. I say, Way up there? I shield my eyes. I let air out through my lips. That's pretty high, I say.

He grins and adds, Three balls to go, last over of the day. Won the match. Straight drives – bam, bam, bam. Clean as a whistle. Right over Markson's head, the tiddler. Almost felt sorry for him. God, you should have heard the crowd. I took the middle stump as a trophy, as you know. They used to let you do that. Built that box frame for it in the lounge room.

Dad gulps the rest of his beer. In the seats beside us, a father and son have been paying attention. The father's smile is fixed, polite, unchallenging. Dad cocks his head to one side. It's true, he tells the small boy. Me.

Dad makes them stand when I need to ease past to go to the toilet. Out of the sun, beneath the concrete structure, the shade is heavy. My belly resting on a bathroom sink, I fill my hands with water and submerge my face. I am cool again and wonder how on earth I'll want to return to my seat. Dad will have gotten in with the father and son. Stuck out his hand. I'm Lawrie, he'd say. Used to play here myself. Tonight at the nursing home Dad will start to tell the other blokes about the boy's favourite player, and have to make up a name because he'll have forgotten.

Lining the walls of the stadium's underbelly are tall tables where beer-drinkers step from foot to foot and talk about this game, another game, the next game they'll come to. Behind them, plaques are fixed to the walls. When I was little, Dad would take my photo beside his plaque every

119

time we visited. He nailed the photos to our lounge room wall next to the middle stump from the Markson match. Me hugging a stuffed rabbit. Me in my togs come straight from swimming. Me, just gone thirteen, my face dotted with acne that I couldn't hide, my face lowered. Don't put them up, I begged him. Love, listen, he said. You've got to be proud.

I go for a wander and locate the plaque beside the steel pole painted with 33A. I consider taking a selfie, or asking one of the drunks to take one for me. Instead I touch a finger to his name: Lawrence 'Ripple' Rivers. I touch a hand to the baby. I hope to feel another kick through warm water, through membrane, through heat and tight skin.

Back to our row of seats and Dad is telling the father and son a story about me, at primary school, being tiny, leading the band. A nice enough memory, anyway, and the other father is smiling. Nothing embarrassing. Dad had wanted to come, I remember. He'd wanted to fold him himself into a front-row chair in our hall and lead the applause that day, all those years after he'd retired from cricket. But he'd been invited to share his story at an awards ceremony. Mum only told me afterwards. He wasn't there at all.

Dad tells me, Like a fly in a pickle jar you were. He zig-zags a hand through the air.

A cheer flares beneath the yellow sun. A straight drive, perhaps.

I remember, he says.

Dots and Spaces

The announcement came from the Honourable Stuart Ryder MP to a press room that was mostly empty on account of the AFL grand final. As Minister for Aged Care and Human Services, he explained that Australia faced an ageing population on an unprecedented scale. Never before had there been such a large population of elderly people, and with so much to offer the young. An untapped resource of wisdom.

Those in need of the pension could apply to be 'Sages' as part of the newly legislated *Old-Age Pension (Wages for Sages) Amendment Act.* Amid soaring unemployment, amid the revocation of veterans' benefits and bulging hospital waiting lists, Ryder had little time for questions.

'No, it isn't at all like Work for the Dole,' he told one reporter. 'At the moment we're pretty sold on Vigour and Rigour. Or Grey Therapy.' He chuckled. 'Next.'

'Minister, might some people see this initiative as exploitative?'

Ryder glared at the reporter with the flimsy hair and steely eyes. 'Surely,' he said, 'this country is great enough to recognise the contributions of its elderly, their wealth of knowledge, their advice to be passed down to younger generations, who are eager to understand the world. Many elderly Australians *want* to stay working. Retirement and leisure just aren't for them. Would the bleeding hearts of this country deny them their right to work?'

★

In the happiest week of her life Iris had been with Marnie, who had finally decided to pack up the things in the house where her late parents had lived for forty-five years. Iris had laid Marnie's mother's knick-knacks out on the lounge room floor, zipping them into plastic sandwich bags to donate to the church fete. The little dioramas made no sense to Iris: a frog asleep on a picnic bench clinked next to a thumb-sized china cup and saucer. Marnie's father had kept a yellow teddy bear whose ears were rubbed free of fur. He'd left behind a green-black emu egg high up on a shelf. Iris put her eye to the hole in the egg where the insides had been sucked away, and Marnie touched Iris's hair on her way to the garage, where the scent of sawdust was in the air. They wrapped goblets in thin pillowcases and taped boxes shut. They toasted Marnie's parents on the back lawn. They ate vanilla slice for dessert. Later, Iris watched the ceiling fan above their bed. She slept well, and in the morning they slid wedding photos and honeymoon photos and christening photos out of their brass frames and arranged them across the carpet in a golden, faded timeline.

Marnie said, 'No one gets a life like that anymore,' and Iris laughed because Marnie was always so *serious* and could never see, the way Iris could, all the wonderful things the pair of them would do together.

But now, all these unspent lives ricochet around inside Iris's body, separate from Marnie, who is still, in Iris's mind, fifty-two years old with a slick of custard on her thumb, bumping the microwave shut with her elbow.

★

Iris pours milk into her teacup, then boiling water, stirring, letting the tea bag steep. She slices potatoes and rests them in water. She uncovers the lamb left over from last night, keeping the alfoil smooth and in one piece so she can fold it up to use again later. She walks to the train alone.

Now assigned to Firm Data Firm, Iris gets the same amount of money in her pension as she received when she was part of Wages for Sages. Back then, her thoughts and advice for young people were available on the wagesforsages.gov.au website. Identified only as Sage 76938, Iris was one of more than ninety thousand Sages across the country saving the government millions of dollars in trained mental-health professionals. Although her colleagues complained about the work, Iris got a thrill every time she sat face to face with a nice young man named Oliver or a nice young woman named Ava. She liked to listen, and she found that her few favourite bits of wisdom (follow your dreams, hang on to your loved ones) seemed to fit most occasions.

Her pension now is the same amount, too, as it had been six months after Wages for Sages, when she was moved to the OzGrandParent scheme, where she was responsible for toddlers while their parents worked, getting around on kitchen tiles on her hands and knees: *a table! a horse! a silly puppy-dog!* Later, she was a white-aproned, in-home Brush Strokes Cleaner, for one of Minister Ryder's more short-lived pilot trials. But as she aged, Iris couldn't keep up with the demands of being a Sage or a toddler's playmate, or lifting heavy rugs to air over clotheslines. So she was assigned to Firm Data Firm, where she has been for six weeks.

At Firm Data Firm, Iris feels like the universe – her sliver of the universe called Marnie – communicates with her through objects in the office. Iris sits at her standard-issue chair, turns on her computer and clicks on the form 68F. A blank page springs open.

She begins to type.

... ...

Iris enters the data, in the exact way their manager, Vic Kloss, taught her. Three dots. One space. Three dots. One space. Ad infinitum. Occasionally Iris gets bogged down by the repetition of it all, but she takes pride in her work ethic, as though it is a pretty object she has carved. She thinks of her mother and her father long gone, who would be proud of this ethic, of this object, too. Each day at Firm Data Firm stunts Iris a bit, but she feels compelled to keep typing.

... ...

Sometimes the dots look like confetti. Other times like very patient insects, in single file with hungry gaps between them.

'All right, listen up, you pack of deviants,' Vic Kloss says, expecting attention as he raps his knuckles on an upturned cardboard box.

Iris glances at docile, beatified Swell Brigham who sits hunch-backed to her left, war-widowed Liccy Emmerich on her right. Vic has a way with words. Vic encourages the old women to bake pies, biscuits and those buttery lemon slices with the coconut icing and leave them in the kitchen for him to paw over at morning tea.

'I don't want anyone taking it upon themselves to slack off,' Vic continues, 'as they say, to rejoice in this lolly-fingered, giggling-gertie, salad-days operation. Mind that you all keep typing. Mind that you meet your targets. Those dots won't dot themselves. Those spaces won't space themselves.'

... ...

Iris has always believed in signs. One time at Firm Data Firm it was coffee grounds at the bottom of a cup she was about to wash up. The message from Marnie: *I am here for you*. Another time it was a ceramic panther the size of a fat baby, perched on top of the fridge. It took Iris the whole day to figure out the wildcat's message: *This won't last forever*. She jotted her messages down in a small notebook as though journalling these words could keep Marnie within her reach.

Marnie is everywhere.

Recognising these talismanic objects at Firm Data Firm crystallises for Iris a sense of purpose. In coming this long distance on the train. On receiving the pension that she manages to stretch twenty-four, sometimes twenty-six, days into the month.

They had both worked at Finegan Textiles: Marnie till her accident and Iris till she lost her job with everyone else when they were told it was closing down. After the accident, Marnie could still mostly walk and talk, and mostly get around okay, but her head injury grew worse. One day, out walking in the poverty of the sunshine and the poverty of their days left together, Iris and Marnie noticed the Finegan smoke stacks puffing and billowing, at work once again.

'Oompa-Loompas,' Marnie said, and that was the end of it.

★

Three hours later, Iris spies a trio of ants on the bench in the coffee room. One of the ants stops. The other two keep moving, pulled towards a white plate with lemon slice crumbs beside the sink. Marnie loved animals, even insects, and here is a new sign. Iris's amazement that Marnie has been able to marionette the movements of actual *living creatures* is short-lived. Of course she's managed to do that. Of course Marnie will do whatever she can to get her message through, and now she's conjured a wisp of air so thin that an ant falls behind its pair of friends and steps out of line.

As Iris returns to her desk, thoughts like flotsam rise to the surface and gather together. All those residuals are suddenly clarified. What would happen, she thinks, if I were to *type something different*?

Deep in the mid-afternoon slump – dot dot dot space dot dot dot space – Swell and Liccy are slipping tiny pink uppers between their lips to stay awake. Iris sits in her chair, feeling puppeted, feeling herself quake. She can't afford to lose the money she earns here.

Still.

Her fingers stroke the keyboard and the usual script comes alive in her mind.

… … … … … … … …

But she is starving to keep Marnie's messages alive. She begins to type.

.. . … .

From Vic's office, Iris hears a barrage of telephone conversation. Vic's boss is Mick and Mick's boss is Dick, all the way up to Minister Stuart Ryder, whose handshake on the day he visited Firm Data Firm was like wet upholstery.

.. .

dot dot space dot

The ground beneath Iris's feet starts to heave and the employees at Firm Data Firm fade. Iris stands, stumbling, one hand on the keyboard with its worn-down full-stop key, its worn-down space bar.

Marnie.

Swell and Liccy and all the others, and Vic, too, are gone. Of course they're gone, because they have no role in the history that belongs to Iris and Marnie.

Iris, seventy-one and frail, stills herself while the thin office partitions solidify into brick, and the dark red scattershot carpet desiccates then re-forms as hardwood planks. Enormous looms break through the floor, shedding their cobwebs and shuddering, suddenly polished and alive. The smell of woollen thread and the stannic scent of combing machines and carding machines that used to shunt and roll and terrify. In the centre of the office where a potted fern once stood is Marnie, occupying the body she was in before the accident. Iris fights her way through the warp and weft of this new place.

She drifts towards Marnie with chaotic, desperate ideas to thank her, to love her, to caress the top of her scalp and her once-more perfect left arm. 'I saw the ants,' is all Iris can say.

★

A deep breath in and Iris wakes to pink and golden light that appears in squares. She pieces those squares together until she thinks she knows where she is. Iris appreciates the order and safety of hospitals. She liked them when Marnie was treated after her accident. She even liked the hospice where Marnie was finally delivered to wait, thin and wool-soft on a bed, for nine days until she died.

She sucks at the spit forming around her mouth and utters her question. 'Is there a nurse?'

The voice of a young man speaks up. 'I'm Toby. I'm not a nurse. But, Iris, how are you?'

She tries to sit up. The movement reminds her of the office, where she'd seen Marnie. Of the motion that tossed everyone out like rags to leave only the pair of them standing.

'Marnie?'

'Is Marnie someone I could call for you?'

'Oh,' Iris says, not understanding.

The young man brings his chair nearer to the bed. 'A good room you've got here,' he says. 'Some of the other ones feel a bit dingy. They told me you'd wake up soon, so I came right in.'

She tries. 'Are you …?'

'I'm here with the My Twentennial Coalition to offer assistance during your recovery.'

Finally, all the queries and secrets are undone. Iris's understanding is now wide and clear.

It is Oliver.

She reaches a hand out to him. What a strange code of events has led her here: from that textile factory to that office and those crumbs and ants, to these squares of light on the wall. Such tumbling inside and outside today. The alfoil from the lamb, she thinks, might not even be flat on the kitchen bench at home.

'Oliver! What a turn-up for the books.'

His throat makes a noise and his face turns into a sign Iris doesn't recognise. She flexes her neck on the pillow then turns back to face him. His red hair is cut fine and neat. She can't remember what haircut he had when they met during Wages for Sages, but he is beautifully handsome now.

'You look like you just stepped off a boat. Or out of a painting.' It's taking longer to say what she wants but, there, she's said it.

'My name is Toby.' He's speaking slowly too.

'Hmmm.' Iris takes a sip of water. 'Yes. I remember you.'

He looks towards the door. 'Iris? Is it okay to call you that? The neurologist will be in soon. You had a fall.'

Marnie had a fall once, Iris recalls, recognising a new sign in this rich and shining place. She saw Marnie fall at the factory.

Iris touches the fabric of a nightgown she's never seen. She makes a fold at the wrist. 'Do I pay you?'

The young man beams and his hair is like a golden pelt in the late afternoon. 'No, ma'am. Fully funded, courtesy of the Minister for Aged Care and Human Services. We'll help you get back to work as soon as possible.'

'Oh, I do hope you followed your dreams, Oliver. Are you a poet now?'

'Sorry, Iris. My name is Toby. But you've just woken up, so perhaps you're a little …'

Absolutely not, Iris thinks. She is no longer dot dot dot.

She glances around for other objects in the hospital room that might have come from Marnie, but none of them means anything to her except Oliver being here, the boy she'd helped with advice as Sage 76938, perhaps having followed his dreams, now reminding her once again of Marnie, of their pair of falls. They are almost together again, at the edge of the world where politicians who are paid to say important things are out of the picture. She and Marnie are panthers, long gone.

Fledermaus

Marlee met Emmett S Ulrich in line at the bakery. She recognised him from the photograph printed on her high school textbook. She stood, frozen, listening to him order a thick-sliced loaf, and she tried to figure out what a man like that was doing in tiny, boring Milford, in the middle of summer.

Marlee studied his face while he counted his money. He had a snowy moustache and goatee and bushy eyebrows. She watched him return the coins to his pocket, frustrated, and pull out a ten-dollar note folded lengthwise. He jabbed it at the air in front of the cash register. He took his change.

On the way to the bakery, Marlee had seen herself reflected in the window of Milford compounding pharmacy. It was the summer after the end of school, and she felt herself peeling away from the cluster of friends who had been so important, but were now dispersing to foreign universities, to P&O Cruises, to the Australian armed forces. In school, Marlee had gone along with everything her friends had done. She'd welcomed it all. When Cassie and Lou had beckoned her into the bathroom stalls at the Bridges Boys' College social and giggled like it was nothing to drop your knickers and hold a conversation and wee in front of someone else, Marlee had tolerated it. When Alexis and Elleni wanted to know what ecstasy would do to them the night before their Year 11 exams, Marlee, who hadn't the faintest clue, had been like, *Sure, I'll be your support person*, and she'd sat across from them at the picnic table in the park with her finger poised over her phone, having pre-dialled triple zero.

'Mr Ulrich?'

'What? Yes?'

'You're on my Drama textbook. At school. I know you.'

She told him that she wanted to be an actor. Emmett's face brightened. 'Ah, wonderful.' He pointed to a neenish tart in the glass cabinet and signalled to the bakery girl for two of those.

'I'm Marlee.'

She mentioned that she'd done well in Drama at Milford State High, and she'd certainly liked it, even if she'd never come top of her class. She had studied his textbook, *The Powerful Player*, since Year 9, and thought it was brilliant. Emmett asked what she was doing now. Marlee told him about her first failed acting audition down in Melbourne, and that she'd been offered a second one, hoping to get a spot at a university in Brisbane.

'And what are your chances, do you think?'

No one had ever asked her that question so simply. Chances were handed out, worn through, used up. 'I hate auditions. I hate how I sound.'

Marlee felt a hand at her elbow. A burly man was pushing through towards the bakery counter, even though there was space on Marlee's other side. She stepped back. 'Sorry,' she said to the man.

Emmett didn't seem to notice. 'You know what?' He held up a finger like he was testing the direction of the wind. 'I think I could help you.'

Excitement grew in her. *Of course you could*, she thought but did not say.

'What if I offered to show you a cracker of an audition piece guaranteed to knock their socks off up in Brisbane? Unusual and frightening in its scope and vigour – and if you like it, well, it's yours.' He tossed his hand up towards the sky. A man used to getting lots and giving lots away. 'Come round one evening. Would that be okay with your folks?' He was in Milford for the week, at his beach house.

'It'd be fine,' she said, knowing she would never tell them. Alexis and Elleni would be proud.

'It's about,' Emmett said, fanning out his fingers, '*bats*.'

Before Marlee could answer, the girl at the bakery said, 'Here you go,' and handed over Marlee's salad sandwich.

Emmett said, 'My wife, Geraldine, is here on holidays as well. I'll make sure she's there, too, so you won't feel strange.'

'I won't feel strange,' Marlee said, recalling the famed Ulrich triad of exercises in Chapter 1 designed to help an actor seek out and inhabit the soul of a character.

'Well, then,' Emmett said, hugging his Vienna loaf close like a newborn. He passed Marlee one of the neenish tarts and wrote his address on the white paper bag. 'Neither will I. Tuesday?'

She watched him walk up the street. She caught a glimpse of herself in the bakery window and she was astonished.

★

Marlee dashed through the house to the back deck and found her brother asleep on the daybed. The sweat from Damien's head blotted a circle on the cushion. Marlee heard the neighbour's chickens shuffling around the yard.

'Oi. Wake up.'

She told Damien who she'd met, knowing he wouldn't understand the significance, or her excitement, or her relief that finally she could stop with all the Lady Macbeth and Blanche DuBois and Meryl Streep in *The Iron Lady* typed up on paper in her bedroom, none of which had been successful in Melbourne. Perhaps this new piece would be perfect for her.

'Sit up. It's about bats.'

'Bats? No one cares about bats.'

'You don't know anything about them,' Marlee said.

'Indeed I do.' Her brother rubbed his hand across the back of his neck and wiped the sweat down his shorts.

'Fine. What?'

'During mating season, the males shine up their testicles so the females can see them from ages away.'

She kicked Damien's feet under the daybed. 'Stop being a sexual predator.'

Her brother screwed up his face, like, *Sis, as if that's something I can control.*

★

On Tuesday, Geraldine met Marlee at the front gate of a timber house on the edge of Milford. There were palm trees in the front yard and yellow lights strung across the verandah.

Geraldine pressed a hand to her chest. '*Geraldine*. Lovely to meet you, Marlee. Did you find the place okay?'

Marlee listened for signs of Damien's car in the distance, hooning back home. She nodded. 'I had a friend in primary school who lived out here, by the beach.'

Geraldine led her around the side of the house, where light from the windows in the second floor illuminated the grass. She put a glass of red wine into Marlee's hand. 'I'm assuming you're eighteen. Emmett said you must be.'

'Almost. Yeah, just about.'

Geraldine grinned, turning away to poke at things on the barbecue.

When Emmett appeared at the top of the stairs, he was dressed in a white shirt and black pants with a scrap of red fabric tied at the waist, like a pirate. He was studying a piece of paper.

'Hello, Marlee,' he called.

He eased himself off the bottom step, as though one leg was troubling him, then took the wine bottle and filled a glass.

'We bought these in Florence,' Geraldine said. 'The glasses – years ago, before we got this house. Before we realised we couldn't have children because we were barren.'

So little happened in Milford. So few adults talked to Marlee in a way that placed her at the centre of their confidence, of their stories. She leant against the table, taking in the potted plants that jotted the edge of a white gazebo. There was lawn the whole way round the house, which sat islanded in the centre. Low fences marked all four sides. Bright towels were draped on the clothesline. A dish of birdseed sat on an upturned bucket. The trees shifted cooler air across her face and neck. She took it all in, happily.

'So,' Emmett said, 'this script came about years ago when we were living in a town in Western Australia that had been overrun by bats. Beautiful but grotesque creatures; no one could sleep. Not during the day, when they make a lot of noise. Not at night, when they make the most noise. Crying and yelling and howling, practically twenty-four hours. An enormous amount of food, too – gorging themselves then shitting on everything. And during mating season, it's even worse.'

Geraldine faced Marlee and snipped the tongs together. 'Orgies, and whatnot.'

'Oh.' Marlee sipped on the wine and decided that she didn't like it, but thought it was important to keep drinking while she listened to Emmett.

'I determined to write a piece about it. I intended it to be part of something longer, a three-act play, about the inhabitants of a town – coincidentally, not unlike Milford in character and landscape – descending into madness over the course of a year. But, Marlee, the play never let me *in*, and at first I couldn't start and then I could. But I couldn't *finish* ...' Emmett plunged his hands left and right through the air as though he was shifting items between baskets. 'But "Nothing will come of nothing", and all that, and it remains *inachevé*. Here. A monologue from the perspective of the mayor's daughter, who is the only person left in town—'

Geraldine interrupted to hand out plates of chicken and blackened sausages. Marlee took the paper.

'Because Marguerite decides to stay and fight the bats, and in doing so ...' They sat. Marlee laid her serviette across her lap. 'She experiences a sort of ... metamorphosis,' Emmett finished.

'I'd love to try it,' she said. 'I'd love to perform something they've never seen before.' Marlee waited for her hosts to start eating.

'So who beat you in Drama?' Emmett asked. 'Who took out the top award?'

Marlee gnawed on a chicken wing. 'Kelsey Bridgeman-Ferguson.'

Emmett thumped the table. 'I don't like the sound of her one bit.' He laughed at his own theatrics. 'Every year?'

Marlee nodded.

Geraldine made a sympathetic sound and straightened the shawl around her shoulders.

'Kelsey wrote a really great essay,' Marlee said, licking marinade off her fingers, 'about the use of the proscenium in *Antigone*, and we had a replacement teacher in third term, and he lapped it up. It's a small school ...' She trailed off.

Geraldine patted Marlee's hand. 'The same thing happened to me when I was your age.'

Emmett rubbed mosquito repellent into his forearms. Marlee saw scars on his skin like something had been cut out. He saw her looking and scissored two pale fingers together in the dark. 'Just cancer. And why do you want to be an actor?'

The truth was Marlee felt good about it. About the confidence she got that first time she was on stage at school, and Lou and Elleni and whoever else from class had come up afterwards, like, *We Had Absolutely No Idea You Were Good, like that was soooooo good.* They didn't expect it, see, and neither did Marlee.

'I like becoming someone else. Another person's skin.' She speared a sausage. Yep. That was the truth.

'Marlee, I am certain I can help you. Did you ever read, in my textbook, the chapter about physicalisation and personification of animal forms?'

She nodded, recalling one example Emmett had given – the William Blake poem that had prompted her Year 8 teacher to drape herself in orange and black striped fake fur and prowl the walkway alongside the classroom, responding to her students' shrieks with ever louder roars until one of the ladies from the office hurried down to tell them that the principal was on his way.

Geraldine topped up her glass. 'What a lark.'

Marlee watched for bats in the trees above them, but could see none.

Dinner was over. Emmett stopped drinking. Geraldine brought out three bowls and three spoons and a tub of ice-cream that she never served up. She ran a spoon around the inside rim, licked the ice-cream off the spoon upside-down, and replaced the lid after each bite. Geraldine swatted at mozzies. They dragged chairs onto the grass, away from the table. They would be Marlee's audience.

'Just a run-through,' Emmett said. He straightened himself, tugging at the collar of his white shirt.

Recently there'd been bushfires west of Milford, and further south and east, but there in the Ulrichs' holiday house, Marlee felt only the dampness of the air, its warm touch. As a child, Marlee thought the fires really were a whole other season, part of the order of things. School holidays, Christmas, New Year's, sweaty afternoons slung across the couch watching cricket on the TV – and bushfires. A few years ago, Marlee and her father had driven west to visit her cousins. Marlee had watched smoke on the horizon. The fires had unsettled her, made her afraid.

'Those nerves, there, Miss Marlee?' Emmett asked, his voice gentle.

'I'm fine. Just reading it.' Marlee waved the script in their direction.

Emmett gestured widely to the empty space on the grass. 'Some nerves – not too many – but a measure of nerves can be just *it*, though, can't they? The thing you need.'

In that case, yes, Marlee thought. She had a measure of nerves.

'Let's see you, then,' Geraldine said.

Marlee would need to coax Damien back out here soon to collect her. In the morning, her mother would offer up a similar story to this one, from her own childhood, and would remind Marlee how careful she needed to be about time slipping away. About the impermanence of youth and the great, dull, unrelenting stain of longevity. Marlee felt invigorated in this secluded yard near the ocean with these people who would surely become her benefactors, her people to worship. Like those teenagers from Lichfield, but less like a cult. All this work in the muggy summer evening. She looked up, and imagined bats in the branches.

★

The audition was five days away. Marlee shut the door to her room and untacked the monologue from her corkboard. She paced back and forth between her desk and the window. In her guise as Marguerite, she rewarded herself with a swig from a carton of chocolate milk every four turns of the room.

> *The night is engraved with howls and cries as sharp as teeth.*
> *Foul cackling comes shiny black through window cracks.*

On her bed lay the in-progress costume. She'd looked online, but the made-in-China ones were the type her friends would wear on Halloween, all pleather dark as coal and stitched-up corsets and knee-high boots, but no judgement, Alexis and Lou. Instead, Marlee cut up her mother's umbrella and sewed the pieces onto the long sleeves of a black top. In Emmett's monologue, Marguerite herself became 'wet-nosed' and developed 'starry-pointed ears'. On her pillow was the feathery hood Marlee was constructing. It had furry ears and a ribbon to tie beneath her chin.

Marlee's mother was posing one of her hypotheticals. In the kitchen, both their faces were a mess of shadow and glare from the pendant light above the breakfast bar. Marlee had her mother's dead-straight brown hair, as coarse as a horse's tail. Her mother squeezed out a dishcloth and set it like a rosette beside the sink while she formulated her question:

Suppose you gave birth to a son and then you had a daughter and they gave you nothing but joy and made you nothing but proud. And they won prizes and were nice to their grandparents and taught themselves how to poach eggs just the way their mother liked. But then they grew up, which you knew was coming, but still it took you by surprise one day, as though someone rang the doorbell and yelled *Delivery!* and the delivery wasn't a bouquet of tulips from your depressed ex-husband but two teenagers who pretended to barely know you but wanted to live in your house. Suppose those teenagers gave you grief for not knowing the difference between Google and Facebook, or for accidentally sending a donation cheque to a politician who was actually anti-gay rights, neither of which made you a bad person. And hypothetically you had read somewhere that it's important to give your children wings so they learn how to fly. And one way of giving your children wings might be to stop driving them everywhere and start encouraging them to pick a career that might make them some actual, human money.

'So, this acting thing, my beautiful girl,' her mother said, rinsing crumbs from the dishcloth under a heavy stream of water. 'Where is *that* leading, hey? And your brother's lack of any sort of direction. How hard can it be?'

Damien swung through the kitchen, shirtless, tickling himself and making monkey noises. He took the stairs two at a time. He called out.

141

'Love you, Mum.'

'Love you, too, Damien.'

★

Marlee accepted her brother's offer to drive her to the audition. She packed her bag into the boot, and they shot off up the street.

'Do you want to practise on me?'

She shook her head. Her guts were churning. She'd already had diarrhoea multiple times that morning. When she thought of all that rehearsal chocolate milk, she felt like throwing up.

'Slow down,' she said. 'Or, speed up. Just do something different.'

Marlee dropped her head to her knees and Damien took one hand off the wheel and rubbed, hard and certain, between her shoulderblades. He dittied the theme tune to *Batman*. Damien followed the map on his phone and Marlee didn't tell him to watch the road. They reached the university gates and wound up a hill covered in ashen-trunked gums. Damien parked the car and spun his keys into the air while she retrieved her bag. They nodded at a pretty girl in a university T-shirt giving directions at the top of the car park. They followed signs. Dozens of kids lined a black-carpeted hallway that was decorated with framed portraits of heavily eyelined alumni.

Damien stopped, pointing to where her bag lay with the costume zipped inside. 'Leave you to it, then?'

'Yep.' Marlee breathed deeply. She'd managed to forget her guts for a quarter of an hour.

He clutched her shoulder. He still had the keys in his hand. They made a sharp jab in Marlee's skin that felt good.

'Break a leg,' Damien said. 'See you back at the car.' Off he scurried, up the stairs and out of sight.

Around Marlee, kids her age chatted and took selfies and burst into laughter. Some paced the corridors, whispering to pieces of paper.

Out, damned spot! Out, I say!

the regulars'd stand aside to let 'em through, just as if they was a – a coupla kings

on the kindness of strangers

Marlee flagged down a passing university helper. 'I'm here for the auditions. When should I change into my costume?'

'No costume required, babe. Christopher and Trish like to see you "as is".'

'Okay.' Marlee picked up her bag. 'Thanks.' She turned and saw a sign, indicating up, for the bathrooms.

This was real life, Marlee decided, taking the stairs two at a time, focusing on her diaphragm, on her stage breathing. This was what it meant to be an adult, no apologies, no one else even *around*, only yourself to rely on, not even Damien, who was surely at that moment being a prowler in the bushes of the car park, too afraid to approach the hot helper girl, but wanting to, so badly. No one else was going to lug that overnight bag upstairs to the bathroom that hopefully had a disabled toilet to accommodate her new wingspan. No one else had stayed up late at night trying to poke black thread through the eye of a needle. Her mother had touched the furry hood on her way to bed, and told her it was pretty but also *a bit full-on*, and called Marlee her beautiful darling girl once again.

In the bathroom mirror, Marlee tied her hair into a low bun and slipped on the hood, leaving her face open and expressive – the face Emmett said evoked his vision of the real and transfigured Marguerite. She powdered her cheeks bronze. She circled a brown eyeliner pencil onto the tip of her nose. She pulled on black leggings and laced up the soft leather boots Geraldine had given her.

Marlee returned down the stairs to the corridor with the framed photographs. The other students in the hallway looked up and said things softly like, *Wow, that's weird.*

'Marlee Hamilton?' said another university helper. The boy ushered her into a small theatre.

On stools behind a tall desk sat a woman with close-cropped red hair and thick-rimmed glasses, and a bald man with a broad smile.

'I'm Christopher. This is Trish. Welcome, Marlee.'

'We see you've decided on an Ulrich piece today. But it isn't one we're familiar with.' Trish paused. '*Marguerite, the Fledermaus* by Emmett S Ulrich.' She looked up. 'Sounds very interesting.'

'*Fledermaus* means bat.'

Christopher asked, 'How did you come upon it?'

Marlee couldn't express it exactly.

'Did you find it on the internet?'

'No,' Marlee said. 'I met Emmett at the bakery, and I told him I was auditioning for this, and he offered to let me use one of his unpublished pieces.'

'Sorry, the bakery?'

144

'Yes.'

'That's quite an endorsement, wouldn't you say, Trish?'

Trish smiled. A low hum was coming from a vent above her head. 'I would.'

The hum turned into a ticking, grating sound. Marlee felt a slick of sweat ride down her belly.

'That's just the air conditioner kicking in,' Christopher said.

Trish asked, 'Would you like to set the scene for us here?'

'There's this girl called Marguerite and she's the daughter of the mayor' – Marlee's words came out in a rush, louder than she'd rehearsed because of the air conditioner kicking in – 'in a town that's filled up with bats. You know, loud and smelly and you can't hear yourself on the phone, and no one can sleep. Anyway, one by one everyone goes mad, even the mayor, and they either leave town or kill themselves. Except for Marguerite, who goes into this sort of weird trance whenever she's around the bats. Until she's the only one left and she turns into a bat herself.'

Marlee raised her black wings to demonstrate. Trish cleared her throat and puckered her lips.

Marlee kept her wings outstretched. 'Oh, and I think I'd be an excellent fit for your university acting program.'

Christopher was nodding. He righted himself on the stool and leant over a notepad. 'Okay, Marlee, we may take notes during your performance. When you're ready to start.'

Marlee was aware of the room's smells – coffee, paint, the tang of a marker pen. She tried, as Emmett had suggested, to summon Marguerite's hometown. Trees overhead loaded with the chaos of low-hanging bats. From that dramatic space, she would burst forth with her first line. Crouched on the floor, Marlee was aware that Trish and Christopher were concentrating very hard on not looking at each other. Marlee's thoughts turned to Lou and Cassie and Alexis and Elleni, who, after a year or so of being in Drama together, stopped saying *We Had Absolutely No Idea You Were Good*, and she was never sure if it was because she wasn't, or because they finally believed it.

Marlee began.

> *Screeching, one of us is screeching, and I am filled with vim and*
> *vigour.*
> *Shards of black-noise, bark-noise, cave-noise, come from the*
> *folded papery parcels.*
> *The bats show shiny, wet-nosed concern for my undistilled grief*
> *And their descent to the ground is as hasty as starfall.*
> *They are stretched with the angular glee of a thousand shrill*
> *lawyers.*
> *In their fine, leathery strait-jackets, I see myself.*

The air conditioner forced Marlee to project her voice from her diaphragm, that was for sure.

★

Damien opened the letter for Marlee one hard, hot afternoon in early January and left it in the lap of the Marguerite costume that he'd stuffed with toilet paper and propped up on the couch. She'd got in. She'd passed the audition. Soon after that it was the trip to Brisbane, and then several trips to Ikea and Woolies for coat hangers and peanut butter and jars of pasta sauce. For a while, Marlee lived on campus in a room with a bookshelf and narrow bed, and a desk carved with semi-revolutionary slogans, beneath a window where giant brush turkeys shuffled about.

They kept her awake.

Marlee started spending time in the middle of the night in the dorm room kitchen (brand new fridge, individually locked pantries, stove with stuck-on egg batter). One night, Joe from Room 3 burst in to find Marlee eating scraps of pear and rockmelon from a plate.

'Hey!' he said, delighted. 'You're nocturnal like me.' A sliver of green showed in his teeth.

In second semester, Marlee felt Christopher's frustration when he became her tutor for the Friday early morning workshop. All the girls in her class were like Cassie and Lou and Alexis and Elleni. Marlee thought for sure Christopher would mention the audition, but he never did. The parts of him that had seemed cool and amused watching her in her wings, following her eyelinered nose, made him now seem harried and exasperated. He was obviously furious with all his students, but Marlee felt his displeasure personally and keenly. She froze to let him pass during warm-ups when classes started at five past eight. She tried to shrink and change. When Christopher saw Marlee scuttle across the stage as Dogberry or Ismene or Betty Parris, her front to the audience like her high school teachers had taught her, Christopher yelled from his stool, 'Your back! Show the audience your back!'

In her dorm room, Marlee sandwiched her head with a pillow. The brush turkeys grunted outside.

One night in mid-semester, the girls who were most like Cassie and Lou invited Marlee to the uni bar after a History of Theatre lecture that everyone else hated but Marlee loved because it meant sitting still for two hours, and because she was soothed by their lecturer's slow-moving, cottony voice.

They met at night on the brightly lit footpath outside the uni bar. That semester, posters all over campus warned female students – the pictures were only ever of girls – to protect themselves from sex pests. Footpaths threaded down the hill through the scrub to the bus station. Reports of students being attacked were either entirely true or largely exaggerated. Marlee felt the collar of her shirt tight around her neck and wanted to loosen it. Where did it end, though, this loosening? She could only go so far. If she left now, Marlee thought suddenly, she could make it back to her room in time to change her shirt, in time to text and cancel the beers. The scent of eucalypts pitched in the air. Marlee felt it high in her nose like fruit rind. She saw her classmates. Tori – the one most like Lou – wore a thin-strapped tank top and tucked herself up tight next to Marlee. Marlee made herself be the first to speak.

'I've never been here before.'

Chloe – the one most like Cassie – cracked up.

'Honestly,' Marlee said.

'We believe you.'

At the door to the bar, a man checked their IDs. Marlee stopped herself from telling the girls this was the first time she'd been carded. They took two beers each to the big verandah out the back. The beer garden was set among trees, with tables bellied through the centre with trunks, stools pulled up, fluorescent lights buzzing above.

'So, Marlee, do you think you're going to be an actor?' Chloe asked.

Marlee shook her head slowly.

'Not even on *Neighbours* or something?' Tori asked.

'I doubt it.'

'Yeah,' Chloe said. 'You're probably right. I mean, about all of us. It's fun, right? But no one actually believes it.'

All around Marlee were tables of students, shrill and sharp. Gold light across the timber planks. Black coats and boots. Leaning over each other, making arguments that blossomed from the residue of tutorial discussions. Marlee yearned for her bedroom, her vase of slender flowers, the photo of her brother and mum set in her wardrobe so she would ration it. She was smitten with the idea that they were missing her. The beer was softening her mind. Tonight, surely, she would be able to sleep. Chloe and Tori touched hands when they talked to each other. They were elastic, they were liquid. Boys from the lecture drifted over to their table and Marlee felt unable to speak. One boy tried three times to ask Marlee a question, his voice growing hotter and louder and closer. Her ear, feeling a bruise. No one was unkind. She was stone, she was composed of straw.

Marlee stood. She pressed her hands to the sides of her face and closed her eyes.

'No way. What? Stay,' Chloe said.

Tori held out her arm and pulled her into a hug. 'No sleep! One more?'

Damien never did anything he didn't want to do. Marlee thought, *I don't want to.* She said it aloud. Chloe and Tori shrugged and blew kisses. No one was unkind.

All semester: more noise. Roommates having sex: Rooms 1 and 7, then Rooms 7 and 4, then 4 and 3, then back to the original formation. Starting at lunchtime when he rose, Joe played hours of podcasts about Tarantino movies and economic conspiracies and melting ice-caps that streamed out of his room and down the hallway. And, yes, Marlee could have afforded to be more light-hearted. To be more tolerant in this shared space. To welcome things like everyone else seemed able to. To make being open and cool her *thing.* Open-minded, open-hearted, show us your back.

But the noise.

The turkeys shuffling, TV blaring. Before university she'd never noticed, but now Marlee was aware of a seam in her mind that let the noise in. Even those noises that she knew weren't there. The high ringing of a bell, somewhere. Scratching. Screeching.

It took a lot of willpower for Marlee to make an appointment at the campus medical centre. The nice bulk-billing doctor tapped details into the computer and lined up his questions. How long had she been feeling this way and who had she told about the lack of sleep and did she know there was no shame in asking for help and did she realise she was brave, actually? Marlee tried not to cry but the pain of trying was hot and cold in her forehead. She could taste only one question: *Why is it easy for everyone else?*

Despite all her efforts, Marlee could not get herself to metamorphose.

★

Damien texted that he was parked outside the dorm. Marlee said goodbye to Joe in the lounge room, who woke up in the late afternoon light in front of the TV – a hostile glow on his white dinner plate. More scraps of food. Joe, irritated, turned underneath his brown blanket and got twisted there. He stayed snug while Marlee made three more trips till Damien's car was full. They drove home with the radio on. News of early summer bushfires scalding somewhere west.

When she and Damien got home, her mother fixed her with a kind look, like, *My beautiful darling girl, twelve months is nothing, not in the grand scheme of things.*

'There's lasagne,' was what she said.

Up in her bedroom, Marlee found that the screeching had stopped. She lay flat on her bed and closed her eyes.

★

Marlee's boss at the Milford bakery was a beautiful Italian woman who sent her home with leftover jam biscuits for Damien and gave her a pedicure voucher for her birthday. She let her keep her phone on in the back room, past the ovens and the dough mixers, and Marlee checked it before she started her shift. A message from her mother to bring home bread. She washed her hands and knotted her apron behind her back.

Marlee lifted a tray of sausage rolls onto a shelf. When she straightened up, she saw a face and for a second she linked it with someone from her time at university. The woman – was she a lecturer, a librarian, the sweet nurse at the clinic? The woman up-ended a bottle of orange juice, then set it upright on the counter, ready to purchase.

'Oh,' Marlee said, realising who it was.

'Yes?' the woman said.

'Nothing.'

'Now, wait, I know you!'

Reluctantly, she explained. 'Marlee. We met last year. I came to your house.'

'Of course, yes, the barbecue. How lovely.'

Coins in Geraldine's fingers. Clink on glass countertop. Marlee's boss chiming in from the back room, *I found the other carton, darling.*

'We'd have you round again,' Geraldine said, 'but Emmett and I are just now selling the place.'

The seaside timber house with the lawn all around. Sweat on the back of her chair at the barbecue and yellow lights strung across the verandah. Marlee would have loved another night like that.

'Oh. Where are you off to?'

'Nothing like that.' Geraldine unscrewed the bottle and took a sip that was dainty. Still, a thin stream of juice dribbled down her chin. She wiped it with her finger. 'Emmett,' she said, 'has been unwell.'

'I'm so sorry.'

Geraldine smiled. 'There was a lot more in life he wanted to do. But we mustn't be ridiculous. We don't get a say in all that, do we?'

A needle of panic as Marlee waited for Geraldine to ask about the audition, about university. Geraldine was precisely the type of person Marlee was afraid of. Everything she'd tried to hold on to had been taken away, and she felt that if Geraldine asked her she'd crumble right there. Cassie and Lou and Alexis – not Elleni, she hadn't heard from her once all year – had wanted to know. But only in the early days of her year at university, and even then only in an *Anyway how are youuuuuu?* kind of way.

Marlee waited, at the cash register, for Geraldine's question to come.

But other people – Milford locals and tourists who brought their children to holiday each summer at the calm water – seemed to appear at the bakery. All of a sudden those customers made up their minds, too, about what they wished to buy.

Geraldine picked up her drink. 'That night in the yard seems so long ago now!'

'I hope Emmett is okay,' Marlee said.

Stepping unsteadily backwards to let another customer through, Geraldine touched a hand to her temple.

At the end of her shift Marlee untied her apron, folded it into her bag, picked up a loaf to take home for her mother, and pushed on the door of the bakery. The air was hot. Summer wasn't over yet. There was still a month left.

Cold Springs

Lily doesn't know what to wear but she's already late. She searches the clothes on her floor until she finds jeans and a black and white striped tee. So she puts those on and goes out to the lounge room and asks her mum what she thinks. Great, is what her mum says, as if surprised to be asked. Really lovely. She asks what time it all starts, and Lily grimaces.

'Chelsea and Tim are already there. I missed the bus they were on.'

'Will you be back in time for the baby?' Her mother lies on the couch, a glass of water within reach. Lily's parents are babysitting for her cousin, who's in town for a wedding. No infants allowed in the Sapphire Marquee of the Cold Springs City Golf Club.

'Not sure.' Lily pauses at the door, noting her mum's pale form. 'Do you need anything …?'

Her mum waves her away. 'I'm fine.'

At the bus stop Lily fishes two plastic rings out of her bag and a necklace to clip on. She pushes her hair to the right, over her shoulder. She hails the bus and buys a return ticket from the driver. Printed on a card next to his fare machine is a sign: *WORLD'S MOST AWESOME BUS DRIVER*. He snaps off the ticket, pretending to read the destination printed there. 'Good for you,' he says. 'Young people, like you, getting into it.'

Soon she's stepping off the bus with a dozen others, spotting Tim first and then Chelsea. At one point Lily had vague ideas about pressing things with Tim, about flirting more. She'd considered fashioning Chelsea into the shape of a cuddled-up best friend. But neither of those – not free and easy high school girlfriend, nor devout sharer of secrets – suits her right now.

They hug and join the crowds marching, yelling, laughing towards Town Hall. At the front are people with signs and flags, chanting. The Grandmas With Grenades group and the Farmers Free Action Coalition and the Lock The Gate people. Half a dozen boys in footy jerseys and green and gold caps joke, wave their signs half-heartedly. Lily recognises their embarrassment.

The first speaker is a woman in a suit who says she met with ministers in Canberra about the earthquakes and came home with 'binders and binders filled with bullshit'. An old man in a brown vest stands at the microphone to recall coming across a 'hug of wombats' who had died from contaminated bore water. Chelsea yells the loudest. Mr Lowe from their high school steps back from a stall selling cold drinks and asks Lily how her mother is. Before she got sick, her mum used to protest alongside Mr Lowe's wife.

Afterwards, Lily, Chelsea and Tim collapse into seats two rows from the back of the bus. It shoots towards the suburbs where dozens of apartment blocks have been built, looking at once strange and also completely at home in the new Cold Springs. In town, the rec centre has a new roof and proper air conditioning. Lily's high school got a makeover – a multipurpose hall was built and the football oval was resurfaced. Way beyond their school's sporting fields, the drilling rigs are statues of light against the burnt-sugar sunset.

'So your mum still has actual cancer?' Tim asks.

'Yeah,' Lily says. 'Ovarian.'

'I'm so sorry.' Tim fixes his gaze out the window of the bus. 'Fucking cancer, hey.'

'The whole thing sterilises the land,' Chelsea says, reading a flyer. She slashes her hand across the air. *Sterile.* 'All that waste? It spills out.'

As shops flash past, Lily is reminded of the video clip that Chelsea sent her last week, with CCTV footage of a woman shoplifting from a convenience store. She saw how the thief pretended to weigh up decisions in her mind, as if checking packets for ingredients or the logo about not testing on animals. The video ran for five minutes, the shoplifter stepping back and forth between the makeup and a stand of birthday cards where she crouched to drop tubs of moisturisers, mascara, lipsticks, a heavy plastic bottle. Lily watched the teenager behind the counter scanning cigarettes and boxes of cereal, never once looking up to notice the woman's bag fattening. The video ended with an appeal for public information, emphasising that this was a family business, with the loss estimated at four hundred dollars.

'That shoplifting video,' Lily says. 'Why'd you send me that?'

Chelsea shrugs. 'It was mesmerising, like, *Quit while you're ahead, lady!* She just kept on stealing the fucking makeup. Didn't you think it was mesmerising?' She presses the bell for the next stop.

Lily noticed the pretend-urgency in the woman's movements and the murmurs at her lips. Going through the motions, even for herself. If someone had seen her it would have looked as though she planned to buy them all along. *I've had this one before. I'll try it again.*

'What video?' Tim asks.

'Everyone's turning on each other,' Chelsea says.

Months earlier, Lily had sat in Chelsea's bedroom, watching her copy and paste notes off the internet about stocking up on tinned food and batteries. Worry had trundled through Lily. She tried to push herself through it.

Chelsea motions for Tim to hop up with her. 'Not to sound dramatic,' she says, 'but it's true. Call me later?'

The bus almost empty now, Lily reads the text messages from her mum that say the baby, Pearl, has arrived. Then: the baby is gorgeous. The baby has vomited. The baby is sucking Bear-Bear's nose. The baby is going to adore Lily. The baby is going for a walk with Lily's dad while they wait for her to come home.

She glances up at a man standing in the aisle at the end of her seat, all grey in trackpants and a sweatshirt rolled up to the elbows. He's older than her dad, but not by much, and Lily smiles at him, the way she's been taught to smile at people who have something wrong with them even if you can't tell what it is.

'Hello,' he says, his voice licking itself on the *lo.*

'Hi.' Lily turns back to the window, willing him gone. Irritation creases her face at the thought of Chelsea and Tim's absence.

Then the man is beside her, dropping into the seat. His left arm, the one closer to the aisle, rests on the bar in front. She'll be trapped now, listening to his story, giving him a couple of bucks. Four or five stops to go.

'Had a good day?' he asks. He slides his hand into his right pocket, a sliver of fabric between his thigh and hers. Chelsea took a steak knife to Lily's jeans right after she bought them, piercing the denim above and below the knee, drawing out the cotton entrails with her fingers.

'Yes, thanks,' Lily says, propped up by politeness.

Even when the man's hand in his right pocket starts moving, like he's searching for something, and even when she realises, as she excuses herself over his knees and stumbles down the steps of the bus onto the verge and tries to force the air into a useful shape around her, that the man, who watched her with a dirty, breathy smile, was masturbating, right there beside her, all the way from Urquhart Avenue through the suburbs with their sickening brown lawns and tethered dogs leaving paw prints on soil that belongs to the CSG company, all the way to Richmond Street, four blocks from her house, Lily is nothing but polite. As the bus drives off, she swallows the panic attack she recognises she's having: that stuck-at-the-bottom-of-the-ocean feeling among the letterboxes and the flame trees and the suffocating sky.

She makes it home, forcing air in through her nose and out her mouth. She stands in the driveway and watches the house. She cannot go inside yet. She will have to face her parents and the baby and not go straight to her room: better to wait here. She rests a hand on the Toyota, driven less and less by her mum now. Last year, after yet another chemo session, Lily woke to find the house empty. The car was in the garage, so she knew her mum had kept her promise not to drive anywhere. Lily stood on the verandah, checking her watch. Hours later a taxi pulled up to the kerb and her mum kicked the door open and eased herself out of the front passenger seat, acknowledging Lily – now running towards her – with a wave.

'Sorry, love, I got caught up.'

'Mum, I thought you had *died*.'

'Oh, love, no.' She shifted shopping bags along her arms. 'There was this man in the train station, a busker. He did all these Bob Dylan covers, but he was *better* than Bob Dylan. Don't know if it was the acoustics or maybe just his talent.' She led Lily back up the steps to the front door, wiping her shoes theatrically, unnecessarily. To go shopping she had worn a long-sleeved blue dress, in spite of the heat.

'What are you talking about?'

'I filmed it, see, and told him I was going to upload it to Facebook. Maybe Bob Dylan will see him and he'll be discovered.'

'Do you really think Bob Dylan gives a shit about some busker?'

'But he was so good. He was *better*.' Her mother set half a dozen kisses on the side of Lily's face. She squirmed away.

'Jesus. Stop.'

Her mum froze, her pinky-pale skin flushing. She used to have long red hair that was for Lily to curl in her fingers and gaze at.

'See?' her mum said finally. She pulled out her phone. 'I filmed it. Just press play.'

'No. He probably wished you'd go away. He probably thought you were weird.' Without meaning to, she glanced up at her mum's headscarf.

Her mother clamped her lips tight, seeming to burn. 'Maybe he took pity on a sick old woman like me. Is that what you mean?'

'You didn't answer your phone. I thought you had died.'

Lily is late now. She takes the steps two at a time and finds her father in the kitchen, pulling a beer from the fridge. He kisses her forehead and asks if she's okay. He rests the beer there, a joke, to cool her down. He offers her a sip and ushers her onto the carpet where her mother holds Pearl in her lap, the baby gnawing on a ring of plastic keys. Lily's father puts his arm around her. He motions towards the baby.

'You used to be that big. I could carry you like this — right here with me. Safe as houses.'

Her mother is holding the sleeping baby on her chest. Lily watches them breathe — her mum and Pearl. Behind them, her father works quietly to clean the kitchen. He motions for Lily to sit with her mother.

Nobody wants to move the baby to the travel cot that's set up in the study. Her mum explains that she made up the mattress and put a stuffed bunny in the corner, but they say no stuffed toys in beds for babies anymore, so she moved it sentinel on the carpet beneath the cot. She had found Lily's old sheets, the pale green set with the clowns.

'Do you remember?'

Lily recalls the fuzz of flannelette sheets in winter, the electric blanket hot on the backs of her legs. 'I remember giraffes, not clowns. Poor Pearl – clowns are scary.'

'All those memories. Everything comes back.' Her mother shakes her head a little. 'But also, strangely, nothing comes back.'

Her mum keeps saying weird things. Ever since the cancer, she's been obsessed with remembering the time when Lily was young. Lily makes herself small among the cushions. She balls up her hand and snugs it inside her mother's palm, trying to be still.

But how physical is Lily's desire for a fight.

'How was the protest today?' her mum asks. 'You used to come to those things with me, helped me carry my signs.'

Lily scoffs. 'What's the point?'

'Sorry?'

'They'll just do what they want with the land and the water, hey? It won't change a thing whether Chelsea and Tim and me, or Mr Lowe or the mayor were there today.'

'I thought we were having a nice chat.'

'What's the point of anything?' Lily asks.

'The baby doesn't ask *what's the point?*, do you, Pearly?'

'And once it's out, it's out.' Chelsea's word: *sterile*. Other words: water table. Waste water. Chemical concentrations. Benzene. Xylene. Paclitaxel. Docetaxel. Cisplatin. Carboplatin. Lily's mum texts people during her hospital stays to ask how

161

they are coping with all the stress in town, smiling big when she gets visitors. Lily thinks her mother could save a lot of energy if she stopped trying to win at everything and everyone. Her mum has never gotten better, only worse. Only the same. 'No offence, but you and your signs made no difference.'

'Hmm.' Her mother's eyes are wet as she fondles Pearl's toes, nested in the jumpsuit. 'Wonder what they're doing now at the wedding.'

For an instant Lily wants to tell her about the man on the bus. But she stops herself. Too humiliating. Too fearsome. Waste of time. She will keep it a secret from everyone. It's as though someone has cut out the man from the bus and fixed him to her insides.

She's almost crying. She sits up and runs her fingertips up and down her mum's arm.

Her mother shuts her eyes. 'Oh, I love that.'

'Remember,' Lily says, 'when Dad got a speeding ticket on our way to Uncle Bill's wedding? And I didn't know I wasn't supposed to tell people, so I announced it at the church — *Hey, everyone. Dad got pulled over!* — and he was so embarrassed.'

'I remember.'

'You were furious.'

Pearl opens her mouth, maybe searching for milk, kissing the air. 'Tell me a secret,' Lily hears her mother beg. 'Pearl and I won't tell. Look. It's just between us.'

'Why?'

'Because I'm your mum and you used to tell me everything. Before there were boys, you used to tell me all your secrets.'

Lily stops tickling and releases her other fingers from her mother's hand. 'There are no *boys*. That isn't a thing.'

'What about Tim? He's a boy. You being careful?'

'Mum, we're just friends.'

'Tell me,' she hisses. 'That's all I care about.'

Lily stares at the baby. Pearl's lips are a rosy fruit. For a few seconds it takes her mind off things.

'Is he good to you?'

'He's not my husband. He doesn't have to be good to me.' Lily sees her mum's horror. 'But, yes. He is.'

Lily touches her mother's blanched skin and lightly feathered scalp. She doesn't wear the scarves anymore – she used to, in the early days, when she still went to big rallies.

'He's not anything. You know that, don't you?'

'Tim?' Lily feels tricked into saying his name.

Her mother says softly, 'You think he's something, but he's not even a blip. This boy, that boy, it doesn't even matter.'

What matters are the flames and the heat and the road trains out on the highways that are impossible to pass at night. It's the farmers selling up and the farmers killing themselves, quietly, while their wives drive to town to shop for Christmas presents. It's the chemicals injected into her mother's veins, teeming in her blood.

'Here.' She lifts Pearl from her chest. 'Your turn. I need to lie down.'

In mid-air, Pearl's arms and legs jerk outwards, then curl back into themselves. She starts to whimper.

'Is it time for a bottle?' Lily asks, but her mother is already stepping around the coffee table, untying her fisherman pants on the way to bed.

Eh eh eh. Pearl fusses.

'Doug?' her mother calls from the bedroom.

'Mum needs you. Dad?'

When no answer comes, Lily eases off the couch and carries Pearl out onto the front verandah to look for her dad there. She closes the screen door behind her.

A tremor.

It shivers through her body, like car sickness. The earthquakes in Cold Springs once seemed so frightening, so cinematic. But now they don't amount to much.

'Coming, Michelle,' her father yells inside. 'Hon? Did you feel that?'

In the distance, the flames from the wells look like solar flares rising up from crystal columns of lights. Beyond the horizon, the man on the bus wanders the aisles. He lurches from seat to seat, from secret-keeper to secret-keeper. And the secret of Cold Springs is not a secret at all, but something under the ground that is so huge it's easier to be mesmerised by it all, to never wonder at what it would mean to just stop. Quit while they're ahead.

The earthquake subsides. Under the silk of the Sapphire Marquee, champagne glasses will have stopped chiming.

'Pearl,' Lily whispers. 'Did you feel that?' In the air, a somersaulting heat. The palm trees in the front yard sway.

They say the Cold Springs boom could last for one hundred years. Lily studies the curled-up baby slipping once again towards sleep. In one hundred years, Pearl will be an old woman, back to her purees, in the scar-tissue white light of a nursing-home sunroom. A carer will be tethered close, patting her hand, talking loudly and slowly about the land and the sky beyond the window.

Lily pictures the boom ending like a dying star.

But that takes millions of years. So she pictures it decaying like cancer, which is still years, yes, but unmistakable.

Brushed Bright Bones

One thing people don't understand about reincarnation is that it's not about whether you're good or bad, it's about whether you're interesting. And I just keep coming back.

This trip I've turned up in Leicester. Again. For my sins. We've got a good enough football team, the Foxes, and I watch them on telly – Mum can't take me to a game because we're poor. Sid's mum bought him a team scarf from the Oxfam on the high street. She thinks this should satisfy him, but he can't explain that getting someone's dirty old Foxes scarf is worse than not having one at all.

The Foxes play at King Power Stadium. Other places people visit in Leicester include the Abbey Pumping Station, which used to pump sewage. We went there last year with Dad when he was in town for the day. It's free, which is why he chose it. All he'd brought for us were two sandwiches from the off-licence. Dakota was teething and Dad had forgotten the gel.

Not every reincarnation is a thrill.

In 1520, I was working the shipyards in Hull. Hard work, very dangerous. One night I met a woman named Anne. She'd come from York to find her brother who'd gotten into trouble gambling. We drank at the Rose and Turtle, eventually moving out to the street. Anne told me that forty years earlier her grandmother had created a scandal. A beautiful woman, she'd been summoned in secret to become the mistress of a very powerful man. He turned out to be Plantagenet, the future King Richard III of England. Five years later, he died in battle.

Anne had a crooked nose and huge bug eyes. Still, one thing led to another and we slept together before daybreak. I left her before she woke – I'm not proud of that. I'm hazy on the details but I may have emptied her purse too.

Right now, Leicester is exciting – the university thinks they're going to find Richard III's body buried beneath a council car park. Dr Nicole Lacey is the osteoarchaeologist on the dig. Last night on TV, Dr Lacey only got to answer one reporter's question ('How does this compare with other archaeology projects you've worked on?'). Sid reckons Dr Lacey would knock me back if I asked her on a date, because she looks like Megan Fox dressed as a scientist. If I looked like Channing Tatum maybe she'd say yes, but reincarnates don't get to select our bodies or where we end up. I didn't choose my mum or how much money she makes, or her boyfriends who leave their greasy takeaway containers on the floor. I'll bet Dr Lacey lives in an apartment with a great view. Everything is clean. The furniture is brushed metal and frosted glass. There are paintings of Venice and girls picking wildflowers. Apple TV and an Xbox. And the milk in her fridge is never off.

In History class, Mr Purcell leans on the ledge beneath the whiteboard, gnawing on a marker. 'Ricky, it's your turn. Answer what you're up to.'

Each trip my eyesight worsens. Reading is hard.

'Evidence suggests Richard III was buried at Greyfriars after the Battle of Bosworth in 1485,' I say. 'The church was demolished by Henry VIII and built over many times.'

Mr Purcell nods but he's surveying the class. They rip paper and tip back in their chairs and slip headphones into their ears.

'Year 10, listen, please. This is happening right here in Leicester.'

I've never come back as a teacher, which is lucky. Not all reincarnations are from birth – most people don't know that either. This time round was. I emerged back when my mum and my grandparents were still speaking. In the maternity ward, Nanny and Pop hooked their fingers into mine. They'd brought a stuffed blue rabbit for me and a bag of Starburst for Mum even though she'd asked for Minstrels. Reincarnations that aren't birth-beginning occur after a near-death experience – it's like you've been tagged in for a wrestling match. I've opened my eyes on a Mexican beach, water in my lungs, gasping, my throat like a salted fish. Brown eyes searched my face and voices called, *Hola! Hola!*

'Mouths closed, please.' Mr Purcell caps and uncaps the whiteboard marker. 'Eyes to the front. This is on the exam.'

At lunch, Sid and I sit on the edge of the oval. The girls' hockey team blurs navy and white like Prussian soldiers bolting from the trenches. Sid passes me a cigarette.

'So you never met him yourself, then?' he asks.

'No, I met Anne. But her grandmother was Richard's mistress.'

'Like a prostitute?'

'More like a girlfriend on the side.'

Sid pinches the cigarette and sucks with his thumb and forefinger against his lips. *Puh, puh, puh*, like the cigarette is a joint. I've said before that marijuana is a disaster for people like him.

'But you saw the bones of Richard III?'

'Absolutely,' I say.

'Cool.'

We head into town. These days most of the shops are food places like Greggs and Pret. There's at least one Boots, and a Costa Coffee where Mum and Aunty Jude meet once a month. They grew up here, but it was safer back then, they say. Not as many angry drunks roaming the streets. Not as many people high late at night who might wander in front of your car.

Sid tries to puncture an empty Coke can with two sticks. A pair of arms for a tin snowman.

'It won't work.'

'Why not?'

'The can's too tough,' I say. It should be obvious.

'We'll see.'

The stick slips and pierces Sid's wrist. He devours his blood. 'Cool. Looks like I tried to kill myself.'

'Kind of.'

'It might scar,' Sid says.

'You got any money?'

'Five quid. You?'

In one of my past lives I ran a travelling magic show: Babette's Caravan of Mystical Wonders and Magical Encounters. This was the east coast of America, 1925, and although Babette was long gone, her name still had traction in certain circles. The governor of Virginia invited us to his mansion, where Bart Brueghel cut out stars in the palms of his hands that healed before the politicians' eyes. Kitty Lee balanced her twin sister, Lulu, on her head, and Lulu's feet dirtied the governor's ceiling. We swallowed waves of gin cocktails and slept on monogrammed sheets.

I tell Sid, 'Nah. I got nothing.'

We slouch on the corner of New and Peacock. The workers at the council offices have less space to park now – that was in the newspaper. Three weeks ago, they photographed the digger plunging into the bitumen and I wondered if the operator had ever done his job in front of cameras before. I've never worked with heavy machinery, unless you count a primitive helicopter in southern Spain.

Everyone was hoping for a body straight away: brushed bright bones showered with champagne under floodlights. But there's just been days of waiting. People talking, pointing, adjusting their University of Leicester hard hats.

How do I tell Dr Lacey it's all futile? They're not going to find the King.

The last time I was in Leicester, I did something shifty, although Sid thinks it's awesome. Two dozen of us were rambling and red from drinking, roaring in the moonlight to the sound of shovels on dirt. Turner, the innkeeper, came along and we loaded the bones into a barrel he'd brought. I sensed drums at my back, a grand and valiant march, and momentum in the frosty air. We rolled the barrel through town and up Bow Bridge. Turner thought I should speak so he called for the cheers to die down.

I began: 'Hear that, lads? Inside this barrel, the bones of Richard III! A nasty bugger, he was. And now His Majesty can float in purgatory and pray for forgiveness until such time as the wood gives way and his sins sink to the bottom.'

I saw my gathered brethren clearly, at a time when my eyesight was far sharper than it is now. The tomb splashed and bobbed on the River Soar.

Now, all I care about is seeing Dr Lacey and hearing her laugh, which is difficult since the trench is taped off from visitors. She wears white work overalls and a mask over her mouth and nose. She rests on her heels in the pit and brushes the ground with tiny movements. Dr Lacey is the youngest member of the dig. In an interview on YouTube she says the best thing about the archaeology department is being part of an amazing team of historians. Sid always pauses the video at 4:29. Dr Lacey wears glasses, like me. At four-and-a-half minutes, her eyes are closed behind her lenses. With hair whipped out by the wind, she's a divine scholarly mermaid. Her accent reminds me of a wife I had in Cardiff, but her eyes remind me of someone else.

University people gather with iPads. Dr Lacey is helped out of the trench. She places her hands on the small of her back and bends. Then she notices us, smiles to her colleagues, and heads our way.

'Aw shit,' Sid says. 'Here's your chance.'

'I'm thinking,' I say.

'Of what?' He glances over at Dr Lacey and grins. 'Oh, wait. I know.'

I sigh. 'They're never going to find him.'

'Tell her.'

'Depends. She'll want to know how I know.' I swing myself up onto the brick wall and Sid follows.

'Nah. They just want to find the body. And if you're right, then − *bam*. You'll be famous and we get to hang out with Dr Lacey.'

In this life, I am a virgin. I think about my former sexual encounters at least sixty, seventy times a day. Teenage hormones. But it's important to be disciplined. Reincarnates have to move past what they *used* to have. I employ the obvious strategies, and hope for an early encounter in this life. It's been a long time between innings, and Dr Lacey has lips like Clara Bow's.

'Mate, she's coming over.'

We've never seen her up close in person. She's a nuclear scientist. She's a disease control expert. She's the starship commander in a science fiction movie. She's something else, too, but I can't figure it out. I rub my eyes.

Dr Lacey says, 'Gentlemen,' and my groin pulses.

'Hi,' I say.

'Hey, Dr Lacey,' Sid says. 'We saw you on telly.'

She rests a gloved hand across her forehead and squints. 'You boys interested in this? You've been here a few times.'

'Have we?' says Sid, bold and chuckling. I want to beat him around the head and push him into the pit.

'We're interested,' I say.

'What's your name?' Dr Lacey stares at me, sweat on her upper lip.

'He's Sid. I'm Ricky.'

'Is that so? We're looking for a Ricky in there too, although I doubt he was ever called that.'

I tell her what I know about the King, but I stick to the facts that Mr Purcell says will be on the exam. Dr Lacey nods when I mention Greyfriars and Henry VIII.

Sid can't sit still any longer. 'Ricky thinks you're wasting your time. The bones aren't there.'

Dr Lacey glances at me.

'You wanna know how he knows?' Sid continues.

I don't try to stop him. It's a harmless thing to tell people – *I've been reincarnated thirty-four times.*

'Ricky's been reincarnated.'

As if released from her freeze in Sid's YouTube video, Dr Lacey tips back her head, and lets out a glorious laugh. 'Reincarnated, hey?'

Sid thinks I'm in. 'Yup.'

I notice a tiny mole beneath her left eye. I could kiss that spot. I could find others, too, our bodies stretched out on the Persian rug in her apartment. I forget Sid is here. Dr Lacey is still and silent, and we study each other. In her face, I see lives I can almost count. I grow tired as centuries whip past and thirty-four journeys burst into life. Icy mountains and a crossbow in my fist. A wooden weather deck lurching on the waves. Fields of poppies crushed beneath my knees.

Last year, I got chatting with a man in the library. After a bit, I told him that I knew him, I really did. He shelved his book and looked away and said, 'I've got nothing for you, kid,' and Dakota was playing up, tearing into the books, so we had to go anyway. I have to remind myself that not all reincarnates feel their lives as strongly as I do. Mine are like engravings.

'Reincarnated? As in, you've been here before?' Dr Lacey asks. 'Like, in a past life?'

I nod.

She smiles. 'Well, I'm a scientist. Scientists don't believe in reincarnation. Sorry.'

'That's okay,' I say. 'I understand.'

'It's great you're interested. But we've done our research and there's a good chance we'll find something.'

Sid's expectations have been dashed. He rises above us on the brick wall. 'But Ricky says the bones are long gone. Don't you want to know where they are?'

Dr Lacey checks around for signs of her colleagues. 'Looks like a good view up there, Sid. Be careful.'

'But then you'd be the one who found him,' Sid yells. 'You'd be famous.'

Sid's used to being ignored. My pasts are the most concrete part of his life. Who cares if you can't see the Foxes play live when your best friend helped draw up the rules for association football in 1863?

I drop off the wall and polish my glasses with my jumper. 'It's cool. Let's go.'

I bring the washing in for Mum from the clothesline that we share with the rest of the flats. Last week someone stole Dakota's pyjamas. I play blocks on the carpet with my sister and tell her a story about a princess who believed she'd swallowed a glass piano. The princess tiptoed around the castle and couldn't bring herself to dance or touch the walls or climb the stairs. She was petrified the piano would break and she'd be filled with broken glass. It was my job to carry the princess from her bed to the garden while she took short breaths in my arms. Dakota loves princesses. She can say *Mum*, *bubble*, *ball* and *milk*. My name comes out like *Icky*.

I slice sausages and pumpkin and switch on the news. Dakota bobs up and down when the opening song comes on.

'Dance, baby.' I reach for her. 'That's it. Dance.'

The first local news item is about the Leicester dig. The camera pans to the car park – probably the most watched piece of bitumen in Britain. Mum thinks the find will generate new pride in Leicester, make the city go back to the way it used to be. I turn off the sound and lift Dakota. I point out the scientists.

'See the people wearing helmets?' I tap her head. 'They're digging in the ground.' How to explain a skeleton without scaring her? Dakota squirms and spills from my arms. She picks up a crust from the floor and puts it to her mouth.

'Yucky,' I tell her.

Mum will be home at ten o'clock. She said Kevin could come round and watch us, but he smells of smoke and Dakota doesn't like him, which isn't Kevin's fault. Things are just easier if I cook dinner for us and do my homework after my sister's gone to sleep. Mum's boyfriends avoid me; they never try anything with her when I'm around. *Careful*, they think. They can see in my eyes that I'm not just some kid.

Dakota palms the television glass. At a press conference, the mayor gestures and the university staff grin.

'That's Dr Lacey,' I say. 'I know her.' Details of past lives slip away so easily; it's impossible to know which parts of a journey I'll need later.

But I get it now. It's *her*.

That's why she's familiar. That's why Dr Lacey thinks she knows where Richard III's body is buried.

Anne had mentioned her grandmother, but the night at the Rose and Turtle was so long ago, and maybe I'd covered Anne's lips as she spoke. A sister looking for her brother in Hull. A lover I robbed. Her grandmother, the King's beautiful mistress, who had revealed where her beloved was buried. The osteoarchaeologist with the thick, strong lenses.

I knew I'd kissed Dr Lacey before.

The phone rings. On the other end of the line, someone slurps from a can. 'Ricky?'

'Sid, oh shit,' I say. 'Guess who Dr Lacey is?'

'What? She's on the news now.'

I focus on the TV screen. Of course it's her, almost five hundred years later, and she's so beautiful. Dr Lacey's lips move and her glasses reflect the flash of the cameras. Maybe the bones made it downriver to Nottinghamshire. Perhaps we can look for them together.

'Ricky, you can't have thrown the bones in the river.'

'Yes, I did, Sid. Listen, she's *Anne*—'

'They found the skeleton in the car park. It's Richard III. Dr Lacey was right.'

But I had climbed the bridge and watched the body fall.

'Ricky?'

I was there with Turner the innkeeper and the drunks who hushed themselves while I spoke. It was my first time in Leicester, when people were quieter and things weren't as busy and police never went to schools and asked to see inside kids' bags. Back then people meant what they said. You could have a cottage with a garden and a dog that licked you on the cheek. Fathers went out to work, and when they came home, the house was warm again.

Yes, I was there. I was. I pushed the barrel up Bow Bridge and heard the bones rattle inside.

For What We Are About to Receive

State Route 18 has the best roadkill. Alison gave me directions, giggling down the phone line like she did when we were teenagers.

'Go past the Lions Club,' she said. 'It's on the left-hand side. Just before you get to that little school, the one with the mural out the front. Of the emus.'

'And it's off the road?'

'Yep. Buster found it on our walk this afternoon. But I shooed him away before he did any damage,' she said.

'Great,' I said. 'Thanks.'

'Don't you want to know what it is?'

'Is it a possum?'

I am Alison's strangest friend.

While Pete rubs his eyes and turns pages on the train home, I cross our driveway and lower myself into the Barina (bum first, breathing evenly, pretending my legs are pressed together like a mermaid's tail). The steering wheel nudges my belly. I rearrange the cushion for my back, and the bath towel that's folded on the seat. Jane, the midwife, said that a good many car seats have been ruined with amniotic fluid, though Pete wouldn't care if I stained the upholstery. The last time I used this towel was to cover my shoulders while I dyed my hair strawberry blonde.

A policeman, hunched in his reflector vest, holds a radar gun beside the road just out of town, and I ease off the accelerator. Even though I know it's eighty, maybe they've changed it since yesterday. Perhaps there are roadworks. A station wagon passes and two kids in the back beg me for a wave. A milk truck sways with a hundred thousand udders, and I almost bring up my lunchtime sandwich at the thought of all that liquid sloshing and lapping about in the stainless-steel vats. Already, each night, I check my nipples for signs of early milk. Jane said it could happen anytime from now, that it's just the body's way of getting ready. In the back of my throat, I taste the Vegemite and the butter and the bread, and breathe deeply till the nausea releases its hold.

Today's sacrifice fell from heaven whereupon a Pajero sent it skywards again. Above is the powerline where it must have scuttled and lost its grip – alarm wheeling through its brain. Up ahead I see the school with the mural; I indicate for five seconds and pull onto the side of the road. Four-wheel drives whip past, but nobody stops to hear the lies on my lips, ready to be born. *Breaks my heart to see them on the road.* Or, *Why do they call it morning sickness, haha, if it lasts all night?*

On his side, his claws curled up, Possum sermonises in the grass: *But ask now the beasts, and they shall teach thee; and the fowls of the air, and they shall tell thee.* I lean in: he's been strafed across the head. His cheeks are bloodied and sticky with grass, but his body is mercifully untouched. Possum is in one piece, and likely only two or three hours dead.

Hunger squeezes my throat. I circle a hand across my belly: a promise, an appeasement. *Not long now.*

Back in the Barina, the Tupperware coffin on my passenger seat could contain anything. If that police officer is still there and he stops me, peers in with his torch, he'd have no reason to ask what was inside. Waiting for Pete at home are two chicken drumsticks glassy with cold fat, tinned eyeball potatoes and congealed waves of gravy. Wedding plate. Wedding cutlery. Pete will eat standing up, then move to the lounge room to watch TV on mute.

As I drive, I send silent thanks to Alison. The baby will be Grace, even though I think the name is too common — eight girls at our church alone have the name. But it was the only one Pete and I could agree on, and *Grace* is what he whispers into my skin at night. I've chosen her middle name, Bernadette, after my great-great-grandmother who had fourteen babies, alternating girl-boy-girl-boy, all delivered in the paddock on the way into town, and all given names beginning with S. That's the story, anyway.

Last night, I dreamt I craved green vegetables: kale, spinach, broccoli. A blooming, a flowering, a nourishing forest. A Babylonian garden within. At church, Grace H's mother drank a green power smoothie every day for nine months. And already now, Grace H, not even nineteen weeks old, is crawling. In my dream, I craved those smoothies, but they were gone when I woke up.

I've looked it up, of course, at work where my computer faces the window. It's not that unusual — some women are even willing to be photographed and interviewed. In Scotland, one woman searched for pheasants hit mid-flight by trucks an hour's drive away. She marinated the meat and served it to dinner party guests. Her friends trusted her as a great cook. Together they all had a laugh, she said.

Even a wafer. I dreamt I craved a communion wafer, pressed onto my tongue while my eyes were closed and I knelt not at the grassy side of State Route 18 but at the altar. I dreamt I could confess to Father Frank.

Blessed are they which do hunger.

Blessed are they which grip the steering wheel on the highway and scan the fiery bitumen.

Our house blisters with light, and I hide the Tupperware in my bag. But it's quiet inside. Pete is asleep in the recliner, tucked up like a foetus. His fingers touch the chicken bones. I resist kissing his greasy mouth. If he wakes, I'll tell him that I ate earlier – a bit of this, a bit of that. Always pear juice. Always carrot sticks during the day, yes. Almonds for the good fats. Cottage cheese for the iodine. Pete sighs in his sleep. He dreams of his baby in a white dress.

I sit on the back steps, where I pray and the knife blesses me till I hold in my fingers the tiny pockets of flesh that look like the oysters Pete and I fed each other on our honeymoon.

In the kitchen, in the dark, images float around me of Bernadette feeding fourteen babies in her farmhouse kitchen. I stand back from the stove and add a pool of olive oil. It's just me and Grace, who wriggles like a fish inside – perhaps she senses the building heat and is curious about what's to come, or she knows that my mouth is watering. It's just the two of us, and our sweet offering anointed in oil that sizzles in the pan.

What You Really Collect Is
Always Yourself

In the summer after primary school, my friend Sadie came to stay with us for eight nights, while her mother went on an all-inclusive cruise to Vanuatu. When Sadie arrived, Mum raised her eyebrows at the palm-sized box of chocolates Mrs Collett gave her. She zipped up the side of Sadie's suitcase where a scrap of nightie had fallen out, and tossed the chocolates onto the kitchen table as Sadie's mum drove away.

Later, after we'd eaten Hawaiian pizza with my little sister Juniper, Sadie and I offered to take slices out to Dad, who was working in the shed. We arranged them the way we thought someone in a restaurant might. We pointed the tips of the triangles together and badgered Mum for what we knew was called a garnish. She wouldn't have indulged me, but Sadie was our guest and it was only the first night, so she dug through the crisper and emerged with a sprig of parsley that we laid on top of the pizza. We stepped out into the night air.

In Dad's shed, the concrete floor was veined with paint and bristling with dust and wood shavings. Plastic zip-ties and nails and screws and a million other bits of metal hung collected in old jam jars, their lids glued to the undersides of rows of shelves so they were easy to unscrew. After Pop died at the start of the year, Dad commandeered his tools. He wanted to restore Pop's yellow Morris Minor. There it sat in the middle of the shed under a bedsheet and a lightbulb on a cord.

'Dad? There's pizza for you.'

I saw his head bump up from a bench opposite the car. He stood, holding a tin and a paintbrush.

'Natalie. Sadie.'

'What are you doing, Mr Simmons?'

He swept a hand towards Pop's car.

'Is that your granddad's?' Sadie asked.

'Pop drove it every day, didn't he, Dad?'

Dad started sniffing, making odd little crying sounds. I fingered the garnish on the pizza as he let out a sob and rubbed his face where a slick of silver paint stuck to his nose. Sadie gaped at me.

'Pop was pretty sick,' I said. 'By the end.'

Dad whispered, 'He was very old.' In the dim light his face looked melted. A patchwork of dark and light. His eyes drooped like commas.

Sadie spoke loudly. 'Mum says she wants one of us kids to kill her before she gets old and loses her mind.'

Dad nodded at Sadie. 'I'm petrified of that.'

'I think Mum just means my brothers and I are really annoying.'

Dad fixed his gaze at a level just below our eyes. He told us that ageing was a disease. 'There are people,' he said, 'actual scientists, who are close to a *cure* for ageing. We humans are nothing more than machines. We are just like cars and aeroplanes that fall apart after a lifelong accumulation of damage. But we can choose to fight it. Scientists already know how to keep bodies alive after death.'

'Like in movies?' I asked.

'It's called cryonics.' Dad was skittish. He seemed to redden and swell.

'Like in freezers?' I asked. 'With your head in ice?'

Sadie let out an almost soundless laugh.

I couldn't disguise my alarm. It felt like I'd never had a conversation with him before in my life. 'What are you talking about, Dad?'

He was watching Sadie pick up a Hungry Jack's plastic novelty cup from a bench streaked with paint. She turned it over and over in her hands. She tried to stop her giggles. I thought of Sadie's mother eating dinner on the cruise, piling her plate with intestine-pink prawns and lettuce shells and globs of mayonnaise, an umbrellaed cocktail resting on the buffet. I wondered how Sadie would describe Dad to her mum, and then I wondered who Mrs Collett might tell. The truth might escape before anyone could catch it.

Mum and Juniper came round the edge of the shed and saw us all standing inside the roller door, beside the front half of Pop's Morris Minor.

'Dad, look. I fixed my gymnastics routine.' Juniper bent backwards, placing her hands on the ground and almost forming an O. Her tight little belly pulsed towards the ceiling. Upside-down her voice came thickly. 'I made it better.'

Dad made a noise like he'd forgotten Juniper existed. 'That's good, love.'

'What's going on?' Mum stared at Sadie and me.

Sadie stared back. 'Um. Cryogenics?'

'Pardon?'

'Dad is telling us,' I replied, 'that he wants to be cryogenically frozen when he dies.'

Mum looked at Dad, smiling. 'Gary. What?'

He swallowed. 'The idea is to keep on living. To just take a pause, while your body is kept alive. From the moment we are born—'

Not joking. Mum got it now. 'Oh, for Christ's sake, Gary. Sadie's here.'

Mum took up a jar of nails in her hand. The insides rattled. Juniper levered herself back to standing.

'I don't want to die,' he said. 'I don't want to leave you all behind.'

'If you love the girls so much then why don't you come in the bloody house and make the gymnastics coaches some Christmas shortbread.'

Dad's blonde eyebrows and blue eyes made him look like a Viking. At last year's disco, Sadie told me that everyone thought he was the cutest out of all the dads. He asked for anti-shine daily moisturiser for Father's Day. He'd recently bought dumbbells and started on about protein.

'Dad?' I said. 'This is a joke, right?'

He shook his head. The silver paint gleamed across the bridge of his nose. 'And if you think I'm going to be buried in some box, you don't know me at all.'

Mum shut her eyes and drummed her fingers against her forehead. I felt Sadie's hand on my wrist, greasy from the pizza. Looking at the Morris Minor, I wondered if Dad had even touched it.

Mum narrowed her eyes at him. 'Do you mean that you want to live forever?'

'Don't you?'

She looked at Juniper and me. She scoffed.

He said, 'This is why I can't tell you things.'

Mum folded her arms. 'And the late night excursions?'

A secret thread revealed itself.

Dad's eyes widened. 'I've only been going to meetings,' he said. 'Life extension meetings.'

I believed him. Sadie couldn't control her giggles any longer.

Mum clapped her hands together. 'All right, Gary. That's enough. Girls, leave his dinner somewhere.'

'It will happen to you,' Dad muttered to her.

At the door to the shed, Mum, trembling, picked up a rag and balled it in her fist. Her face was fixed like she was trying to hear a sound from far away.

'It will happen to us all,' Dad said, much louder than a whisper.

I washed up. Sadie and Juniper wound tea towels around their hands. Sadie dropped dishes she said were dirty back into the water for me to do again. She asked Mum if she could use the phone.

'Do you miss your mother?'

Sadie shrugged.

'Well,' Mum said, 'don't stay on too long.'

'Why not?'

'Who knows how much they charge out at sea.'

Sadie rolled her eyes at me. I guessed it was a boy she

was phoning and I guessed he was not on a ship, not out at sea.

Juniper dipped her tea towel into the sink. She took aim at my legs. Dad had taught us the whipping trick.

'Juniper? Don't,' Mum said, passing the cordless phone to Sadie before she left the room. My sister spun the towel and reached back and flicked the wet corner onto my thigh.

'Mum!'

Sadie started dialling. 'Don't dob,' she told me.

A couple of nights later, Sadie shuffled in bed beside me. She sat up and cracked her knuckles against her face. She knew I hated it. She knew it would wake me up.

'What do you think he's doing out there?'

'Who?' I said, knowing.

'Your dad. He's been in the shed all night.'

I pulled the doona closer to my face, but left a gap so I could still hear. 'You're obsessed,' I said.

Sadie's hairy legs rubbed against mine. I'd recently thrown a packet of razors in the shopping trolley, no eye contact, and Mum had paid for them with the rest of the stuff, and left them in the shopping bag for me on the kitchen bench. I used a different razor each time, which I didn't think Mum had figured out yet. She kept buying them, wordlessly.

The pop and crick of the joints in Sadie's knuckles again. 'Aren't you curious?' Sadie whispered.

I readied my feet at the bottom of the bed and kicked where I knew Sadie's feet would be. I had no idea Vanuatu would feel so far away. I missed being alone in my bedroom. I missed standing naked in front of the mirror after a shower. Rubbing moisturiser on my legs and chest. Inspecting myself. Studying signs that I was changing. Logging a voice that assured me I was bony and ugly. Dad had it – aloneness – out there in the shed.

'Not really,' I said.

I stood outside Mum and Dad's bathroom, desperate to be by myself. That day, in the hours between lunch and dinner, Sadie and Juniper began conspiring against me. Lots of things were on the table to be mocked. My excessive handwashing. My cold feet in bed. My unrequited crushes at school. Michael Moroney, who told Sadie after the sports carnival that, sorry, he only liked me as a friend. My smallness, everywhere. Juniper, only three years younger, calling me *Dwarf Hat Rack*, and Sadie laughing, saying, *That's good!*

I left them picking at a board game in the suffocating heat of the lounge room. I planned to take a cool, lengthy, very adult bath in Mum and Dad's ensuite, during which I would form a rock-hard tumour of wrongs that would feel good to mull over. Sadie still had three nights left of her stay. Maybe they would notice I was missing. I was about to enter the bathroom when I heard voices behind the door.

'You must have done something,' Mum said. 'People don't get sacked for no reason.'

'He didn't give me a reason. What difference does it make?'

I slunk into the doorway of their walk-in wardrobe, where I was still able to hear.

188

Dad said, 'Justin thinks he can get me a job.'

'Who's Justin?'

'We have the life extension meetings at his house.'

'For fuck's sake, Gary,' Mum said. 'We don't have the money for you to be this weird.'

She stalked from the bathroom and out into the hallway. Dad started to follow, but stopped in front of a low window that led to the front yard. I watched Dad for a moment with the late afternoon sun behind him. He tapped a finger at his belt, then ducked his head around the door frame to give me a wave.

'I love you, Natalie,' he said. 'I love both you girls.'

'Did you lose your job?'

'I need to go out.'

'Where?'

'To see a friend.'

'Which friend?'

'Justin. You don't know him. He's a doctor.'

'Can I come?' Just me and Dad and the open road. Maybe we'd stop at a servo somewhere for milkshakes.

He rubbed a hand across his face and through his hair. 'Yeah, okay.'

Through the house together and I shut the front door behind us. But as soon as I did, it opened again. Sadie.

'Who's that?' Dad stood on the front path.

'Where are you going?' Sadie asked.

'Nowhere.'

'Can I come?'

'No.'

'Why not?'

Dad put his hands on his waist and leant around me, pointing at Sadie. 'Quick. You'd better bring your mate too.'

Dr Justin Berryhill lived in a plain house. There was a skinny letterbox numbered with black stickers and a short, steep concrete driveway leading to a garage. Two storeys, flat-faced except for a small awning above the door. Not curtains but towels in the windows.

Outside, Dad said, 'You can ring the bell, Natalie,' like I was three years old. 'This is where we have our meetings.'

Footsteps coming down inside and then the door opened. Dr Justin Berryhill was tall and thin with glasses. He had a painful-looking Adam's apple above the neck of his yellow polo shirt. He was younger than Dad.

'Hi, Justin.'

'Gary, welcome. Just got off work.' They shook hands and pulled each other into a hug that left a gap where their hands were linked.

'This is my daughter, Natalie. Her friend, Sadie. They wanted to come for the ride.'

Justin took us up the carpeted stairs to the lounge room, where I saw the printed side of the towel I'd noticed from the car. It said: *Players Hold All The Cards.* Another one draped over the side of a stereo, fixed with a lava lamp, showed a tiger prowling. On an armchair, Justin plucked a remote control from under a departing cat and silenced a game show.

'Take a seat.'

On the couch, Sadie sat cross-legged, taking up room, happy to be on an excursion, hungry for it. This was all a cruise-ship buffet for her. I was prickled with irritation.

Dad chose another armchair. I watched him trying to smile, nodding like he was finding a beat.

'How was work?' he asked.

'Good, good.' Justin kneaded his armrest. He regarded Sadie and me, then pointed to the logo on his shirt. 'At the moment I'm down at the Plaza. Doing security. Head of.'

'The girls here are interested in what we're doing. In the ASCI and the CLA in Blacktown.' Dad cleared his throat. 'And here, with plans for the new cryonics facility.'

Sadie looked at me, like, *Interested is a bit strong.*

Dad used to talk about the footy, about that bastard Geoff Toovey. We'd go to the drive-thru at the Criterion every second Friday night and I'd help Dad load a carton of stubbies into the boot, and he'd exchange a couple of sentences with the guy on shift about that arsehole Des Hasler too. I couldn't imagine Dad saying *bastard* or *arsehole* now.

'Are you a real doctor?' I asked Justin. He pursed his lips and jerked his thumb up to a frame on the wall behind him.

Dad said, 'There are all different types of doctors, Natalie.'

Justin held his hands up. 'I wouldn't be where I am today without some serious formal qualifications. Not possible.' He scoffed. 'So you're interested in what your dad is doing?'

I told him it sounded like a bit of a joke.

Justin didn't blink. 'More girls than guys have undertaken the procedure, did you know that? Globally speaking.'

Sadie looked up at the *Players Hold All The Cards* towel, her expression strange. 'So cryogenics—'

'Cryonics,' Justin corrected.

'—is where you freeze a body so the person doesn't die?'

Over on his armchair, Dad and his smile swelled. 'Bit more complicated than that. But, yes, under certain conditions the brain and other cells are able to be shut down and the decaying can be reversed. Later on, not too far down the track, we believe technology will be so advanced that parts of us can be revived.'

'But you'll be all alone,' I said. I imagined heavy steel doors hissing open and bodies defrosting, stretching, blinking. 'How much does it cost?'

I wondered when our money would run out. I knew Juniper's teeth needed fixing and she'd go nuts without her gymnastics lessons.

Justin steepled his hands. 'Look, Natalie, some people care about sports cars and satellite dishes and jet skis. What Gary and I and a bunch of people in the ASCI and the CLA care about is eternal life. We want to return to a world where "dead" doesn't technically mean "dead", and we can pick up where we left off.' He opened his palm out towards the things in his lounge room. The cat returned. Its claws went to work on Justin's armchair fabric.

He addressed Sadie and me on the couch. 'You girls, Gary, want a drink? Beer? Whatever you want – I've got, like, some cans of Fanta in the fridge. Sadie – did I say that right? How about I show you something in the freezer.' He paused. 'And, no, it isn't a body.'

Dad chuckled.

I nodded when Sadie suggested getting me a drink too, and she followed Justin into the kitchen.

Silence. 'Dad?' I pleaded with him non-specifically. I'd figured out that Dr Justin Berryhill wasn't likely to offer him a brilliant new job with a BMW and a pay rise.

Dad shushed me gently. 'Years ago we didn't think hand and face transplants were possible.'

The fact that Dad retained bits of information like this felt perverse. I mouthed, *Let's go*. I wanted to mouth, *Des Hasler. Remember?*

I heard Sadie shriek. 'Get your hands off me.'

Dad and I sat up. I beat him to the kitchen. Justin stood beside a kitchen chair, his hands up high. Sadie's hip was keeping the fridge door open.

'What happened?' Dad was shaking.

'I was *just* getting the girls a Fanta ...' Justin pointed to two orange cans on the bench behind him. 'And I went to show her the scientific thermometer I keep in the freezer by way of explanation about—'

'And you grabbed me.'

'I did not.'

Sadie looked at me. 'He grabbed me. He touched my boobs.'

Dad was upset but I knew it wasn't just about this. I could see he was thinking hard and it was something like, *Can't anything just be good?*

Justin pursed his lips and shook his head. His face reddened. His eyes were small and dark and wet. 'No way. No fucking way.'

'Ah,' Dad said, clapping his hands together the way Mum did to stop ugly things getting out. 'We should probably go anyway. Sadie, you all right? Okay, then.'

I held her arm at the elbow. The open fridge door began to beep. None of us went to move Sadie out of the way.

Justin grabbed a Fanta can and waggled it like evidence. 'Christ, Gary. That wasn't anything. You should have told me you were bringing other people.'

Dad let Sadie and me walk in front of him down the stairs. Our shoes were loud and fast on the thin carpet.

'See you soon, Justin,' Dad said at the door. 'Maybe at the thing at Leanne's place.'

'Gary—'

'It's fine. Thanks, Justin. Bye.'

Dad let himself into the car first. After a few seconds, he leant over, looking old. He unlocked our doors, we buckled ourselves in and he drove. We would need to make a stop for the bread and milk Mum was expecting.

'Sadie,' I said from the front seat. 'Tell Dad how you make things up like that all the time at school.'

'What?' she said.

'Natalie!' Dad said.

'Admit it.' I turned around and made eye contact. 'You were out of the room for ten seconds.'

Sadie sat with her arms folded. Lights from Justin's neighbourhood – a neon 7-Eleven, a do-it-yourself car wash, a laundromat – quivered over her face.

I hissed, 'Tell him.'

Dad tapped the wheel. 'The important thing is that everyone is fine and you got to see where I go to meetings. And, Natalie, maybe it will help you and your mother understand my wishes.'

Mrs Collett drove up on Saturday. On a day trip to one of the Pacific islands, she'd bought dolphin-shaped salt and pepper shakers for Mum and wooden hibiscus brooches for Juniper and me. She held out a stubby cooler.

'Gary around?'

Mum nudged me forward. 'I'll take it to him,' I said.

'Thank you for having me,' Sadie said. Our first words to each other for days.

Mrs Collett touched the sunburn on her nose. 'Yes, thank you very much. Even when you're at different schools, we'll still make the effort, won't we? Your turn at ours next, hey, Nattie?'

As sharp as a wet sting to my skin. *No way.*

Once Sadie had gone, I took off for the back of the house, kicking past the clothesline, round to the side of Dad's shed. I tossed the stubby cooler up onto the roof, but it bounced down to the grass. I stood panting. Go for it, Sadie, I thought. Go off and get pregnant, or get popular, at your rubbish high school where no one wears the same shoes and everyone drops out anyway. My uniform – the woollen forest-green dress with the tartan collar – was hanging in my wardrobe. I didn't have to see Sadie again, at all. Mum and Dad wouldn't notice either way.

★

I promise Mum and Juniper that I'll be back, my mind already shifting to the rest of the school fete plotted out in bright plastic and wide swinging skeleton metal on the bottom oval of the primary school that, five years ago, used to be mine. Juniper is fourteen now and gossipy and smart, taut and focused. As her older sister, I'm mostly irrelevant. Juniper wants a little sack of White Christmas to eat before she takes to the stage with the other cheerleaders. Mum has tried telling her that this will likely make her feel sick in her tight leotard, already blossoming with sweat beneath her armpits, only minutes to go before her club's routine to 'I Love Rock 'n Roll'. But she refuses to listen.

Mum is crouched over. She plucks at Juniper's stockinged legs.

'There's a bee,' Juniper is saying.

'Do you have to be so dramatic?' Mum says. 'There's no bee.'

'It's a bee. Get it out.'

'You're not getting anything to eat and there's no way anything got into your stocking.'

Down on the oval, past the heavy dip of the yellow slide where the operator is handing out hessian sacks, Sadie and I once buried a shoebox full of treasures from the depths of our fish tanks, treasures from the dregs of her mother's makeup bag, from Dad's jars of spark-plugs and oily washers. Into the box I'd placed wooden dolly pegs, novelties that Mum preferred even though they were no longer practical. Sadie and I collected it all when we were only seven or eight, when we first became friends. I itch to see the trove again, but part of me doubts the box exists. I'm buoyed by the idea that I could have made the whole thing up. Not just the miniature fluorescent castle that my goldfish looped through and over, but the shoebox itself, and the wet soil and the holes in the ground that Sadie and I gouged out with spoons. If I'd made it up, I wanted to know, how did that idea start? Where did it come from? Why would I do that?

'I'll be back,' I tell them. Mum shades her eyes with her hand. She smiles at me.

The sky is blue and clear. Juniper worried about the weather for the fete all week, just about setting herself alight with panic, Mum had said while she twisted threads of elastic through her glittery braid. On the oval a lamb at the petting zoo bleats brokenly. A woman's voice calls out, *Never took me hunting!* A father lifts a baby onto his shoulders.

Then, at the top of the concrete steps, I see her. I pretend I don't.

'Natalie.'

I toss my head and try to look confused. The sun is in my eyes. I let my eyes go past her.

'Oh!' I say. 'Hi.'

We give each other a dinky little hug. Everyone at my school does this at the beginning and end of breaks, and to say goodbye at the end of class. The teachers had a staff meeting about it, apparently, about the messages it sends about inclusion and exclusion among teenage girls, and the time and energy it sucks out of our brain space.

'Can't believe how long it's been since we went here.' I swallow hard and Sadie doesn't answer, almost as if she hasn't heard. We haven't been at school together since Mr Jacobson's class in Grade 7.

'Do you remember,' Sadie finally says, 'that teacher who used to be a singer and then quit teaching and went to Antarctica? She liked a poem I wrote once. She used to say nice things and make everyone feel good, and then she left to be a scientist.'

I nod. 'But surely that was a lie. The Antarctica bit, I mean.'

Sadie grips herself, just above the elbows. Five years on and she is beautiful and tall. Her breasts are even bigger now. She was the first to get them in primary school. The other girls – a netball-skirted group of friends and tormentors – harassed her every day, lurking behind her to find evidence of a bra through her school shirt.

She reaches into a paper bag looped around her wrist, pops a lolly into her mouth and accordions the wrapper with her hands. She has big square fingernails painted red.

'Do you like any of your high school teachers?' I ask. 'Any good ones?' I sound like an uncle at a barbecue.

'I guess,' she says. 'That's a weird question.' Sadie takes her phone from her pocket and rubs it down the front of her skirt. 'What's been happening?'

'A fair bit, actually.' I start to tell her things. I move myself up a high school social bracket, invent a Grade 12 party that was pretty chill, but then turned wild. I lie and say that the cops showed up, three of them storming through the lounge room, showing mercy by the end, one even accepting a serve of nachos in a plastic bowl as a peace offering. I make up an art prize, hint that I might win, paint myself into the role of a deliberate and admired outcast at my expensive, progressive single-sex high school for girls who want to be oncologists and lawyers.

'Mum's boyfriend is a cop,' Sadie says. 'I don't think that happens. With the nachos, I mean.'

I shrug, searching the oval. I find the father with the baby on his shoulders stitching his way across the green grass. 'I guess the cop who came to the party wasn't your mum's boyfriend.'

Sadie rolls her eyes. I wish there was someplace to lean on, but Sadie's claimed the railing. I realise I haven't had any water since breakfast and the forecast said thirty degrees. My head feels grainy and dry.

Sadie looks at me properly for the first time. 'How's your dad?'

'He's good. He lives in Shorewood now.'

When I visited him, I found myself comparing his third-floor flat with Justin Berryhill's upstairs lounge room, with Justin's towels for curtains. Outside Dad's front door, someone had left a plastic bucket half-filled with grass clippings. We sidestepped it, him first, then me, nothing to say about it. His flat inside was bright and ordinary. A fat recliner sat in the corner facing a bookshelf, and a table and chairs that used to belong to the whole family was wedged into an alcove in the kitchen. There was no room for the yellow Morris Minor in his garage downstairs. Mum took care of it, housing it at her brother's property, promising to leave the car covered and protected till Dad wanted to start working on it again. Surely Mum knew the car would be at Uncle Al's forever. But, for once, she didn't point it out.

'Is he still ...'

'A bit weird?' I try to laugh. 'Still alive. Still talking about dying. But he's good.'

Once, in the Morris Minor with Dad and me as his passengers, Pop took a corner too quickly and the door swung open right there at the intersection. It was *funny*, Pop had said. Why couldn't we see that?

At Dad's flat that day, he showed me the brand new mincer he'd bought and the juicer he'd gotten secondhand. He put on some music and I rested my feet in his lap. After a while he rubbed them like nothing had changed. I sensed things he wanted to ask me. When was the last time he and I had been alone together, with no Juniper springing up around us like a foal, without Mum telling us all to hurry, to calm down, to stop our nonsense? Even the afternoon to go see Justin had been invaded.

I stare at Sadie. 'And your sister?' she asks.

'Juniper'll be up on stage any minute. She's a cheerleader now. Under-15 state champions.' I deliberate over my watch for a few seconds. I feel Sadie getting ready to leave. She digs out a scrap of lolly from her teeth and swaps her long hair from one shoulder to the other.

'Listen,' I say in a rush, 'have you heard anything about me?'

Sadie stops inspecting her fingers for loose strands of hair. 'Like what?'

A swelling and roiling in my belly. 'Do you remember Michael Moroney? From primary school?'

'Yeah, you used to like him.'

'He's been telling everyone that I—'

Introductory bars of Joan Jett cascade from the stage onto the oval. I picture Juniper cradling her arms over her head, raising a leg to land lightly beside her ear. When she bounds onstage, grinning, she will be a brown curl of muscle.

Sadie is asking me something, but the PA system is too loud with sounds that are tinny and thin and filled with gaps. *What's he been telling everyone?*

'That we had sex.'

She pauses. 'I hadn't heard anything, actually.'

'But you know Michael Moroney's friends,' I say. 'His friends go to Wakefield too.'

Sadie looks me in the eye. 'Yeah, but they're pigs and I couldn't give two shits what they say.'

And she sounds so much like Mum, fierce and calm and confident, when she and Dad split up. When Mum's surety was like a spell.

'It isn't true. That isn't what happened,' I say. 'I told him not to.'

Bile in my throat. The humiliation, again, at all the things Sadie might know.

She nods. She leans her hip against the railing, like it's five years ago and she's holding open the door of Justin Berryhill's fridge.

'I believe you,' she says.

The house party with the police officer scooping corn chips from a bowl dissolves and a different party comes into focus. I'm wedged between Michael Moroney's washing machine and the laundry sink and Michael's cold fingers are kneading my breasts and then poking down the waistband of my shorts and he's sipping beer from a bottle and talking me into it and yelling to his mates out in the hallway, *Come here and say that haha* and *Yeah, I bought more, just give me a sec.* He can hear them but he can't hear me. By the time I've figured out how far away I am from Sadie, with her can of Fanta, shrieking *Get your hands off me* at Justin Berryhill, it's all over.

Michael Moroney does not go to Wakefield. He sleeps in a shared dorm at Trinity College where his walls are postered with Messi and Ronaldo. When he finishes school he'll take up a contract with Liverpool FC Academy Under 18s and buy a Jeep for himself and a titanium watch for his nutritionist who makes sure Michael eats right and treats his body well. Michael is home for the weekend but his parents are at a murder mystery party. A chance thing, really, after all these years since primary school, that we'd run into each other at the Exeter Street Caltex, where he said he'd add me on Facebook straight away and invite me to his party, which was BYO and no pressure.

There are grains of laundry powder on the tips of my fingers and I'm thinking of Michael's mother and whether she does all the washing in their house and whether she ever pushed Michael around in the washing trolley like my mum used to, laughing, warm soft towels under me and a collection of pegs in my lap like treasures.

Acrobat

Dr Butler started talking about the next phase of the operation. He typed fast, using only his forefingers.

'The next phase?' My knee quickened with pain. My mind seized up.

'The next stage, obviously,' he said, 'is physiotherapy, which will be longer than we perhaps thought.'

'Like, how long?'

Three weeks ago, Dr Butler had located the cysts in my knee and spent an hour scraping away fifty per cent of my ACL. Afterwards, I'd spent the same amount of time vomiting into a kidney dish in a recovery room that had a view of the river.

Dr Butler tapped the backspace button. 'Hard to say.' He held it down and peered at the screen. On his desk, like a trophy, was a rubber patella with the tendons exposed.

'And would I be covered?'

'As I said, six to twelve months of physiotherapy, if you want any chance of regaining full movement.'

I remembered what I'd already paid him. Then I multiplied it and kept multiplying it. Brad had told me not to get my hopes up about how soon I'd be back to normal.

I perched on the edge of my chair and reached for the walking stick.

Tap tap tap on the keyboard. Dr Butler glanced up. 'Do you want the girls to organise it for you?'

'I'll ring you back tomorrow.'

I left Dr Butler and his slick offices and limped towards Flinders Street station past Fed Square. I was getting pretty good at using my walking stick, but strangers still stared – I was young and female with a fat right leg inside jeans I couldn't face taking off. I'd hired the metal walking stick from a hospital chemist. Brad said it would be cheaper in the long run to start our own walking-stick factory and sell them to Sudanese child soldiers.

'Cheaper for who?' I'd asked, folding the receipt inside my purse.

Yesterday, Brad's boss told him that he needed to be more flexible. More prepared to fail in the pursuit of holistic organisational goals. Brad said it made him feel like his job was precarious.

'So? Suck it up,' I said, thinking of our online bank balance since I first went to see Dr Butler. The red line for *money out*. The green line lagging behind: *money in*. 'Be more flexible.'

There was a hamburger stand at the edge of Fed Square, a head-sized fibreglass burger spinning lazily on a spike from its roof. School was out; students in Brad's old uniform reclined beneath the television screen, fixated on their phones. When I was small, my parents brought me here to watch the tennis. I remember the scuba blue of the court, the punctuated hits and sighs and cheers coming from the screen, and the glacial white of the players' polos sliding into view on the big screen.

I'm not going to try to tell you what I saw next was normal, but at first I thought it was an ad for something – another way for a company to stand out from all the noise. I was watching the schoolboys, shot through with a memory of teenage Brad jumping down from the tram to meet me after class, when I noticed a woman give her daughter a pat on the head, their faces turned to each other. The girl was skinny, in pigtails and a dark red leotard with short, sequined ruffles for a skirt. Two ruffles on one side, but only one on the other, like its pair had been ripped away.

The woman placed a black hat on the ground and the girl ran towards the big concrete structure that housed the television screen. She started climbing up the side. And, yes, it had my attention, but at the time I didn't think it was truly that strange. I had stopped to rest anyway. Lately I'd been carrying all my things around in a backpack, but I'd grabbed a handbag on my way to Dr Butler's because I'd been so sure of good news. I wanted to feel normal again. But the shoulder bag was too unwieldy, so I sat down and leant my walking stick on the edge of the garden. I twisted the strap of my handbag around my good leg. Anyone wanting to steal from me again would, frankly, be choosing the right person.

A few others were noticing the girl too, this small creature in a leotard scuttling up the side of the screen, finding footholds and handholds, trying one or two out and rejecting them, but mostly seeming to know her way to the top. And then I saw that there was a line, a wire, strung from the top of the screen to the top of the building opposite, four storeys high. There used to be a museum there, or an art gallery.

'Ladies and gentlemen!' The mother's accent was European sing-song-something. A voice for cursing out a window. I thought it was a black dress she was wearing, but it was a cape, nipped in at her throat. She tottered in sparkly slippers. 'Welcome! Up there is my daughter, Mila, a world-class acrobat. What you're about to see may shock and surprise you, but hopefully inspire you.'

I gathered my hands in my lap. 'She's going to walk it.' I glanced around. I'd said the words aloud, not meaning to. But this seemed like a thing to watch with someone else.

Mila's mother indicated the open mouth of the velvet hat. 'If you're charmed by Mila, if she thrills you, if she makes your belly turn topsy-turvy, then please show your amazement with a coin or two or three!'

A pair of women on the seat beside me clapped half-heartedly.

'That is so dangerous,' murmured one. 'That's child labour.'

The other addressed the sky. 'They must really need the money.'

'If you can't afford to have kids then you shouldn't have them.'

'Maybe they didn't know till they had them.'

Brad and I agreed children were too expensive for us, too expensive for the world. That operation, twelve months ago, had been cheaper than my knee. That doctor kept a set of rubber fallopian tubes pinned to the wall behind him. And I left feeling no great pain, feeling no different, and I didn't vomit once.

I saw then that Mila's mother's slippers had once been stilettos, but that the heels were gone. Without them, the shoes couldn't flatten to the ground and she had to walk on tiptoe.

She cupped her hands around her mouth and shouted. 'Are you ready, Mila?'

Mila gave an Olympic smile, nodded, raised her arms and pointed a toe onto the wire. I gasped and the women beside me did too. The boys in their striped ties panned their phones up to start filming. Mila's mother kept her focus on the ground, didn't watch her daughter's steps along the wire, instead nudging the hat with the toe of her shoe, grinning at me and the other strangers. Twenty or thirty of us dolloped in groups between the hamburger caravan and the screen.

'No way,' I whispered.

The two women balled up their food wrappers and tucked them into the garden before they left.

Above us, Mila flexed and tricked her toes along the wire. She held her arms out for balance. She was a thin red scrap testing the air. Alongside her, the Yarra meandered, its surface crawling with car-sized rubbish collectors like water beetles. Flinders Street station was a golden medallion sinking into the river bank. Inside the station, there were more sleeping bags than train services now.

'What if she falls?' The cut in my knee, the incision where Dr Butler had sent his scalpel, worked its way back into my mind.

Mila's mother was by my side in an instant. 'Ah, but she will not,' her line went. 'She has been an acrobat since the day she could walk. Why, Mila could stand on her head before she could talk.'

'She's quite amazing.'

'Do you have children?' For some reason the woman motioned at my walking stick.

'Yes.'

The woman liked my lie.

'Two daughters.'

'Ah, then you understand little girls.'

'They tackled me when we were playing soccer at the park,' I continued. 'So, my knee.'

Mila's mother skipped over to the hat and brought it back, beaming. 'Lovely,' she said, offering it to me. 'Perhaps you would like to show Mila your encouragement?'

'Mine are at home. With their dad.'

'Lovely.'

I pictured a pair of daughters somersaulting off the couch. Two little fabrications in leotards stretched tight across their bellies. 'We've never thought about taking them to gymnastics. A bit dangerous, maybe. And all that body-image stuff, you know? But this, I mean, with your Mila. It makes me think.'

Mila – she must have been five or six years old – was more than halfway across the wire. She pointed her toes, her pale legs, with each step. Half a dozen tourists took photos from low angles so they could be in the shots too. I knew for sure then the girl would make it. No one takes a photo on their phone of a child acrobat before she falls. This woman, her mother, had it all under control.

I steadied myself to standing, gripped the walking stick and took a step away from the black hat with its clutch of coins.

But I'd forgotten the handbag looped around my left ankle, there so I'd feel the tug if someone tried to mug me again. I fell suddenly, awkwardly, shamefully onto my right leg. And the walking stick did nothing, and the jeans covering my compression bandage did nothing. I hit the concrete. Pain torched through my knee, an exquisite sharpness, metallic and loathsome. The yowl from my mouth was clownish. One second I was on my feet with the black hat and the golden sun in my vision – a vague thought that Brad and I might be able to afford to go out for burgers later – and the next I was sprawled face-down, my arse high.

I couldn't remember the dimensions of my own body. But I could picture Dr Butler typing on his keyboard, my name back in his system as he grabbed the rubber knee and scooted on his wheeled office chair around his desk.

Now.

Here.

See?

'Oh,' Mila's mother said. The word got swept away at the end as though she was turning to look for help, or glancing up at her daughter.

I saw Mila's mother above me through tears. Tremendous pain was working to distil my life to two pinpricks of time. Nothing else existed except the two moments in which I had lain face-down on concrete with my heart dopplering against my ribs.

The spangled knife, the velvet hat.

The opiated man, the spangled acrobat.

In the first, I had a cheekful of cold concrete while the man who had mugged me jogged away. In the second, the concrete was warm. In both, my head was packed with fear.

'Your bag, my darling,' Mila's mother said. 'You tripped over your bag. Can you call your husband?'

'I don't know.'

'And, oh, already with your leg and the walking stick.'

'Did she make it?'

'Wait there – I have to go. Here is your bag.' She laid it by my hand where it crumpled like a shot cat.

I remembered how Dr Butler had told me that women are more likely to injure their knees. Not a weakness, he said, but a predisposition. We jump to the ground with our legs straighter than men. When we menstruate our muscle tissue becomes elastic. Maybe we pivot when we shouldn't. Dr Butler showed me a clip of a Russian gymnast landing after a complicated aerial manoeuvre.

I began to sob.

From across the square came the freefall of a cheer. Mila must have made it across and then down to safety. I guessed she was getting cuddles and high-fives from those tourists, and from her mother.

I felt around for my bag, but it was gone.

Deer Lane

The boy lives on Deer Lane, which Jen discovered when she looked through the paper folders in the school office. Confidential information is supposed to be stored electronically, in databases, but in the last week of the school year she slipped into the storage room next to the trophy cabinet. There was no interest from anyone, no spark of suspicion. On the boy's file next to his photo were the names of his father and mother, and Jen forgot them, quickly and deliberately.

Today she wakes after lunchtime. She has disguised the fatigue and excess of six weeks' school holidays with a short and flimsy wraparound, a dress that sticks to her thighs in the heat. Polyester floral with a spare button still sewn to the inside tag. It cost fifteen dollars from a shop beside the train station. An observation: the cheaper the better. The silk blouse she bought herself for her birthday receives fewer comments from the boy, less interest. Doesn't mean she'll never wear the silk blouse. But his preferences are interesting.

Her car is new. She has money now, her teacher's pay-cheque regular and decent. When Grandpa died, the car that had belonged to him and Gran went to her, and she sold it. It was a hefty Falcon without power steering, slow to react, even though Gran made it seem easy when they'd driven Grandpa to appointments for his glaucoma. He would concentrate on finding a song on the radio they'd all like: it was a job he could do, eye patches on, fingers on the dial, not needing to see.

Now, in her bright blue hatchback, Jen slows down from eighty ks and chooses a parking spot on a vacant block next to a service station, a street away from Deer Lane. She turns off the engine and gets out. It's January and the body of the car is hot to touch. She gazes around at the scrub set back from the road. A wolfish word, capitalised, comes to her: *Rural*. A few houses cower behind fences that look unfinished, or perhaps were never properly started. Three trucks, one after the other, hurl their violent bulk around the bend. The short grass bakes on the vast empty blocks and a coiny stink drifts from the river. How did such a handsome boy emerge from a place like this? She doesn't waste time on it. She wants to touch him and be touched by him.

For months she has been firm with herself. But this morning, temptation pulsed through her.

One day in November, after the first bell to signal the end of the period, in the spare minutes before Jen's next class showed up, the boy stopped a metre away from her. The others pushed past and out the door. The boy's feet were planted wide, his bag tucked between them. Poking out of one unzipped side were a water bottle and the thin tangle of earbuds. She loved to see him talking. He lifted a long brown arm to point and Jen felt desire like something wrenched from her. She knew how to draw him out with easy questions. Where would he like to visit?

'Dubrovnik. It's in Europe, on the Mediterranean. Where bits of *Game of Thrones* are filmed?'

'Yes, I know Dubrovnik,' she said. 'But it isn't on the Mediterranean.'

'It is. Isn't it?'

'No. The Adriatic.'

'Well. That's where I want to go.' His smile came as unexpectedly as rainwater tipped from a hat.

The second bell rang. Jen felt a shiver through her. The boy lingered till students from her next class arrived and she waved them over, not at all happy to see them. 'Hello, early birds!' she called.

Perhaps she would tell him, another time, that she had visited Dubrovnik, three years ago. In the centre of the old town, a crowd of people gathered around a man with enormous birds on his shoulders. The birds were red and green and blue, reptilian. Beaks like scythes. Eyes like beads. A woman paid the man, who placed the smallest bird, the size and shape of a pineapple, onto the bare shoulder of the woman's daughter, a teenager in a bikini top.

In Dubrovnik, the doors of tiny restaurants were lit with spherical lamps. Jen trotted out her Australian accent but no one was interested. She ate alone, ordering plates of fried squid and briny octopus salad.

Back in Australia, in this regular life – the one she imagines she'll have for a while – Jen dares herself to jog ten kilometres every day. She dares herself to run out of fresh food in the fridge, to work the end of a pen through a hole in her pocket and into her thigh during assembly. To flirt, listlessly, with a co-worker after a staff meeting. To eavesdrop on details of her students' teenage parties, imagining herself there, whole and young on the cold lawn. To say the boy's name aloud while she lies on the lounge room floor. To bite her fingernails down to the quick. To live, each week, on only thirty dollars' worth of groceries. To only sometimes wear a bra. Reuse her underwear, no washing.

All that money she saves, maybe she'll go back to Dubrovnik.

The late afternoon heat scrapes at her. Jen leans in over the driver's seat, grabs her phone, goes to Instagram and finds the boy's account. She stares at a photo of him in board shorts at the bottom of a water slide. Sometimes she scrolls through other kids' feeds, though none as closely. Most of their accounts are public despite the pleas from the cyber-crime consultants. She is careful not to double-tap on a photo, moving gently through half a dozen images that are new since yesterday, and then on to the ones she recognises.

Images, evidence of what they do in their spare time. The idiotic things these kids get up to repulse and excite her. Their gluttony and recklessness with food, their attempts to swallow spoonfuls of cinnamon: it makes her feel physically ill. That the body should be contaminated in this way, that they do not understand what all these threats can do – it disgusts her. They think the body is endless, is reliable. That it has a membrane.

An observation: it may happen today, or another day, or never.

Another observation: before she became aware of her body as a thing the boy desired, she knew herself to be dumpy and uninteresting. She wasn't wrong: how you know yourself is how you really are. But she became aware of his attention, like the slow twisting of the dial on her grandparents' old car stereo, tuning into a radio station. First: noise, chaotic and undesired. Then: electric clarity.

Three years ago, at a point high up on the red brick wall that circled the old town of Dubrovnik, Jen stood with a tour guide. As her fellow tourists milled around at the brick ledge, she asked the guide a question about the war. The man said it was difficult for people to talk about and he turned away, towards the water. He said one more thing: *There are no simple answers.* She wanted to know where people stood now, what he'd observed about citizens' allegiances and grudges. But the man refused to answer and Jen left the tour early. *Don't be a guide and take my money if you feel that way*, she thought, but didn't say. *Don't pretend people don't love to share the worst things they've seen and done.*

The trucks have disappeared completely when she notices a man on the other side of the road. She watches him pulling a dog on a leash, like, *Stay cool, buddy.* Jen knows he will walk to her, and it unlocks a familiar feeling.

The man – he's at least sixty – pauses. 'You need a hand?' he asks.

'No, thanks.'

His face is marked with acne scars. 'You sure? People often say no when they mean yes.'

She shakes her head, feeling her ponytail brush the back of her neck, a sensation charged with a memory from her youth: the pace and leaps of jumping in volleyball. That lightness in the air, sun on the court, bare legs, short skirt. 'I don't.'

He laughs and it surprises her. The dog sits heavily to the ground. It hooks a leg around to scratch, misses its neck and topples to one side. The leash pulls taut. The man swallows a burp, touches his chest. 'Are you lost?' he asks. 'What number you after?'

'Just pulled over for a rest.'

The man scratches the side of his nose. All his fingernails are too long. The pores on his face are visible in the folds of his skin.

'Yeah, see,' he continues, as though she hasn't spoken, 'it's a bit odd. The street is sort of divided into two—'

'I'm not lost.'

'—and the river cuts back just there, behind the scrub. Confuses some people.'

Jen feels a gust of sandy-hot wind around her legs. 'Maybe the river did confuse me.'

He grins, like he's in on the joke. 'Nah. You look too smart for that.'

'Maybe.' She points to the service station. 'They do food?'

He nods, flicks his fingernail across the tip of his nose. 'Leave you to it.'

Once, at a conference, Jen sat during lunch with two colleagues – a pair of frumpy women, best friends Kylie and Sally. Kylie had just started seeing a man who sold gym equipment for a living, and when she was halfway through her burger and chips, Kylie rang to tell him not to worry about dinner. She would be full after all this food. Jen held her fork. She couldn't stop herself rolling her eyes. Kylie was making a point for her new boyfriend about the sort of person she was: a woman with limits. Sacrificial. A modest appetite. Jen pictured Kylie's boyfriend working out on one of those cross-trainers in the shopping centre, in that ridiculous soaring way. She pictured him ending Kylie's phone call and trying to make a sale.

Jen chooses a sausage roll and eats it standing up beside the drinks fridge while the service station attendant watches. In the bathroom she seeks out the edge of a toilet door and rolls her forehead across it, harder each time. Her groan invades the bathroom. She places one hand on the outside of the door and one on the inside. Hears footsteps. She opens one eye, just for a moment. A girl in a bright polo has entered. Jen presses the edge of the door against her temple, a cool lick of white. Rolls. Sharpness creases down her face, then dullness. Both are beautifully gratifying.

'Are you okay?' The girl has spoken.

Two things existing at once. 'I'm fine. Thanks.'

The girl must be about sixteen. She wears a long pair of brown plaits, black leggings and roughed-up sneakers.

'You been on school holidays?' Jen releases her grip on the door. She takes a step towards her.

'No, I work here. My shift starts soon.' The girl doesn't move. Perhaps she doesn't like going to the toilet with someone else in the bathroom. Understanding this, Jen plans to wash, then leave.

In the mirror above the sink, she sees crumbs from the sausage roll around her mouth and lines down her forehead. She scrubs her hands till they are red.

It's dusk by the time she leaves the service station. The sky is a spell. A band of melon orange has appeared and above that are swirls of pink the colour of tongue. Jen locates her car on the vacant block, on the little bend. It is still so hot. Sweat pools in the bones around her neck and shoulderblades, and in her sandals, between her toes. Parked on slightly sloping ground, her car looks abandoned. She wants to see the boy. She wants to go home. She wants to see the man, wants to pat that dog.

In Dubrovnik, she had visited Paola, the Croatian girl from her bus tour. Paola had fallen ill in Dresden the week before: she thought she might be pregnant but didn't want to take a test while she was away from home. They'd swapped addresses and mobile numbers on their final night together on the bus. Paola vomited into Jen's lap and Jen helped her into the shower at their next hostel before bathing herself. The next day Paola caught a flight from Berlin back home.

Paola's house was white and two storeys high. An old man was on the roof on all fours, hammering, bent over the tiles. Mountains rose behind the house like folded stone. The hull of a blue boat was chocked up on bricks in the front yard, pricked on all sides by bunches of cactus. Paola's brother David answered the door. Finding her way to their house had been easier than Jen had imagined, and this was the first thing she told David, a teenager, perhaps sixteen or seventeen years old, after he'd said something in Croatian and she'd been unable to answer.

'Is Paola here?' she asked. 'I'm her friend. Is she okay?'

David left her standing on the front stones. The clear and close hammering on the roof continued. David returned to ask for her name, this time in English. He seemed very unsure of something.

'She is sleeping.'

'We were on our trip together. I came to see if she's okay.'

Jen has not showered today and would love to take a swim in a river far nicer than the one behind the boy's house. She guesses this river is a place where all kinds of things turn up.

From the boy's letterbox she thinks she sees a few shabby buildings set a hundred or so metres back from the road. As she makes her way closer, though, feeling light raindrops on her skin, she realises that the three or four stepped, angled roofs are actually part of the one house. She eases through a corrugated iron gate. Several steps from the gate is a front door and next to it a narrow window, glowing violet – a television is on. Light pulses as the images change. She raises a fist to the door.

A sound from the river makes her pause. Beyond the boy's backyard an outboard motor drones through the water, its buzz rising and falling like breathing.

The boy's house is not what she'd expected.

But: *there are no simple answers.*

★

David hadn't understood why Jen had turned up uninvited, and perhaps Paola hadn't either, but in the end David ushered Jen in to wait with him in the lounge room. Time passed, Paola slept, and Jen steered her mind towards David on the seat beside her.

If the boat is still buzzing in five seconds, she dares herself, she will leave.

Inside, through the thick and frosted window pane, a figure moves like a fish underwater. She could reach out and catch it. It is him, surely – told in his slender height, in his sharp posture. She holds her breath. There's a rush of laughter, more fish floating behind the glass, but she recognises none of them. A dull, overpowering dread rises in her. The boy is not alone. And what if she knows those others who are with him? Louder types ready to flare up and crash through the front door with their vulgar questions.

The road is empty. Jen pulls her keys from her pocket, pokes the sharpest one through her second and third fingers, and is relieved to see her car. Across the windscreen white bird shit is smeared like a handprint. Dozens of stars are pinned in the sky above; she is far from the city. A voice cuts through from where the grass dips away on the passenger side. 'Did you find something to eat?'

'Jesus, fuck.' Her hands fly to her throat. It's the man with the dog, not on a leash this time but in his arms. 'You scared me.'

Nestled against the man's chest, the dog looks tinier and scrappier than she remembers. It looks up at its owner, waiting for him to speak. The man says, 'You didn't come back so I thought I'd keep an eye out.'

'On my car?'

'You don't live here. It's getting dark.' He's beside her now, both of them less than a metre from the roadside.

Jen pulls on the handle. The click of the door. 'Where do you live?' she asks him.

'On Isherwood Road. A woman – oh, twenty-five, twenty-six – went missing round there a few years ago near the river. Like I'm saying: it's dark.'

Jen imagines herself buckled in, radio on high, eighty kilometres an hour out of this place, feeling in control because she will be back with him tomorrow: it will be a new day with the boy, a new year, and the gleaming desire right at her centre will still be there. The dog growls at something Jen can't see and she dares herself to touch its nose. She nods at the man, taking care to smile, knowing the smile will be seen, even in the dark.

He reaches forward with his spare hand, towards her waist, and pats the fabric of her dress. 'What do you do? For work?'

She freezes and he releases her. 'I'm a teacher.'

'You're kidding! None like you when I was around. I wouldn't have been able to concentrate. Excuse me, but I wouldn't.'

'Good,' she says. 'Good that you were here to help. No harm done. All safe now.'

She can still hear the sound of the outboard motor as she climbs in and locks all the doors. The outside has been flensed away and her bright new car is a membrane. The man motions for her to wind down the window, but she only switches on the radio, and finally he steps back. She pictures Grandpa with his hands over his eye patches and Gran with hers on the steering wheel, shifting the long heavy car back towards home.

This Will All Be Recorded

Layla cries. Chats to herself. I wake the morning too early, back to sleep. Day for uni. Shower. Pack lunch and jumper for Layla. Water. Honey. No fruit in the house. No fruit. What sort of mother. Why can't I just. Don't say *can't*. Say *how can I*. That's what the lady at the clinic said. Don't say. Kiss for Mummy. Layla turns her head. Points at the lounge room. Mess from the night before. Torn book. Mouldy towel. Coffee table sticky. Carpet prickled with crumbs. I should clean before bed. Mop arcing white through the grime and then a hand on hip and a smile at the camera. Wake up fresh and new. But at night I can't stay awake. I can't not worry. Don't say *can't*. How can I not worry. Say *how can I*. How.

Out the door and down the steps. One, two, three. Layla wants to walk but walking makes her cry. Up, up. Nappy bag, lunch bag, uni bag, purse. Layla. Kiss her dreamy head. Lips on her hair, near her ear. Forgot to brush her teeth. Forgot to check the fridge is shut. Forgot her hat, my water, the library book with fines ticking over like pages through fingers. Down one, two, three.

Lecture hall. Laptops and teenagers sleeping in and

coming in late and iPhones with turquoise cases and protein bars and five-dollar takeaway flat whites on desks like totems. PowerPoint slides and Times New Roman and *This will all be recorded, so no need to take notes. Please ask any questions you may have* and *In 1925 before the Great Depression* and *Maxwell Perkins wrote* and *Zelda died in a fire in a hospital* and *Any questions?* How can I. Did Zelda wake up when she felt the smoke? Was she strapped down, with a leather one for her mouth? Did they have money, lots of money? Enough money. Some money. More than nothing money. How can I. *Any questions?* A trickle of bodies, books folded up, students treading stairs. A boy holds the door open for me. Do I look. I can't look that. How can I possibly look that old?

I'll do my work at home. I'll buy fruit on the way. I'll practise my interview techniques. I'll practise pretending Layla never gets sick. That there is no Layla. That there never was and I'm free as a bird and yes I'll take extra shifts and call me as often as you need and I'll never say no and I can be there in half an hour, carrying only one bag containing zero nappies. But Layla is. The hospital in Newcastle has her name on file and her fingers greased the glass door at Centrelink and her little voice has hummed R-O-B-O-T watching *Play School* while she bobs in the thinning dusk.

Analyse two authors. Analyse three authors. How the author uses literary techniques. How the author introduces the subject in such a way as to. How the author makes money. How Fitzgerald how Faulkner how Franzen take half a cup of frozen peas and a stock cube and turn it into a soup.

Vegetable stock is a vegetable. But she won't like it. And I'll be annoyed. Big sighs. Teeth grinding. Layla mussing hands through hair. Banana. She wants. Anything that I haven't cooked. A banana. How the author positions the reader to feel sympathy for. Banana isn't a meal. You can't just live on banana. Don't touch that. Please. Mummy's books. And I've prepared. Well, that's it. That's your dinner. I'm not going to be one of those mothers who. Taste it. Please. Try it. It's got vegetables and it's good for you. Oh, fine. Here. Peel it. Eat it. Eat.

Wisdom is the principal thing; therefore get wisdom, and with all thy getting get understanding. Work is the principal thing. Food is the principal thing. Standing at a restaurant counter and ordering a large and an extra and an also and a dripping, heaving, garish thing is the thing. Watching Layla plod, primate-toddle, slippery-slide scrabbling, stranger-meeting. Say hello. Be gentle. One at a time down the slide. A chip for you, love. Is the thing.

Layla wakes. Cries. It's too dark in her room. It's too light. It's too cold, too hot. She lifts her face. Pink and wet. Her right eyelid is stuck shut. No no no no. Open. Wash it out with salt and water. Someone to hold her still. While I take a shower, brush my hair, wash the dishes, buckle sandals. Someone to take Layla to the park and go spin spin spin on the dragon and someone to laugh with when the kookaburra steals her hot cross bun right out of her tight little grasp. Face washer in the laundry. Layla wants it back. Pink and wet as she plucks it from the basket and stretches it above her head. Hat. Yes, a hat. Time to go.

Analyse how the author pretends her shirt is supposed to look that way.

Doctor hands. Layla waves. Wooden tongue. Ask the question. I have a job interview. I have to. Can I? *It's up to you.* How can I make it up to me? How can I make it up to her. The girl at reception doesn't ask for my card. *It's all fine. That's all done.* It's free, is what she means.

I kiss Layla. She likes the girls at the centre with their black fingernail polish and blue fringes, fresh out of high school where those weren't allowed. Silent beg. Fixed smile. Chat fast and light. Please don't look too closely at her eye. Analyse the motifs of sight and blindness. What might Fitzgerald's eye represent? Lower Layla to the ground, her face at the teenager's knees. Off you go. Find the dollies. Wave bye-bye. One hour, two hours. Let my phone not ring. Let them not send her home.

At the job interview it's me and him and her and him. And, now. Hello! The hours are not fixed. *We can't guarantee you hours. We can't guarantee you times.* Don't say *can't*, say *how can we make it fair.* Here. You'd be working here. Sweep hand around papered office, room dividers, desks topped with telephones. Murmurs over styrofoam and fingers on keys tapping. Fluorescent bright, low ceiling, hardly pressed shirts. *Are you prepared to ask the tough questions? Are you prepared to be ignored? Hung up on? We'll give you a call.*

Sun slides over the pavement. Bus stop where a small boy toys about with shopping bags on his arms. An action doll. A figurine just bought. Plastic feet bump my leg, step step step up my arm. He's okay, I say. I've got a daughter.

Boy unfolds the doll's arms. Plays peek-a-boo. Says to his mother, *He's got eyes like strawberries.* Says to me, *Look.*

Imagine Layla's eyes. Face to face with the girls at the centre while they pick the nail polish from their thumbs.

Afterwards: the park. We'll go spin spin spin on the dragon.

My phone rings. Yes. And. You got the job. The job the job the job. Yes. You got the job. You.

Joiner Bay

I'm a runner. I don't get pocket money for jobs or just because. Dad tells everyone how if I run ten ks he'll give me five bucks. If I get a PB I get five bucks more. We have the rowing machine and the weights and the bench press in the spare room now. I've been running more lately, and someone else, like a psychologist, might say it's because my best friend died. But people can say what they like, and they still won't know the truth, even if they believe it. Even if they tell other adults while I'm in the room. My best friend's name was Robbie. You don't need to know his last name, because nobody cares about that. But what you will care about is that he killed himself, and you'll care how he did it: with a cord and a beam to hang from, which means he probably broke his neck, and then he probably stopped breathing. That's the order of things.

Last night I set my alarm for four-thirty. When it goes off, I get up and take a piss without turning the light on. I get dressed and have a sip of water, only a sip, so I don't get a stitch. I used to listen to music with my headphones in but one night I was almost hit by a car — my fault — driven by the school librarian. Our town, Lusk, is pretty small, and Mr Rigby didn't seem annoyed that he'd almost been in an accident with a student. He didn't yell. He motioned me over to say that I had three library books overdue and they'd soon start attracting a fine. I liked him a lot after that. I found the books in my room and went to school to hand them to him and he said, 'What? Put them in the chute.'

After Robbie died, Mr Rigby never tried talking to me about suicide and I liked him even more after that.

So, to be able to hear the traffic, I ditched the headphones and now I have to listen to my thoughts.

I'm going to run ten ks and show Dad my Strava when I get home so he'll give me five bucks after breakfast. I'll run my usual route into town, past the murals along Dartmouth Street and out to Joiner Bay, where they want to build a big coal port that might kill everything in the reef. Not much we can do about that, Dad says, and I agree. It'll be tied up for years, anyway, and there's a lot to be said for seeing how things pan out, and not getting too worried about stuff we can't change.

I pick up speed along our wide, dead-quiet street as I head towards the murals that Lusk is famous for. The first is of a horse and carriage, and next to that is the mural of the train driving towards you, but the perspective is all off so it tugs at your guts and makes you feel sick. The Lusk family who founded our town is painted in the next one against the back wall of the church. Gilbert Lusk and his three sons are sharp and mean in an oval frame like a brooch. The smallest son looks like a total murderer, as though he killed a family up in the hills and then wiped his hands and sat down to dinner with his dad and brothers. Without music to listen to I have the same thoughts each time, and there's nothing I can do to come up with new ones.

I run. The sky lightens. The sun rises above Joiner Bay, which is shaped like an embrace, with two arms of rocky hills reaching into the water. The flowers on the trees are white and pink and yellow. There aren't many houses out here. Set back from the road is the caravan park with a post box and a telephone booth out the front, and a fibreglass pool with a waterslide that gets jammed with kids during summer.

After Robbie killed himself in our shed, Dad said, 'Isn't it strange, Jake, that he brought that cord with him?' Dad likes having a mate to talk to, and that's usually me, and he always says exactly what's on his mind.

I'd already thought about the cord. 'Maybe he didn't think we had one in there.'

'We don't,' Dad said.

'He must have known.'

At least one night a week Robbie came over to chat with Dad and me while we exercised. He wandered around, inspecting the equipment, cradling dumbbells. He knew we had a rowing machine and a bench press and a whole range of beams to choose from, painted dark green. Now, when people at school talk about caring for each other and about preventative measures, they're not talking about having no beams, or no access to cords. Every single person in Lusk has a theory about why Robbie killed himself. Theories they've hunkered down with and won't let go of. They've all used their imaginations very hard, sipping smoothies in the cafe in town and sharing their imaginations with someone else. They've locked the front door at night and sat at the kitchen table, bobbing a tea bag up and down in a thinking way.

I stop for water at the fountain and rinse it through my mouth, spitting it onto the road. I still haven't seen anybody on foot in town this morning, only a few utes and delivery trucks. I pause the Strava so my time is still good, and I think about Robbie. He was short. He had bad breath. He liked watching Formula One racing and soccer on TV. He went to church. He had two younger sisters he spoilt with those glittery kid magazines from the supermarket. Robbie liked that I was nice to the twins and he made me promise I'd help them when they got to high school. The week before it all happened, he followed me around the library at the end of lunch, bored, slipping books out and putting them back spine-in. He found a hardcover about celebrities who died young and he kept on coming back to the shelf to read it. He showed it to me. I think I thought it was funny.

Lusk is hot. Even in May. Even at five in the morning. I press restart on my phone and spring from the balls of my feet towards the hill that will take me to the water. Years ago, Robbie and I sat on the sand at Joiner Bay for pretty much the whole month of January to watch a movie being filmed on the peninsula. They'd built a pirate ship with sails and cannons and a mermaid on the front. We ate fish and chips and mucked around in the water. Robbie reckoned we should swim out to spy on the actors, but we never did.

And where was I when Robbie fished out the spare key from the drainpipe and entered the shed? Where was Dad? We'd gone for a sunset run, on our other regular route, in the opposite direction, past the war memorial and out to Opal Bay. Dad promised me ten dollars for a PB. We came home through the front door, and I took off my sneakers and T-shirt and Dad passed me a water bottle. He did some high knee-jumps on the tiles. He stretched out his hip flexors and tossed me the TV remote from under the couch. I watched a bunch of things – about how to catch black bream with river prawns, about how much a three-hundred-year-old jade pendant is worth, about athletes who almost died when they took steroids in the eighties.

We ate dinner. I folded the ten-dollar note into the envelope in my desk drawer and went to bed. While I was asleep, Dad went out to the shed to use the rowing machine. He found Robbie and made the phone calls and stayed up all night. When I woke up, I saw Dad crouched beside my bed, wet from the shower. My muscles were tender after a dreamless sleep.

He said, 'Mate.'

My first thought was that he'd injured himself. Still sleepy, I leant over to check his legs.

'My little mate.'

Robbie was heavy, Dad said. Heavy and peaceful. That last bit Dad made up, as if I didn't have the imagination to know what happens when your neck breaks and you suffocate in the dingy light outside your best friend's house. Robbie's trouble was with his church, someone said. His trouble was with a new girl from school. A clutch of older boys. His trouble was with his father, always distant and gloomy, who seemed to rally himself better after Robbie's death than he ever had before.

On the footpath winding up the hill, I dodge dozens of jackfruit that have split open. They are fat, fluorescent, mammalian. I see and hear the ocean. I try to steady my breath in through my nose and out my mouth. The coal port out on the water is more solid than a simple idea. It's an unshelved book, harbouring secrets. What's to stop me right now from running into the ocean? Endorphins, according to Dad. The shed is empty now and we don't go in there but endorphins will protect us both.

I reach the halfway point at one of the outcrops overlooking the bay. I press pause and reach for my toes. My theory about what stopped Robbie from doing it at his own house were his sisters: cross-legged on the floor of the bedroom they shared, peeling stickers from the magazines and placing them like medallions down their legs. That's all I've come up with – he didn't leave a note. Back at school after the funeral, I checked the library shelves for spine-in books, thinking maybe Robbie was into clues and secrets, even though he'd never talked about clues and secrets with me. I turned a corner and saw Mr Rigby standing in the 200s. He held a stack of books. They looked like props.

'You need anything?' he asked.

'I'm right, thanks.' I didn't want to lose track of the shelves I'd checked.

'You still go running?' Mr Rigby asked. A couple of students wriggled past us down the aisle, heading for the beanbags.

'Yeah.' I thought he was going to tell me to be careful.

He said, 'I went to church with Robbie and his family.'

I held my breath.

Mr Rigby nodded. He tapped a finger against one of the books in his hand. 'Here.'

The book was called *Striding with a Singular Heart*. On its cover, a silhouetted woman in running shorts sped towards a marbled mountain.

'Be careful with that dust jacket. It's old.'

I'm jogging down the hill, breathing deeply, holding myself upright, and Robbie makes his way into my mind, where he hangs like a teardrop. A watery breeze picks up the smell of the ocean. The endorphins are setting in and I start the timer again. I shake the blunt, numb ends of my fingers. The book Mr Rigby lent me said that some people think running is like praying. It isn't difficult to turn running into praying, or to turn disbelief into faith. It isn't difficult to turn sadness or confusion into the slim white nerve of a cord looped and fixed around a beam.

Orbit

Dad used to tell me that if our dog, Kato, ever got into a fight with the Doberman down the street, I should never under any circumstances step in and try to break it up. He made me promise that I would run away, because Dad said even though Kato loved me, if I got between them, they would rip me up. Dogs were dogs and, in the middle of a fight, Kato would forget who I was.

Nowadays my best friend is Krystal, but this morning we were running late and Miss Chester wouldn't let us be excursion buddies. She said, 'Oh, honestly, girls. It won't kill you to go with someone else. You're not getting married.'

As we cross the road, Miss Chester tells us to find our buddies and hold their hand. Matthew looks across at me and hovers his hand near mine, and I don't want to touch him either. Behind me, Krystal is stuck with Samir, who always does his school work, but never says boo to anyone because he doesn't speak the language.

Miss Chester doesn't want children. Not ever. Krystal asked her two weeks ago when we found out that Mrs Romano the Music teacher was pregnant and hadn't just been wearing all those flowy dresses for fun.

Krystal said to Miss Chester, 'Is that because we're like your children?' And she snorted and said that it was because having children is very risky and she'd never get any peace and quiet and she gets enough of us ratbags at school, thank you very much, and who is Krystal? Her mother? Then Nate asked what about Mr Chester, which is what our teacher sometimes calls her boyfriend even though they're not married. Miss Chester said that Mr Chester would love children. But he wouldn't be bloody having them with her.

'Aren't you supposed to compromise when you love someone?' Nate said.

She turned her back on stupid Nate to write on the board and said, 'Yes. But not like that.'

In the middle of our excursion to the Orbit, Mr Chester shows up. I don't know it's him at first – I think it's just a man in an Arsenal jersey who lives in Stratford. But then Miss Chester says, 'Russell?' and her face looks like the time our headteacher, Mr Walcott, burst into the classroom when we were making lots of noise because the DVD player wouldn't work. And I remember that her boyfriend's name is Russell.

'Russell. What are you doing here?'

He lifts himself off the park bench beneath the Orbit. He walks through the lines we've made with our excursion buddies – just ploughs on through, as though he doesn't even see us in our fluoro vests – and stamps right over to Miss Chester. I wait for him to give her a big kiss but instead he yanks her arm behind her back and she says his name again and she topples to the ground.

★

Mum says they shouldn't waste millions of pounds on things like the Orbit, and that politicians shouldn't be allowed to do whatever they want with everyone's money when loads of people are starving in Africa and even in the north of England. Now that the Olympics are over, she's sure nobody will want to go to Stratford for fun, and what are they going to do with that big empty stadium? When I'm older, I'm not going to pay any tax except to buy computers for schools and hospital equipment for babies and food for animal rescue centres.

But I wanted to go on the excursion, so last week I asked Dad to sign the letter during an advert break for *Fifth Gear*.

'What's this, then?' he said, reaching for his glasses.

'Miss Chester's taking us to the Orbit.'

He shifted around in his recliner and the cat fell from his thighs. He skimmed the paper. 'That thing ...' he said and I thought it was going to be exactly the same as what Mum said and I wondered if adults only marry people who agree with them. 'It's quite interesting, isn't it? Like someone's had a bit of fun with Meccano.'

'Mum doesn't like it.'

'Hmm,' he said.

'Can I go?'

He put his left hand under the paper to make a table, and wrote his signature on the bottom of Miss Chester's letter, the 'P' from Paul looking like a pregnant lady who's about to pop. By then *Fifth Gear* was back on, and he'd already taken the glasses from his face, and Milly was stalking her claws back onto his thighs.

At the Tube station this morning, Catie forgot her Oyster

card and Miss Chester was furious because she told us that she wouldn't be responsible if anyone came unprepared. But Miss Chester had no choice, and paid for Catie's ticket, but she's going to stay with her till her mother picks her up this afternoon so she can be reimbursed.

The Orbit has a long name that is the name of the man who built it. But everyone just calls it the Orbit, even Mayor Boris Johnson, who's very keen on it and seems to want everyone else to like it too. On the video we watch on the bus, Boris is wearing bright yellow: just like the letter home said, we have to wear fluoro vests and hard hats in case bits of steel fall on our heads. Krystal's vest is too big for her, and mine smells.

Our tour guide is a man called Eric who looks like he's just come from an action film. His hair is cut spiky, even though it's grey and he must be as old as my dad. He says he's delighted to see us. Excursions always start like this, but by the end Eric will be rubbing his forehead and telling Miss Chester that he doesn't know how she does it, day in day out, haha.

'Now,' Eric says. 'Has anyone seen two thousand tonnes of steel before?'

Samir puts up his hand, which means Jordan does too.

'Well, boys, you probably *think* you have, but not like this.'

Eric asks Miss Chester to go first: what does the Orbit remind her of?

'I think it looks like a rollercoaster.'

Krystal whacks me with the back of her hand because that's what she said when we got here.

Eric nods and says, 'Yep. A lot of people say that. Anyone else? There are no wrong answers. It's art.'

'Maybe some chains?' Madison says, putting her hand up at the end of her sentence so our teacher won't yell.

'A musical instrument,' says Jordan. 'But from the future.'

Matthew says, 'Like an alien spreading DNA over its host.'

'A rocket,' says one of the Smith twins.

'A rocket, hey?' Eric smiles and frowns at the same time. He stands back and shades his eyes to look up at the steel. 'Pretty weird rocket. But yeah, I suppose. Could be.'

After we've been to the observation deck at the top, and Krystal and I can't find anywhere to carve our names, and the view of the stadium is okay but also a bit boring because you can look at it on Google, Miss Chester says it's time to go and we take the lift to the bottom and we burst out into the sunshine.

'Find your buddies for lunch,' she says.

Krystal forgets the bit about Samir being her buddy and she crash-tackles me with a hug. Krystal's cousin's girlfriend was a dancer in the Olympic opening ceremony. She didn't get paid anything, but she got to keep her costume and go to heaps of secret rehearsals. Mum and I watched the ceremony until I fell asleep, but they showed all the best bits on telly for weeks. At one point, enormous pipes came up from the ground and that was the Industrial Revolution. It was way better than the opening ceremony Miss Chester showed us after Mr Walcott had words with her and went back to his office and she finally got the DVD player to work. Three afternoons a week, Miss Chester puts on movies because it's good for those of us who are visual learners, and also sometimes she needs a rest. We've been watching old Olympic Games because that's our theme for the term. During the movies, Miss Chester sits up the back and stares out the window with her fingers on her lips.

★

I'm thinking maybe the man in the red jersey lives in Stratford because he's sitting on a bench, while everyone else is wandering around and taking photos and drinking from water bottles. People can only come to the Orbit for a few months before they close it again. We're lucky to be here.

'Russell,' Miss Chester says as he walks towards her. Russell wants to have children, but he won't be bloody having them with her. Russell doesn't look like someone's dad. He's younger than Miss Chester, and skinny and tall.

'What are you doing here?' she says.

At first I wonder if Russell is meeting us for lunch, which could be interesting. Nate and Lewis will hassle him about Arsenal and why he doesn't go for West Ham. Maybe with her boyfriend around we'll see Miss Chester smile. Maybe Russell will buy everyone a Coke.

He takes Miss Chester's arm and yanks it so it bends around her back. 'What's this I fucking hear about you and Joel Price? Don't fucking lie to me.'

Next to Krystal, Samir seems to understand every word and his mouth opens and shuts over and over.

'Russell,' Miss Chester says and he steps into her so that even though he's skinny and she isn't, she stumbles and lands on her back. Above her, Russell lets go of her arm, but he doesn't help her up. Now he takes hold of her face and yells her name, once, twice, and he can't stop.

'Joanne, you're a fucking liar and I always knew you were.'

'What are you talking about? Get off me!'

Nate tiptoes towards our teacher on the ground, her skirt bunched up around her thighs and her top undone at the bottom.

'Miss?' Nate says.

Krystal's fingers bite into the skin on my arm.

★

We catch the Tube. We meet the tour bus. We are given safety vests and hats. Lewis doesn't want to wear his and Miss Chester tells him he doesn't have a choice. Wearing them is non-negotiable and Lewis will have to catch the Tube all the way back to school on his own and explain to Mr Walcott why he's back so early. So Lewis puts his vest on, but doesn't do it up like you're supposed to and he tosses the hard hat in his hands. Miss Chester shakes her head but she must decide that Lewis isn't worth the trouble because she leaves him alone.

We climb some stairs. We take the lift. We dance around in front of the huge mirror that makes my face and body go lumpy and fat and then watery and skinny until it could be anyone's face and body. Eric shows Catie how to look for Boris Johnson hidden in a map of the park. Eric answers my question about how much the Orbit cost. He tells Nate not to run. He reminds him that there are other people who are interested in the Orbit too, children younger than we are, and a woman with a pram and an old couple who hold on to each other and keep their hard hats on the whole time.

When Russell pushes Miss Chester to the ground, she isn't wearing a hard hat because we had to leave them inside. She falls on her back first, then her head hits the ground and that's what makes the sound: a thump like food falling from a table. A Christmas turkey maybe. After Russell yells in her face about being a fucking liar, he seems to be waiting for Nate to go away, and waiting for Miss Chester to say something. I want her to scream back at him. Maybe she doesn't even know who Joel Price is.

'Miss Chester.' Krystal's voice is shrill and her fingernails are hurting my arm.

'Miss Chester!' I yell. But yelling is as useless as tits on a bull because I don't combine the yelling with a roundhouse kick to Russell's face, or a punch in the kidneys. I can't move at all.

In the sunshine, people who were drinking from water bottles have stopped. The woman with the baby has scooted to the other side of the footpath and isn't looking back. There's a family wearing matching baseball caps, and the dad stands in front of his daughters and calls out, 'Hey, stop! Leave her alone!'

Russell pauses for a second, keeping his fingers on Miss Chester's face. She has her hands wrapped around his arms but can't pull free. With a leg either side of Miss Chester's body, Russell makes it look like she is a thing on the ground that he has chased and hunted and might even kill. Miss Chester showed us a movie like that one afternoon, when she closed all the curtains except at the window she wanted to look out of with her fingers on her lips, and the narrator explained why a lion might kill another lion. Animal documentaries are good for visual learners. So are documentaries about space shuttles and Vikings in ships.

I think of Kato and what he looked like after Vamp the Doberman attacked him. Kato's neck was shredded and shiny with muscle and blood and bone. I'd done the right thing, running back to get Dad. He told me so in a shaky voice before he backed down the driveway with Kato in pieces on the back seat.

But Miss Chester is not Kato and Russell is not Vamp, and I should help her. A lot of people in our class don't like Miss Chester because she doesn't always know what she's doing when she comes to class and she never gives out stickers like Mrs Romano the Music teacher. But I like that she told us about her dad getting electroshock treatment when he was a teenager, and that she yelled at the older girls who tipped all my books into the bin and threw my bag under the cafeteria stairs.

The man in the baseball cap has left his daughters and shouts as he stalks towards Russell. Russell sees him and takes his fingers from Miss Chester's face, and this is over now. It's over. It's over and I won't tell Dad about this part of the excursion. I won't tell Mum that I agree with her now, that the Orbit is a waste of time and space and money we don't have. Russell's hands hang by his sides. Miss Chester tries to get up and she kicks her boyfriend in the shins. Russell leans in close over her body and lifts a fist and hits

243

her across the mouth. He punches her in the cheek. I look around but the Olympics are over now, and all the cameras are gone.

★

We close the curtains. Mr Walcott smiles and introduces Mr Johnson, who will be with us for a few days until Miss Chester is right as rain. After our headteacher leaves, Mr Johnson says he doesn't know why we're watching this, but it's what our teacher left. He presses the remote and the DVD player works first time. It's a movie about the Olympic Games in Berlin, he says. Krystal slides her book onto my side of the desk and rests her hand on mine. Mr Johnson sits at the front and tilts his chair to the side so he can keep one eye on us and one on the movie, which is in black and white with loud music and no talking. It starts with the leaves of a tree dangling in the water and then its branches make shadows on the ground. The boys at the back are fed up already and Mr Johnson threatens us with a morning of writing instead of a morning of watching a movie. I put my head in my hands and I imagine Miss Chester in the hospital right now, staring out the window with her fingers on her lips, wondering why no one, not even Eric the action film star, made it all stop.

Caius Atlas

The baby-name book is the size of a pack of cards. It was left on top of a bin outside the port. I picture a pregnant woman reading it, circling her belly with her palm, looking up to see the ferry arrive, the ferry that will take her back to England. She's been on holiday, beside a clean, warm beach in France. Maybe she left the book because she'd found the perfect name, or maybe she and her husband could never agree. Maybe the baby never arrived.

I take the book back to my tent to read. Eritrean names aren't listed, but I write *Almaz* on the inside cover. The book recommends that parents find a suitable middle name, and I like Temperance Ophelia and Claire Adelrune for a girl. For a boy I've chosen Monroe Carlisle and, my favourite, Caius Atlas.

Once, I helped deliver a baby in my hometown. In between pushes, the mother rested on all fours, fear in her eyes. She knew what was coming and she gripped her own mother's hand and tried to come up for air. She squalled and shuddered and screamed for a day and a half, and the baby – the bones of its skull making the shape of a diamond inside her – lingered too long. The mother was blood-sore and ready for peace. At the last minute, like a passenger waiting for her ferry to arrive, the baby put down her book and looked up. I was that baby. A blind and slippery sea creature that pulled itself out. And my mother let go of my grandmother's hand, rocked on all fours and wept before she died.

It's starting to darken outside in the Wasteland when I hear voices. I shouldn't sleep in the afternoon. I should study my book and think about my future as a midwife in England, or concentrate on picturing the Queen and squirrels and big football stadiums. When I do it's like I'm in England already, pulling myself up onto a bright red bus with a book under my arm, on my way to university.

Abel rushes into my tent, head low, his voice firm. 'You coming? Let's go.'

Through the flapping tent door, I see dozens of people shuffling towards the port. They're better dressed than Abel and me, in scarves and coats.

'Who are all these people?'

'Locals,' Abel says. 'They're on our side. See, Almaz? Not everyone wants us dead.'

He gives me a sign written in black. *WE ARE HUMAN.* He takes my hand and pulls me outside.

The factory owners bury chemicals in the ground next to the Wasteland and they lock the back doors of the lorries that go in and out. If I had a son here named Caius Atlas, I wouldn't be able to stop him playing on the poisoned ground, and the soles of his feet and hands would be blistered and then maybe scarred forever.

I hold my sign high.

Abel grips his in both hands. *STOP THE VIOLENCE.* He reckons the police took his shoes. They slice through the rows of tents at night and tip our bottles of water out onto the road. Yesterday one snatched up a boy's football, bouncing it from hand to hand. Curl-shouldered, the little boy drooped, knowing what was coming. But the policeman, without saying a word, let the ball fall to the ground, grinning as he dribbled it back and forth between his feet before he lobbed it back. The boy let the ball roll past and stayed silent. The policeman's smile faded.

Ahead of us in the night, the port is lit. Last week I counted ferries, lined up like pigs at a trough.

'There aren't as many,' I say.

'We only need one.' Abel's grin is brassy.

Crowds push past before I can reply. *GIVE US DIGNITY.* We walk. The locals chant but I can't catch all the words. On our side the voices speak French, English, Arabic, Urdu. A lot of the migrants say they have family in England – if so, why wouldn't they help them get there? I have no one behind me and no one in front. When I'm in England I'll learn to ride on the Underground. I'll write letters to nobody and post them in a red box on the corner of my street. I'll go to a football match and cheer for both teams.

'That's where we jumped the fence,' Abel tells me.

Abel and his brother say they came *this close* to boarding a ferry last week. The police ran after them, charging till the group of men scattered. The ferry was too quick. But the fence is easy to climb with only a bit of barbed wire at the top. The men ran across the road, saw the ships up ahead. This was the closest they'd ever come. They felt alive, Abel says, and they would do it again.

'Again!' someone yells, and the chant at the front of the group starts up.

Abel and I don't talk about how we will never see each other again. On a bright street in London, I won't be looking for the faces I once knew. I've already forgotten the faces of people who've escaped, those who have disappeared. When lorries slow to a stop on the long road into the port, packs of men check to see if the back is unlocked. One or two of them climb in. No one says goodbye. The others simply shut the door and run off, hoping that next time will be their turn. I need the Wasteland to last just long enough.

Facing us now in a long chain are policemen in bruise-blue. Their plastic shields fit tight as shells, batons by their side. They expected our decaying lot.

Abel's brother Sammy arrives breathless and jogs beside us. *WE WANT FREEDOM.*

'Another three hundred this week,' he shouts over the noise of the crowd. 'They're going to do something about us soon.'

'What can they do?' I shout back. 'They give us nothing.'

At night the men fight with cigarettes and bottles in their hands. They're hungry and dull and desolate. Sitting in the opening of their tents, they heckle one another. Tomorrow, though, they'll offer a brother a fork, a sip of water. A man Sammy knew, practically still a teenager, lay down behind a reversing lorry. I picture his arms folded across his chest and the dimness behind his eyes before the first nightmare tyre touched his legs. Some can stand the waiting better than others.

'They can destroy our tents – all of them, in the middle of the night.' Abel counts on his fingers, answering me. 'Take our water. Bring in more dogs. Close the port.'

'What are we supposed to do then?' asks Sammy.

'We will get there, brother,' Abel says. 'We'll try and try. Charity people will keep bringing us food. There'll be ferries just over there and lorries with doors we can open.'

We've heard some lorry drivers leave their doors unlocked deliberately.

A teenager in an orange shirt strides towards Sammy. In his right hand is a thick broken branch reaching up to rest on his shoulder. He could be whistling. His three friends in caps and sweatshirts have weapons too.

'You.' One of them points. Sammy raises his chin.

The boy in the orange shirt finishes the thought. 'You stole the gun.'

He swings the branch onto Sammy's cheek and I catch him as we fold to the ground, thinking, *Here. On the ground, Sammy, you're in pain. This bit of grass, sit down. Bury your fingers in it. No chemicals here.*

Abel rushes his brother's attacker.

'Police,' I say from my spot on the ground. I point at the protest up the road.

'We're done here,' the boy in orange says, stepping backwards, waving his branch at the night sky. 'You should go find the gun. Then you give it back.'

'Jesus, Sammy. Your whole face,' I say.

He wails low, in swells, into my shoulder.

'All right, all right, Sammy.'

Abel and Sammy came up through Lampedusa a year ago, where they said a local woman gave them bread. When her husband came home, she swore in Italian and chased them from her yard.

Abel doesn't remember being born like I do, and he says his mother doesn't know if he and Sammy are alive. Stuck here among mud and pools of blankets and broken crates, my body feels like a used and dirty thing. I watch pregnant girls sway to standing from the gutter, trying not to touch the poisoned ground. In England, I'll be the one to help them, kneading my hands over their bellies, nodding when I find the top of the uterus, counting the baby's size with my fingers. But here I just watch. I don't want to deliver anyone's baby in the Wasteland.

★

When I delivered myself on the floor of my parents' house, the world was swollen with light and agony. I was outside of my mother's body, trying to help her stay in one piece, saying *breathe breathe, that's right breathe*, but I was also inside being a nuisance, tilting my head back until my forehead met my mother's opening, getting stuck, forgetting that the first person you need to save is yourself.

I grew up beside the sea. The earth beneath our house seethed as though it were waiting to be sucked back in at any moment. The ocean water had been corralled into a concrete rectangle and I went there, to the swimming pool, carrying a dry dress to walk home in. The first day I tried to swim, I assumed my body would know what to do the instant I hit the water, like all the boys backflipping from the concrete high above me.

One of them noticed me hanging on to the side and he struck out to me.

'Hold your arms like this,' he said. 'And your legs, like this.'

'Don't tell me what to do.'

The boy's head was a slick hard melon beaded with water. He reached for my leg. I kicked his hand away and I plunged down, feeling like I was breathing evenly. My head filled with constellations. Month after month I spent at the pool, pushing my limbs away, calling them back again. From under the water, I saw the boys passing overhead like birds.

★

The walls of my tent are stitched in several places, stretched tight with repairs. I shut myself inside as best as I can, reaching for the baby-name book and searching for my name, knowing what it means, knowing it isn't listed. Yesterday I circled Viola, Rosetta, Calliope and Magnus. I touch the space on the page where my name should be.

'Almaz?'

Abel unties the rope and enters, stooping.

'Sammy's okay. He's with the others now. We'll fix it tonight.'

'What's happening tonight?' I use my finger to mark the page.

'We're going to stand up for ourselves.'

'And try for a ferry?'

251

'Tonight this is more important.' He takes the book from me.

'Do you want to die here? Do you want to get arrested?' I ask him. The French have offered us refuge but France is not the goal. I grab his arm. 'Do you want to *live* here?'

Abel's face is polished with sweat. I see him as a little kid scrabbling along a street in Massawa, the thin bones of his legs churning along the paved road, pummelling the air, taking flight, beating his brother home for dinner. His mother sighs through a dry smile and fixes Abel's wriggling form onto a chair. At the table, he looks towards the Red Sea and spoons fish into his mouth.

'You must deliver yourself,' is what I say out loud, just to me, though Abel is there. He edges his hand along the top of my thigh.

'Is that right?' He wants to have sex with me again, doesn't care if I get pregnant. And if I stay here in this filthy tent that's what will happen and I'll be no closer to anywhere. Here, it's better to be attached to someone than to be alone. But now there's more than the space in the tent between us. More space than the salty channel between here and England. Abel is a dark sculpture, wet and marbled in the dusk. I touch his forehead. I think, *You'll never leave.*

'Here,' I say. I toss him the packet of biscuits the aid workers brought us this morning. 'Have these.' I stand and grab the book on my way out.

★

A woman at the service station hoses the concrete while she drinks from a glass bottle. She stares at me and yanks on the hose and it whips behind her like a snake. I cross the car park, a stretch of bitumen muddied at its broken edges. Six or so lorries are parked, some with their doors open. A man with a shaved head like Abel's talks on a phone and smokes. Another balances on the edges of his naked feet, trying to wedge something off the bottom of his boots. I choose a lorry with a Union Jack on the door. I have to believe there's a driver inside who will take pity on me, or, more likely, ask for something more. And I'll give it, but I will arrive in England whole. Delivered. When I leave the Wasteland, the bones of my skull will finally settle.

Other girls have done it. Girls I used to know at the Wasteland did it for a lot less – a bit of dinner or a coat or even just a proper shower. Smart girls square the days into a calendar on the back of a piece of cardboard and keep it close. They circle the digits and avoid the men on the most dangerous days.

'Hello?' I thump on the passenger door, stepping up to peer in through the window.

★

I pocket the euros – five notes folded in my hand – and walk the forty-five minutes to Decathlon. Inside I choose a grey wetsuit, hand paddles, flippers, goggles and a zippered plastic case that the teenager behind the counter assures me is watertight. I slip the baby-name book inside the case and hand over the money.

'Wetsuit on the ground. Step into it,' he tells me, banging the register shut with his palm. 'With the legs like this.'

He watches me leave.

At the beach, on the edge of the water, you can see the white cliffs across the Channel that look like the teeth of a whale. No one can tell me why they're white. One day I'll come back to those cliffs carrying a baby of my own, little Caius Atlas with his fingers wrapped around my thumb. We'll point things out to each other, like how France looks so close it seems we're separated by nothing more than a lake. Just a line of water on a map you could swim across, pulling yourself up onto the beach on the other side, waving back at where you've come from.

Acknowledgements

When I was a child I spent a lot of time at the Toowoomba public library. I stayed there for hours alone, or with my mother or my sister. My family let me read and write whatever I wanted. It's a thrill to have something of my own published now, all these years later, after being drawn down from the upstairs kids' section to the grown-up books on the ground floor. My reading and writing was also encouraged by many teachers. Particular thanks to Miss F Scott and to the late Mr C Yeabsley for energising my interest in telling stories.

I'm really grateful to the team at UQP. It's been a privilege to have you on my side and see my book take shape under your guidance. Thank you to my publisher, Madonna Duffy, for your enthusiasm for my manuscript, and to Josh Durham for designing the beautiful cover. Thank you to my brilliant editor, Ian See, who has shown me incredible wisdom and kindness. It is such a pleasure working with you.

Warm thanks to my friends and colleagues at QUT for helping with early story drafts, for attending events I read at and for believing in my writing. My progress on this manuscript has been aided by a QUT fellowship and mentorship with the terrific Ryan O'Neill – many thanks –

and a shortlisting in the 2016 Queensland Literary Awards. My gratitude also to the marvellous Brooke Davis.

Thank you to members of my writing groups for your time and generosity. My deep gratitude to Andrea, Madeleine, Sikwasa, Bettina, Kathy, Kim, Les, Mhairead and Sarah R for your support.

Special thanks to Kate and Sean, to Emma and Mirandi, to Andy, to Sarah K for years of friendship and encouragement, for your sharp and good eyes.

I've been writing these stories over a period of about five years. I'm so lucky to have friends and family who care about what I do and who let me ask them random questions by text message about bits in my stories that I hope they'll know the answers to – thank you, I love you.

I am indebted to friends and family for babysitting my daughter to give me time to write. Endless gratitude to the Haddons, Simpsons and Elverys.

Love and admiration forever to my sister, Jiselle. To my parents, your faith in me means the world. Thank you, Mum and Dad, for giving me a wonderful childhood. Thanks for letting me read and read and read.

Thank you to Simon and Harriet, the loves of my life.

★

Versions of the following stories have appeared online and in print. Thank you to the editors of these publications.

'Trick of the Light', published as 'The Elements', *Kill Your Darlings*, 10 November 2014; and *Award Winning Australian Writing 2015*, Melbourne Books, 2015.

'Replica', *Award Winning Australian Writing 2013*, Melbourne Books, 2013; and *Prizing Diversity*, Thames and Hudson, 2015.

'Pudding', *The Big Issue*, Issue 491 (Fiction Edition 2015), 14 August 2015.

'La Otra', *Lip Mag*, 28 June 2016.

'Love, Listen', *Yen Mag*, 11 September 2015.

'What You Really Collect Is Always Yourself', *Review of Australian Fiction*, Volume 21, Issue 1, 2017.

'Acrobat', *Shibboleth and Other Stories*, Margaret River Press, 2016.

'Joiner Bay', *Joiner Bay and Other Stories*, Margaret River Press, 2017.

'Caius Atlas', *Griffith Review 51: Fixing the System*, 2016.

Also in UQP's short fiction series

PORTABLE CURIOSITIES
Julie Koh

Winner, *Sydney Morning Herald* Best Young Australian Novelist 2017

Brilliantly clever and brimming with heart, these twelve stories combine absurd humour with searing critiques on contemporary society – the rampant consumerism, the casual misogyny, the insidious fear of those who are different. *Portable Curiosities* is an unforgettable collection by a significant new talent.

'Cutting-edge writing in many ways.' Maxine Beneba Clarke, *Guardian Australia*, Best Books of 2016

'Koh is a gifted satirist who makes wonderful use of language … in this clever and highly original collection.' *Age/Sydney Morning Herald*

ISBN 978 0 7022 5404 8

PERIPHERAL VISION
Paddy O'Reilly

**'This is a great collection, which also burns
an impression on our imagination.'
Debra Adelaide, *Australian Book Review***

In her second collection of short stories, Paddy O'Reilly takes us into the fringes of human nature – our hidden thoughts, our darker impulses and our unspoken tragedies. By turns elegiac and acerbic, but always acutely observed, *Peripheral Vision* confirms O'Reilly as one of our most inventive and insightful writers.

'A writer of considerable poise and ingenuity … O'Reilly's imagination is never predictable, and her readers will thrill to the kinds of strange harmonies she composes.' *Age/Sydney Morning Herald*

'Stellar … worth it for the staggeringly good "Procession" alone.' Charlotte Wood, *Weekend Australian*, Best Books of 2015

ISBN 978 0 7022 5360 7

UQP